THE LIGHTHOUSE

FIVE ISLAND COVE, BOOK 1

JESSIE NEWTON

COPYRIGHT

ISBN-13: 979-8621108243

CHAPTER ONE

Robin Grover picked up the basket with the red-and-white checkered cloth, her tears filling her eyes and almost flowing down her face. She would not cry yet. As soon as she saw Kristen, she wouldn't be able to hold back the tide. But she still had a fifteen-minute drive and a five-minute hike before she could release the emotions.

"Ready," she said to herself, looking around the office where she ran events. The house sat empty during weekdays, with Duke off on his fishing boat until at least one or two in the afternoon. During peak fishing season, he didn't come home until the fish dried up, sometimes for days at a time. He'd been gone for a few days, and Robin expected to hear from him by evening.

The boxes on her planning table could wait. For once,

the anniversaries, birthdays, and family reunions of the rich and famous could simply *wait*.

Joel Shields had died, and surely even heaven had paused for a moment to welcome him home with open arms.

His wife, Kristen, was still here, and Robin had quickly collected all of the woman's favorite things, tied them up in ribbons and cloths, as if that could erase the stunning pain of losing someone you loved.

Her emotions hitched again, and Robin laced them behind a brave smile and clenched her fingers around the handle of the basket. She moved, knowing that for her, doing something helped her tame the urge to scream and beg to know why. Yes, staying busy had often kept her mind off the more unpleasant things in life.

She made it behind the wheel of her SUV, and she managed to drive across Diamond Island on autopilot. She wasn't sure if the lights she went through were green or not, but she didn't get hit, so they must have been.

Kristen and Joel Shields had lived in and ran the lighthouse on Diamond Island, the largest of the five islands that made up Five Island Cove, for almost four decades. Located off the coast of Connecticut, north of Martha's Vineyard yet west of Nantucket, Five Island Cove was the epitome of a quaint New England life. South of Cape Cod, the islands were nestled right in the center of the triangle made from some of the most popular vacation destinations for the rich and famous.

Once the celebrities and ultra-rich had discovered the islands, vacation homes, weekend getaways, and tourism had soared.

Robin had lived on Diamond Island for her entire life, and while she often thought she would've liked to have seen more of the world, she couldn't imagine living anywhere but on a mound of earth surrounded by water. She loved the sound of the waves as they washed ashore. She adored the way the sun glinted off the water. And once she'd married Duke Grover, she'd had all the lobster and soft-shell crab she could want.

Gratitude for the life she'd been given streamed through her, and Robin allowed a tiny trickle of tears to slip down her face. She sniffed and swiped them away as she pulled into the small parking lot at the lighthouse, somehow there already.

The water in front of her undulated as it usually did, and Robin watched it for a moment. The sun shone today, and it likely would for many more days to come, as they'd just come into spring and were well into April. The flowers had started to peek up from their winter naps, and Robin couldn't wait for the rose bushes along the edge of this parking lot to bloom.

Joel had planted all of them, each a different color, until a few years ago. He'd planted a pink lemonade variety for her, and Robin tensed from head to toe. She exhaled and rolled her neck, trying to get some of the tightness to go. She felt suffocated with grief, as if someone was leaning against her windpipe and she couldn't get enough air.

She found she couldn't quite get out of the vehicle, and she peered up at the lighthouse through her window. She'd thrown an absolute bash the day Joel and Kristen had retired from their post here. Their son, Rueben, had taken over the job of making sure the glass was polished, the light beamed out into the darkness, and that ships and smaller craft navigated these waters safely.

Diamond Island was aptly named for its shape. It also sat at the head of the other island, with the cove they created on the opposite side from this lighthouse. This side contained more cliffs, more rocks, and more wind. Oh, the wind could steal a breath from a person before they could identify the thief.

The flag on top of the lighthouse didn't seem to be flapping too hard, but Robin could see Alice climbing the ladder one cold day in November to replace it. The job had to be done from time to time, and all of the Seafaring Girls had had to do it at some point.

A shaky smile touched Robin's mouth. Her friends in the Seafaring Girls had been Robin's lifeline. They'd been as close as sisters, sharing clothes, shoes, and stories for so many years. She'd slept at Alice's for a couple of weeks one summer when the fighting with her mother had become unbearable for both of them, and Alice had come to Robin's the moment the funeral had ended.

Alice had replaced the flag with great triumph, and

the other girls had clapped and whooped for her. She'd been the bravest of them back then, and Robin wished she hadn't let so much time go by since talking to her.

Rueben lived in the lower two levels of the lighthouse now, but Robin could still see herself knocking on that deep, navy blue door around the back of the lighthouse. Kristen would always answer, and words didn't even need to be said before Robin stepped inside. Sometimes she went alone, but usually, she came to the lighthouse with her sisterhood.

Memories of the four girls she'd been best friends with growing up streamed freely now, and she wondered if anyone had alerted them of Joel's death.

"Probably not," she said to herself, still looking at the clapboard white lighthouse. It looked like Rueben had painted it recently, though Robin knew he had not. She would've noticed such a chore, as it took scaffolding and time to get the entire lighthouse as gleaming as possible, and the job was done once a year.

She'd seen no scaffolding in her last few visits to Kristen and Joel, and come to think of it, she hadn't seen Rueben or his wife either.

The roof of the lighthouse was the same navy blue as the door around the back, and the whole structure stood tall and proud, right on the edge of the island. Robin remembered the first time she'd come here, and she'd felt like she could see clear across the ocean to another continent.

She couldn't, of course. But she'd felt both powerful and small in that moment, and then she'd met Alice Williams, also at the lighthouse for the first time. Then another girl came. And another. Kristen had led a sea adventure group for girls for years, and Robin couldn't even imagine how many lives she'd touched through the Seafaring Girls.

In that very moment, she once again felt both powerful and small. What had she done with her life? Had her time on earth meant anything, to anyone?

Her chest tightened, and she hated the feeling of teetering on the edge of a steep cliff, about to fall off. She'd felt like this when it had been her turn to replace the flag on the top of the lighthouse, like one misstep and she'd go tumbling down. The stakes back then had been steep, sure. But now, they felt astronomical, like if she didn't choose correctly, everything would shatter.

She drew a deep breath, reached for the basket, and got out of the car. Step one, and she'd done it.

When Rueben had taken over the lighthouse, Kristen and Joel had moved into the cottage up the hill a bit, and Robin glanced at the minivan parked as close to the path as a vehicle could get. She remembered the day she'd gone with Kristen to buy it. The day Joel hadn't been able to get into a vehicle that stood higher off the ground, but he also couldn't stoop down to get into a sedan.

Cancer was a cruel master, and Joel had suffered with it for five years before succumbing to its unrelenting grip.

She sniffled as she started up the path, keeping her eyes on the asphalt at her feet. Step two, get moving. Done.

"I was wondering when you were going to get out of that car."

Robin looked up to find Kristen standing on the path, wearing a black sweat suit that seemed like it had been tailored just for her.

Their eyes met, and Robin wouldn't have been able to hold back the tears then, even if she'd wanted to. "Kristen," she said, her voice breaking. The woman was twenty-two years older than Robin, but age didn't matter right now.

"I should've known you'd be the first to come. Joel's been dead less than twenty four hours." Kristen's smile shook on her mouth, and she looked out toward the ocean.

Robin stepped toward her, her vision blurry from the tears. "I'm so sorry. I won't stay. I just brought you a few comfort items." She reached Kristen and folded back the checkered cloth. "Those chewy Werther's you like so much. A new visor, because I thought you might like to sit on the upper deck and watch the waves." She glanced up at Kristen but didn't want to make eye contact. "And of course, cookies."

Always cookies. It had been the cookies that had first bonded the two women together, and Robin couldn't look at a cookie of any variety without thinking of Kristen.

She practically shoved the gifts at Kristen and then latched onto her, the embrace awkward with the basket between them. "I'm so sorry. I loved Joel so much." Her voice was little more than air and a squeak, but she didn't know how to make it sound normal.

There was no more normal without Joel.

Kristen moved the basket and hugged Robin properly, both of them crying. For some reason, when Kristen wept that validated Robin's feelings, and a sense of relief and belonging flowed through her.

A minute or two later, Kristen pulled back. "Okay." She wiped at her eyes. "Let's take this to the deck."

Robin nodded, clearing the water from her own eyes and face. She looped her hand through Kristen's arm as they turned and walked back toward the lighthouse. They went through the navy blue door and climbed up instead of down, emerging onto the upper deck and winding around to the side that faced the water.

A sigh moved through Robin's body, and she asked, "What do you need help with?"

"Nothing," Kristen said as she sat in one of the chairs on the deck. There were only two, and Robin had sat up here with Kristen countless times before. "Joel had everything planned, right down to the day the funeral should take place." A small, fond smile sat on her face as she looked at the waves. "He wanted it on a Saturday so people wouldn't have to take work off to come."

Robin nodded as she sat. She leaned forward, keeping

her elbows on her knees. "I can go to the funeral home with you, Kristen. You shouldn't have to do that alone."

"Jean is here," Kristen said softly. "And Clara is trying to come."

"Oh, okay." Surprise moved through Robin, and she couldn't help asking, "You want to go with Jean or Clara?"

Jean was Rueben's wife, and she'd thrown a literal fit about moving to Diamond Island and living in a lighthouse. She'd cried for a solid month after she'd arrived, and she'd gone to the doctor to get on anti-depressants after she'd gained thirty pounds in the first year they'd been here. She went back to Long Island where her parents lived for long stretches of time, and Robin would be surprised if Jean had the fortitude to go to the funeral home with her mother-in-law.

"No," Kristen said. "I don't want to go with either of them." She looked at Robin, and a quick snort came from her, followed by a laugh. "Jean didn't offer. And Clara's still trying to get a flight in."

Clara was Joel and Kristen's daughter, and she also lived off-island. Like a lot of people, she'd left Five Island Cove as soon as she could, and Robin hadn't seen her in years.

She wasn't sure what had driven Clara away. Robin loved the big, summer homes of the rich who only came in the warmest months. Robin participated—and sometimes planned—all the small-town traditions that made Five Island Cove the gem that it was.

Every island had its own charm and celebrations, and each was only a short ferry ride from the others. They created a crescent in the vast waters, with the cove coming ashore on the biggest of the islands, Diamond Island.

There was great seafood and other delicious restaurants, most of them family-owned for generations. The picturesque Main Street had picture-perfect shopping, which had only gotten better as people with more money helicoptered or sailed in for their retreats on the island. Why Clara hadn't liked that, she wasn't sure. People paid a *lot* of money to come to Five Island Cove, and yet some of the people who'd grown up here wanted to run from it.

"So I'll go with you," Robin said, smiling. She reached across the space between them and took Kristen's papery hand in hers. "And I was thinking…"

"Here we go," Kristen said, but she squeezed Robin's fingers. "You and that brain of yours."

Robin ducked her head, not quite brave enough to say what was on her mind while looking at Kristen. "I think I should call all the girls. Get them back here for the funeral."

Kristen's grip on Robin's hand increased, and then she let go. "They won't come."

Robin looked up at the pain in the older woman's voice. "Sure they will," she said. "You and Joel meant a lot to us."

"You might get Alice and Eloise," Kristen conceded.

"But if you can get Kelli back here, you'll be lucky. And AJ? You'd have worked a miracle."

Robin had always liked a good challenge. At the very least, she'd never shied away from one. "Well, I guess it's time to work a miracle."

CHAPTER TWO

Eloise Hall reached for her phone as it rang, the last grades for the semester about to be finished. She just had one more class to go, and she'd be free until fall semester.

"Doctor Hall," she said.

"Eloise," a woman said.

A rush of memories filled Eloise's mind with that voice. Slightly high, always a bit on the self-important side, but with a foundation of kindness. "Robin?" Her heart started beating in a strange, syncopated way. She hadn't spoken to Robin—or anyone from Five Island Cove —in a long time. At least five years.

Too long, Eloise thought, as she had in the past. But she'd done nothing to bring the once-close group together. It was always Robin or Alice that did that, and

Eloise shouldn't have been surprised to get a call like this out of the blue from the power blonde.

"Yes," Robin said. "How are you? Did you know you're very hard to get in touch with?"

"Am I?" Eloise sat back in her luxury office chair, her grading forgotten. She pictured Robin from their youth, the image of the pretty, perfect, perky blonde girl a very hard memory to get rid of. Funnily enough, Eloise had never been jealous of Robin, though she'd been very popular. AJ had always had the most boyfriends, but that was because she wasn't afraid to sneak off with the boys in the dark and do things Eloise hadn't done until college.

"Very hard," Robin said with a smile in her voice. "It's so good to hear your voice."

Eloise didn't know what to say, so she said nothing. She'd spent the last twenty-seven years in college, as a matter of fact, as she'd attended Boston University after leaving Sanctuary Island, one of the islands that made up Five Island Cove, gone on to get her doctorate at Harvard, and then returned to BU as a professor.

Biology she knew. How to have a conversation with someone she hadn't seen in years she did not. Her mind niggled at her that she did know Robin, almost as well as she knew her own self. Still, it felt like the five years stretched until a chasm existed between them, with Eloise on one side and Robin calling to her from the other.

"Anyway," Robin said, filling the silence. "I'm calling

because Joel Shields passed away, and the funeral is next Saturday."

There was no invitation there, but Eloise heard it anyway. "Oh, no," she said, her past marching through her mind now. Damn Robin for opening that door. Eloise pressed against it from the other side, but it would not close all the way. "That's terrible news. I knew he was sick, but..." She let the words hang there, because while she'd gone to visit her aging mother a couple of years ago, she hadn't thought much about the Shields' since she'd heard the news of Joel's cancer.

"Yes," Robin said. "And I really think the five of us should be here for Kristen."

Eloise recognized that tone, even if she hadn't heard it in over two decades. This was the take-charge Robin. The one who would not take no for an answer.

The five of us.

Once, the five of them had been Eloise's saving grace. The only place she felt safe, loved.

Eloise sighed as she turned in her chair. "I don't want to come back there," she said. The reason why was a whole new door that Eloise would not let open, not even for a moment.

"Just for a few days," Robin said. "Your dad isn't here anymore, Eloise, and I'm sure your mother would love to see you."

"You should've been a lawyer," Eloise said. Not many people knew Eloise's number one reason for leaving and staying away from Five Island Cove was her father. The door in her mind started to inch open, and Eloise shoved mightily against it. Only a few people knew what life had been like behind the closed doors of the beach cottage where Eloise had grown up with her parents and brother. Garrett had left the islands almost as quickly as Eloise had, and she twisted the key on the lock on that door in her mind.

"And Wes hasn't stepped foot on the island since your divorce." Robin was one of those people who knew the finer details of Eloise's life, a fact she really wished wasn't true right now. At the same time, Eloise thought someone should know the finer details of her life, and while she had friends on campus and neighbors on her street, no one truly knew her the way Robin did.

Point two taken. Eloise really had no reason not to go. "I have some work—"

"The semester ended today," Robin interrupted. "So you're probably sitting at home, finishing up your grades and wondering what you're going to do with all your free time."

"I am not sitting at home," Eloise said, looking at the final class's worth of grades. "And I have plenty to keep me busy." Knitting, and her cats, and...

Suddenly a couple of weeks on Five Island Cove didn't sound so bad. At least she wouldn't have to say she had no plans for her break should someone ask her on her way out of the building that afternoon.

"You could stay with me," Robin said. "I know you don't like going back to your mom's place."

A third blow to Eloise's flimsy tower of excuses sent it shattering. She drew in a long breath to make a big show. "I don't know, Robin."

"Please," the woman said next, and Eloise's defenses dropped.

"You don't play fair," she said.

"Kristen needs us," Robin said. "And if that means I have to play dirty to get everyone here, I'm going to do it."

"You've talked to AJ?"

"Not yet," Robin hedged.

"You called me first, didn't you?"

"Kristen needs us," she repeated, which was code for You're a softie. I knew I could get you, and that will help get the others.

"Fine," Eloise said. "But I'm bringing both of my cats, so you better have somewhere for them too."

"I can handle two felines," Robin said coolly. A moment later, a shriek came through the phone, and Eloise should've known it would sound. But she'd forgotten Robin's tendency to scream in excitement, and she startled, her heart pounding furiously now.

"Oh, I'm so excited, Eloise. We can go to Mort's like we did growing up. And I'll make the chocolate chip banana pancakes that won the fireman's cook-off, and we'll go to the beach and talk about everything."

Everything.

The word inspired fear in Eloise's heart, because she didn't want to talk about everything. Some things, in her opinion, *shouldn't* be talked about. Some secrets were worth keeping. "I need to finish my grades," she said. "And look at flights. I'll text you, okay?"

"I knew you were doing grades," Robin teased.

Eloise managed to smile. "Yeah, but I'm not doing them at home."

"I know," Robin said. "I called you at the university." The pure triumph in Robin's voice wasn't lost on Eloise.

She rolled her eyes, though she did love Robin. "I'll talk to you later." She hung up and stared at her laptop, that last class taunting her now. She acted like she would be really put out with a return visit to Five Island Cove, but maybe it was time. Maybe she could finally put to rest the simmering secrets that she kept in the beach house not even Robin knew about.

Maybe a bit of excitement bubbled through her too. She didn't have any plans for her break, though she had been looking forward to attending her power yoga classes at a more sane hour. And that was when she realized her life had been reduced to knitting, cats, and a half an hour of power yoga at five a.m.

Maybe she could just look at airplane tickets for a few minutes before she finished her grades...

CHAPTER THREE

Alice Kelton tossed another swimming suit into the open suitcase on her bed. Frank's phone rang and rang, and he did not pick up. "Of course," she muttered, ending the call before his voicemail could demand she leave a message. She wanted to hurl the phone through the window, load up everything she owned, and get on the jet back to Rocky Ridge, the smallest of the islands that made up Five Island Cove.

It would probably take Frank at least a week to realize she'd even moved out. He worked in the city during the week, only coming home to grace everyone with his presence on the weekends. As it was Monday, and he'd left last night, Alice wouldn't be missed for days.

Even when she was in their sprawling mansion on their immaculate grounds, she wasn't missed. She hadn't slept with Frank in over two years, as the man couldn't keep it in his pants, and she didn't want to get another disease, thank you very much.

Divorce was not something she had considered for very long, though the idea did occur to Alice from time to time. But Frank liked having her here in the Hamptons, simply so he could drop sentences like, "My wife runs the charity that helps disabled veterans," or "Back home in the Hamptons..."

Yes, Alice had married way up, and she'd paid heavily for it.

"Mom," Ginny said, drawing her out of her personal pity party. She didn't allow herself to fall into such episodes very often, because she knew what kind of bed she'd been getting into twenty years ago, and she'd been making it and remaking it every morning since.

"Yes, dear," she said, pulling her thoughts and feelings back from the precipice where they'd been dangling.

"Do I need my computer? How long are we going to be at Grandpa's?"

"I don't know," she said. "But yes, bring your computer. You'll need to finish up the term, at the very least."

Ginny didn't look pleased about missing the last two weeks of the term, but Alice honestly didn't care. Out of the twins, Ginny definitely cared more about her grades than Charlie, who had struggled with math since the third grade. Alice had been the one at the kitchen table with him night after night. Alice had been the one to hire the private tutors. Alice had been the one to police the time the kids spent on electronic devices, how much allowance the twins were allowed to have, and how many electives they could take and still be considered academically sound.

Frank expected the children to get into Ivy League schools. Frank expected peace and quiet when he came home. Frank expected children who didn't act like children. And when they'd become teenagers...Alice had taken to bribing them to get them to act the way Frank expected.

Alice had given everything to him. She reached up and patted her mousy brown hair, reminding herself that no, she didn't particularly like Frank Kelton all that much. But she had married him, and he'd provided a life of luxury for her that few could even imagine.

She smoothed down the front of her slacks, noting how empty her stomach felt. But she couldn't eat, because women Alice's age could hardly eat anything or they'd gain weight. And Alice could not go above a size eight. The front of her slacks wouldn't be flat then, and she was determined to stay in the skirts and pants she'd spent a fortune on. Then she could stand up in front of the library board and demand ratings on their video sections, be admired and looked at longingly by the other trophy wives on her street, and get nominated for another term as the HOA president.

All in all, though, Alice did not care about any of it. She wanted a bowl of lobster mac from the run-down, nearly condemned shack on the south side of Diamond Island, with plenty of butter and breadcrumbs. Her mouth watered just thinking about it.

She tugged on the bottom of her sweater as she walked smoothly into the hall. "Charlie," she said. "You're packing, right? The jet leaves in a couple of hours."

Her son did not answer, and Alice braced herself for an argument. Charlie loved to argue, and if he could get the grades, he'd make a fine lawyer, like his father. He didn't get flustered by confrontation the way Alice did, and she really just wanted to open his door and find his neatly packed suitcase waiting by the door.

Life was rarely how Alice wanted it, though.

"Charlie," she said again, knocking on the door. She tried the knob, but he'd locked it. "I hate it when you lock the door." She pressed her face right into the seam where the door met the jamb to speak to him.

A moment later, he opened the door, and Alice fell back. He wore a sharp look on his face, and Alice couldn't count how many times she'd seen those same slanted eyebrows on her husband's face. "I'm coming, Mom," he said. "You literally told me twenty minutes ago about this stupid trip."

"It's not my fault you do not answer your phone," Alice said, lifting her chin. "Had you picked up the phone when I called earlier, you'd have had plenty of time to prepare."

"I was talking to Jessica."

"Ah, Jessica." Alice put a smile on her face, because

she didn't need to push Charlie further away. "And how is she?"

"Great," he said in a deadpan. "She was in crisis, Mom."

"Oh? What kind of crisis?"

"The kind where she got a B." He rolled his eyes. "Her parents are seriously so uptight, and she was *crying*."

And surely Charlie had made Jessica feel all better. Alice cocked her head at him, hating the question in her mind. She didn't want to speak it. She disliked making things awkward between her and the children, but some things just needed to be said.

"You're not having sex with her, are you?"

"Mom," Charlie said, rolling his whole head now. "No, okay? *No*. Stop asking me that."

"I will not stop asking you that," Alice said. "You're fourteen years old, and you shouldn't be having sex."

"I'm fifteen," Charlie said. "And—"

"You won't be fifteen until next week," she said. "Trust me, I know when you came out of my body."

"Mom, gross."

"Gross?" Alice cocked her eyebrow at him and smiled. "Jessica could get pregnant if you're doing...that."

"We're not," he said. "Besides, I've talked to Dad about this a hundred times. I know how to not get a girl pregnant."

"That is so not comforting," Alice said, true worry striking her heartstrings. "Using a condom during sex is still having sex. You know that, right?" She didn't like Frank talking to Charlie about sex. What was he saying? *Use a condom so you don't get a girl pregnant. Don't be stupid about it.*

That was all fine and good—unless he was telling Charlie that so he didn't get caught. That sex with a condom was like not having sex at all. Frank would do whatever it took not to get caught, as Alice knew only too well.

"Mom, can you please stop?" Charlie reached for something next to the door and shoved his suitcase into the hall. "Please. I already have a headache, and you've already ruined my fifteenth birthday."

"I can't help it if a close, *personal* friend passed away and the funeral is near your birthday," she said. "Besides, Della makes a delicious chocolate cake, and it's not like we're not going to celebrate at all."

But she knew what he meant. He didn't care about having a party with her and her seventy-five-year-old father and the new wife he'd married a decade ago. Charlie wanted a shindig in the expansive basement, where he could have his friends over and they could eat pizza and drink soda, shoot baskets or pool, and watch movies.

She reached out and ran her hand down the side of his face. "I'm sorry about your birthday."

He wore a growl on his face, but he said, "I know, Mom."

If only he knew how much she'd protected him from. How much she'd do to make sure his life was as easy as possible. She picked up the suitcase and turned. "Okay. I'm going to put this in the car."

"I got it," Charlie said. "And if you leave yours in the hallway, I'll take it down too."

Alice smiled at him, wondering what she'd done to get such a good son. Especially from a sperm donor like Frank. "Thank you, dear. I just need to finish up a few things."

She turned and went down the long hallway to the master suite. Alice could keep her composure in front of people like a pro. She'd had twenty-five years of experience. But behind closed doors...Alice sighed and slumped against the door behind her.

All the way to the floor she slid, curling her knees to her chest. Her step-mother's chocolate cake sounded like heaven about now. Once, Alice had once thought her mom could fix anything with a hug and a huge pitcher of lemonade.

Chocolate cake and lemonade did not fix marriages, though. They did not fill the lonely hours Alice spent by herself in a seven-thousand square-foot house that had no soul. They did not bring back the dead, as she knew so well.

Flashes of her fifteen-year-old self filled her mind like bright pops of light. Choosing the flowers. Following the casket into the chapel. Singing a song with her brother.

The way the wind whipped at the cemetery. Going home. Making dinner for a father who didn't come home that night.

And then she'd gone to Robin's, where she'd always been welcome, where some sense of normalcy existed, even if her mother could pick at a person until they snapped back. That night, after the funeral, there'd been no picking and no snapping.

Robin's mother had made fish tacos, and they'd all cried together. She'd told Alice to come any time she needed to, and she'd said she'd talk to Alice's father about not leaving his teenagers home alone.

Acting quickly, she flipped the switch to turn off that line of thought. Instead, she focused on Kristen Shields, the woman who had guided Alice through so many tumultuous times in her life, including her mother's death.

When Robin had called, Alice's first words were, "Of course I'll be there." She'd started an email to their pilot before the phone call had ended, and the flight was scheduled on their private jet for later that afternoon.

In truth, Alice couldn't face the thought of another week trapped in this house by herself. The walls of her life had been pressing ever closer the past month or so, and Alice needed an escape. She might not have thought she'd find it in Five Island Cove, but that was the direction she was being called at the moment.

And while April wasn't the warmest time of year for a

visit to the islands, she was going. And she was taking the kids. She might tell Frank later in the week, but she might not. She hadn't decided yet.

Her phone chimed, reminding her she really needed to finish packing, and she got to her feet. Smoothing down all that had rumpled during the past five minutes, Alice stepped over to her suitcase and looked inside. Five Island Cove had stores and quaint little shops, and whatever she didn't have, she could buy.

The cove had become a haven for the rich and famous over the past fifteen years or so, and Alice had found herself listening to friends at the high teas around the Hamptons talk about the homes they were building on Sanctuary Island or Pearl Island. Alice had said nothing, though most of the wives knew she hailed from Five Island Cove.

Since so many wealthy people visited the islands now, she knew she could find whatever she needed should her fancy slacks get dirty or ruined. So she zipped up the suitcase and set it in the hall before going into the bathroom to make sure every eyelash sat in the right spot. She slicked on lipstick and collected her purse from the drawer in her dresser, the motions done out of habit now. Every piece of Alice got put in the right place before anyone ever saw. Always.

In the kitchen, she found Charlie and Ginny sitting at the counter, both of them absorbed in their phones. "Ready, guys?" she asked cheerily, as if she'd been planning this little outing to a brilliant tropical island for months.

The twins got up but didn't speak, and Alice supposed that would have to do. She smiled brightly at them, wondering if they could see through her façade. *Probably*, she thought, keeping the grin hitched in place. "Charlie, do you want to drive?"

Hope lit his face. "Really?"

"Really." She took the keys out of her purse and handed them to her son. "You're not going to kill us on the way to the airstrip, are you?" She laughed as he rolled his eyes and ignored Ginny as she complained that Charlie got to drive more than she did.

After all, Alice was very good at ignoring the things that bothered her, and she could deal with Ginny when they arrived at the ridge, miles and miles from the concerns and worries of this insufferable place.

"ALICE!" ROBIN'S VOICE LIFTED ABOVE THE OTHERS, AND Alice's pulse picked up. She hadn't realized how comforting a kind voice could be. "Alice, over here."

She turned to her right, and the sight of the petite, blonde woman brought a smile to Alice's face. "Robin." She veered to her friend, almost forgetting she'd brought two surly fourteen-year-olds with her. "This way, guys," she added as an afterthought.

Robin balanced on her tiptoes, because she'd never grown much over five-foot-two inches. And she hadn't changed a bit. Still blonde, with perfectly blue eyes. Robin had never had many blemishes, and she didn't now either. She didn't struggle with acne, or hair that didn't poof perfectly the way she'd wanted it. Now, with the current styles, her hair fell straight down her back, and it looked kissed by the sun itself.

She must be starving, Alice thought as she reached Robin and the two hugged. Robin had been trim and tan and talented in high school, and she still was. The woman looked like she'd barely graduated from Cove High, without many wrinkles, crow's feet, or laugh lines. Alice wondered how much she'd spent to keep her skin smooth, and she was dying to ask her how many calories she ate every day.

As if on cue, her stomach growled, and Robin pulled away, the joy on her face very real. "Are you hungry? I bet we have time to grab something."

"I'm always hungry," Alice said with a laugh, as if she were kidding. She stepped back, remembering how tight she needed to keep her real thoughts laced. "Guys, this is Robin Golden, one of my friends from high school." She indicated her children, who had been properly trained to meet princes and presidents. "Charlie and Ginny," she said, smiling at them, a stream of pride moving through her as they both put a charming smile on their face.

"Nice to meet you," Charlie said, reaching out his hand.

Robin glanced at Alice, clearly impressed. "And you."

"Ma'am," Ginny said.

"Okay," Robin said. "I'm the same age as your mother." She grinned at the twins. "Now come on. I know just what your mother wants to eat." She beamed at Alice, that knowing glint in her eye exactly the same. No matter what had happened over the past twenty-seven years, it hadn't erased their bond.

Alice felt like she'd changed a ton, and likely Robin had too. But in this one moment, they were seventeen again, and they could communicate without words.

"Lobster mac," they said together, and the laughter that spilled from Alice's mouth afterward was probably the first real laugh she'd made in at least a decade.

CHAPTER FOUR

Kristen Shields entered the office her husband had kept in their small, cliffside home. She'd rarely came in here while Joel was alive, and now she faced the task of cleaning out the cramped space.

Joel could probably be labeled a hoarder, as the entire back wall was stuffed with bookcases that had papers, books, notebooks, and receipts spilling from them. The thought of looking at each thing in this office and deciding to keep it or not brought a powerful wave of weariness to Kristen's entire being.

As if the Good Lord above knew she couldn't face such a thing alone, knocking sounded on the door behind her. She'd barely turned when Robin said, "Knock knock."

Kristen paused and took a deep breath. She and Robin had remained close over the years, and she appreciated the woman the shy, only-made-of-legs girl had grown into. She did want Robin to accompany her to the funeral home, because Jean had left the island that morning, and Rueben didn't know when she'd be home. And Clara—

"Hey," Kristen said, cutting off the painful thought of her daughter. She pasted a smile on her face as she entered the living room, where Robin stood clutching a white paper bag in her fingers. She still ran every morning, and she seemed to have made Kristen's house part of her workout, because she still wore a pair of black leggings and a black jacket that clung to her curves.

"Look who I brought." Robin's smile seemed made of marshmallows and cotton candy—so utterly sweet—as she moved to the side to reveal another woman.

Kristen's breath caught in her throat, choking her. "Alice." Her hand fluttered up near her throat, the tears coming instantly. "Oh, come here, child."

Alice's eyes gleamed like wet glass as she crossed the room and embraced Kristen. She pressed her eyes closed, remembering everything about this girl. The way she'd braid her hair to try to make it more interesting. How she'd shown up one night at the lighthouse with a bright red face, a rash that had come on suddenly after a facial mask gone bad. The academic scholarship she'd earned to Harvard, and how she'd supported her husband through law school by working at a family law firm until her children were born.

"How are you?" she managed to ask through her

memories and emotions. She stepped back but kept her hands on Alice's shoulders. "You're so bony."

Alice reached up and wiped her eyes, glancing at Robin. The two of them were almost cut from the same skin, though Alice certainly had more of an image and reputation to maintain. "I'm not bony, Kristen," she said, and she seemed so...refined. Like she knew exactly where to put every word, and exactly how to enunciate it as it came out of her mouth.

"We brought those lemon tarts you like," Robin said, moving into the kitchen while Kristen and Alice looked at one another as if they'd never met. Kristen knew better than most how much time and circumstances could change a person, and she hardly recognized the woman in front of her.

Alice was so unhappy, and Kristen had seen that inside her before. She'd also seen her radiate pure joy, and she desperately wanted that woman to come out.

As Robin bustled around the kitchen, unloading the plastic containers holding the pastries, Kristen asked, "How are the children?"

"Good," Alice said, her voice a bit too high. "Good. They're with my dad and Della today." She nodded and looked around the living room. It too held too many things for its size. Kristen had never minded the clutter, the extra furniture, the single path through things to the hallway. Until now.

"This is such a lovely place," Alice said, so much falsehood in her voice and eyes that Kristen could only stare at her.

Did people believe her when she spoke like that?

She shook herself, trying to find something else they could talk about. "How's Frank?" Kristen asked.

Darkness gathered across Alice's face, but she swept it away with little effort. Instead of answering, she sucked in a breath. "Is that the picture of us on the sailboat?" She moved away from Kristen and picked up a framed picture sitting on the bookcase. "Oh, wow," she said, laughing. "It is."

But even her laugh sounded fake.

She looked at Kristen and held up the picture as if she'd never seen it. "Remember this day?"

"Of course." Kristen stepped around the end table where Joel had kept all of the many remote controls. She didn't even know what they all did, and she'd have to sort that out too. She took the picture from Alice and gazed down at the five girls smiling for all they were worth. "It was our first successful launch."

"My shoulders hurt for days after that," Alice said, still chuckling. At least she seemed more real now. More like the self-confident girl that had pulled and pulled to get the sailboat out into the current.

"Lemon tarts," Robin announced, and Kristen started to put the picture frame back in its spot. It wasn't hard to know where to set it, because she wasn't the world's best housekeeper, and she hadn't dusted this bookcase in at least a month. Or a year.

So the blue piece of paper stuck partway under the books that provided the backdrop for the Seafaring Girls caught Kristen's eye. It had no dust on it and looked as if someone had put it there quite in a hurry.

Alice moved into the kitchen, but Kristen took a moment to set the picture frame down and pick up the paper. It was folded in the traditional way, into thirds, as if someone was getting ready to put it in an envelope and mail it off.

She had no idea what she'd find as she unfolded the paper, because Joel had so many writings and scribbles lying around the house. He'd had a real affinity for words, and he was constantly putting down poems or words he liked, stuffing the papers into every drawer and crevice he could. He'd studied four languages over the years, and he'd made flash cards of the signs for American Sign Language.

Words fascinated him, and when he'd started the chemotherapy treatments, she'd found a vocabulary app for him to help him keep his mind sharp despite the drugs.

The paper made a crinkling sound as she opened it, and her eyes scanned the words at the top quickly.

Kris,

I have to tell you something, and I don't know how.

A letter. Kristen loved the nickname he had for her,

and she'd often received letters from her husband throughout their life together. She'd open them while he smiled at her, secrets in his gaze that would be revealed as she read about their trip to New York City he'd planned or the anniversary dinner at Pearl Island's premier restaurant.

But the more she read this letter, the faster her heart raced.

I haven't always been faithful to you. There were many things pulling my attention from you, from our marriage. The sea, the school, the lighthouse.

They'd both done more than tend to the lighthouse, which was a part-time job at best. Joel had coached recreational baseball and worked at the high school, coaching girl's track. His personality was perfect for coaching, because he possessed a no-nonsense approach to guiding teens who didn't want to be guided, tempered with his more artistic, writing side.

Kristen had worked with the township of Five Island Cove, teaching and training girls to be masters of the sea, from fishing to sailing to everything in between, in the Seafaring Girls program. The day that program had been canceled had been a terrible one for her, and if she were being honest, without Robin, she'd have drifted a lot more than she had.

She read over the words again, not sure what Joel had been trying to say. The pencil was obviously old, most of it smeared slightly in some way. When he wrote this, surely he was just feeling like he hadn't connected to her in a while. They'd been through years where it felt like they were two ships passing in the night, both of them working to make ends meet, keep the lighthouse functioning, and maintain their family dynamic.

Kristen pushed away thoughts of her Clara, who hadn't yet confirmed that she'd be returning to the cove in time for the funeral. Joel wasn't a god, and not everything had been perfect between them. He yelled too much. Drank sometimes. Had very strong opinions.

Clara had butted heads with him since the age of two, but surely she'd come to the islands for the funeral. He was her *father*.

She read the letter for a third time, the chatter of Alice and Robin in the background and fading fast. They'd ask her what she was reading in a minute, and she needed to refold the paper and join them in the kitchen.

But when she saw the erased words beginning a new paragraph in the letter, she couldn't help tilting it to try to get a better idea of what her husband had written and then erased.

After several long seconds of struggling, her brain finally seized onto the three words there.

And another woman.

The breath left her body; the blue paper fluttered to the ground; a moan came from her mouth as she reached for something to steady her.

"Hey," Robin said, appearing in front of Kristen. "Are you okay?"

She should've just nodded. Tacked that smile back on her face. Joined the others in the kitchen. Drowned her feelings in lemon curd and crumbling pie crust. They'd simply think she was grieving her husband, and she could deal with this in private.

She looked down at the ground, where the blue paper had landed, the top and bottom flaps sticking straight up.

"What's that?" Robin bent to pick it up, her hand extending toward the blue page as if in slow motion. And Kristen couldn't stop her.

CHAPTER FIVE

R obin read the letter, some of the life and warmth inside her draining away. "What does this mean?"

"I don't know," Kristen said. "I haven't seen it before."

Robin looked back at the words, trying to put them in the right order so they made sense. "I haven't always been faithful to you. There were many things pulling my attention from you, from our marriage. The sea, the school, the lighthouse."

She looked up as Alice joined them, stirring her coffee. She peered over Robin's shoulder, reading the note herself, though Robin had just read it out loud.

"You were probably just busy," Alice said. "I don't see Frank very often. Out of our sixteen years together, I think we've been together maybe two or three years total." She looked at Robin, who didn't comprehend such a thing.

But she seized onto the idea and ran with it. "Yeah,"

she said. "Duke can be gone for a while sometimes, when the fishing is good." She looked at Kristen, who stood absolutely still. Her face had turned a strange shade of gray, and Robin's worry tripled.

"You should sit," she said to her, folding the paper and tucking it under her arm. "I'll get you a treat and a cup of coffee." She helped Kristen over to the armchair, her curiosity shooting through the roof. "Did you know what he meant?" She straightened and went into the kitchen, placing the blue letter on the counter and turning back to make sure Kristen hadn't fainted.

Kristen shook her head. "We did have some very trying years, there for a while."

"Everyone does," Alice said with a sigh as she sat on the sofa. "In fact, I didn't even tell Frank that I was coming here." She gave a light laugh that Robin could tell covered something deep and painful. "And I brought the kids with me. Not that he'll really care."

Kristen and Robin both looked at Alice, who hid behind her coffee cup for a few seconds. Robin had no idea what to say. Alice had seemed to love Frank in the beginning of their marriage, but she obviously wasn't overly fond of him now.

"He works in New York, right?" Robin asked, still puzzling through the letter from Joel to Kristen.

"That's right," Alice said. "Big, fancy lawyer." Her voice slurred slightly, and Robin strode over to her.

"What did you put in your coffee?" She took the cup

from Alice and lifted it to her nose. "Alice. This is mostly vodka."

Alice reached for the cup, but Robin held it out of her reach. "No, it's far too early for this much alcohol." She took the cup back into the kitchen and rinsed it down the sink. "Where did you even get it?"

"I know where Kristen keeps the good stuff." Alice giggled again, and Robin wanted to throttle her. Didn't she know they were here for Kristen? This wasn't a vacation where she could get drunk by ten a.m. and someone would take care of everything—including her two teenagers.

Robin shook her head in a tight back-and-forth movement as she started opening cupboards. Kristen shouldn't be drinking either, as she lived above an uneven path that bordered cliffs. She found the vodka bottle in the cupboard next to the refrigerator and she stepped over to the sink.

"She is no fun," Alice said.

Annoyance shot through Robin as the clear liquid went down the drain. "Someone has to be responsible, and I can see it's not going to be you."

"I'm responsible," Alice said, her light brown eyes flashing. She was on a plane reserved for the wealthy and royal, and Robin had no idea how to talk to her anymore. She reminded Robin of her mother, who held herself on such a high pedestal, no one would ever be able to reach her standards. Robin knew she'd never been able to.

"I do everything around that house," Alice continued. "Frank's never there, and I'm the one doing the homework, and teaching the twins to drive, and managing everything." She stood up and stalked toward Robin.

Robin glared at her as the last of the liquid left the upturned the bottle. "Drink on your own time. You have to take a ferry back to Rocky Ridge and drive back to your dad's."

"Nope," Alice said, popping the P as she leaned into the counter. "I got a hotel here tonight. The kids are staying there for the week. My dad's going to take them out on the sailboat in the morning."

"Oh, well, in that case, you should've stayed with me." Robin didn't really want to subject her family and house to Alice's scrutiny, but she had to offer. "Eloise is staying with me too, but she won't be here for a few more days." She capped the empty bottle and placed it in the recycling bin.

"I'd be happier in a hotel," Alice said, and Robin believed her. A stitch caught in her breath at the same time. When Alice had trouble in the past, she'd come to Robin's house, not a hotel.

"If you change your mind—"

"He cheated on me," Kristen said, and both Alice and Robin looked at her. They exchanged a glance, but otherwise, Robin didn't dare move.

"What are you talking about?" Alice asked, some of her ultra-shine sliding back into position.

"That letter," Kristen said, shooting to her feet too fast for a woman her age. "Look. Come look." She sounded frantic, and Robin met Alice's gaze again. Her worry was explicit, and Robin's own anxiety lifted.

"Right here," Kristen jabbed at an empty line on the page. "He erased it. It said, 'and another woman.'" She straightened, the letter in her fingers now. She waved it, sending it crinkling. "He cheated on me."

"Where?" Alice asked, and Kristen showed her again. Alice peered at the paper, her eyes narrowing and then widening. "Wow, look at that."

Robin really wanted to see it, so she joined the other two women at the counter. She didn't want to believe them. Joel Shields had been like a second father to her, and she'd held him in high regard her whole life.

There was no way he could've cheated on Kristen. She looked at Kristen, who wore anguish in every line of her face.

She studied the paper again, and she too could see the words. *And another woman.* Written and then erased. A letter never to be finished.

"When did he write this?" she asked.

"I have no idea," Kristen said, running both hands through her hair. Some pieces of it stuck up haphazardly, and she looked around wildly. "It could've been sitting there for a week or a year or a decade." In the next moment, a primal yell came from her mouth, and she reached for the glass sitting on the counter.

"Kristen," Alice yelled, but Robin just got out of the way. Kristen hurled the glass against the cabinet, and the glass exploded into thousands of tiny shards.

"Okay, we'll deal with this later," Alice said in a very business-like tone. In her world, she probably had a servant to clean up things like this. "Come on. To the lighthouse."

"Yes," Robin said, grasping onto the symbol of safety and security. "Let's go to the lighthouse."

Kristen wailed, the sound quickly quieting into more subdued crying, but she allowed Alice to lead her out of the cottage. Robin panted, taking in the ruined lemon tarts and the pieces of glass on the blue paper.

The small space crammed with too much furniture threatened to smother her. The old paint on the walls seemed dirtier than she'd ever seen it. All the papers, the files, the folders, she now viewed as weapons.

A scream gathered in her stomach, coiling and tensing like a tornado did. She'd been in this house so many times, and she'd never noticed all the ugliness of it.

She turned and left it all behind.

She did not follow Alice and Kristen down to the lighthouse, but instead marched further into the trees, pulling her phone from her pocket. She often ran along a path lined with trees like this, the tall thin trunks that would soon be filled with leaves. Robin took comfort from them every morning, but today, the trees were only made of wood, representing fences in her life that Robin still hadn't been able to scale.

She'd called AJ twice already, and the woman hadn't even had the decency to answer the phone. Kelli had answered the first time and said she'd call Robin back in fifteen minutes. But she hadn't, and she didn't answer Robin's second call.

Panting and with burning calves, she tapped to dial AJ again. "Come on, AJ," she muttered, keeping the anger very close to her heart so she wouldn't have to feel too deeply. "Answer the phone."

AJ did not answer, and her chirpy voicemail further irritated Robin. She hung up without leaving a message and immediately dialed AJ again. "I swear, if you don't answer—"

"Robin, hi," AJ said, as if Robin hadn't tried to call her three times already. "What's up?"

"What's up?" Robin barked into the phone. "Do you even know what we're dealing with here?"

Of course she wouldn't. AJ never was the one to stick around and deal with the aftermath of a situation. She was the girl who snuck off before drama happened and returned only minutes before it was time to go home, often carrying her shoes and once with her shirt on backward.

"I'm sorry?" AJ asked, her voice definitely cooler.

Robin breathed in through her nose, the way she did when dealing with her fifteen-year-old. "AJ," she said, forcing a measure of kindness and cheer into her voice. "Poor Kristen is just...she needs us. She needs *all* of us."

AJ said nothing, and Robin had forgotten her carefully constructed arguments for why she needed to get on the next plane to Five Island Cove.

"If you could find a way—*any* way—to get here for the funeral, she would appreciate it," Robin said.

"I'm covering a story in Miami this week," AJ said.

"So you know Joel Shields died."

"Yes."

"How?"

AJ sighed as if Robin were being difficult on purpose. "When you called the first time, I did a search. Nothing ever happens there, and it wasn't hard to find the news."

"He wrote the obituary himself," Robin said, a bit of fondness creeping into her voice. Kristen had said he'd planned everything, right down to when and where to have the funeral, to make things easier for her.

Now, Robin didn't think so. Joel had planned everything for his own funeral out of guilt. He didn't want Kristen to have to do anything for him once she learned the truth about who he was.

"Yeah, well, I could tell," AJ said.

"What does that mean?" Robin asked.

"It means it was the biggest load of lies I've ever read," AJ bit out.

"AJ," Robin said, shocked. AJ had never said anything bad about Joel. She'd left the island for college, sure, just like a lot of people. But Robin had never gotten the impression that AJ didn't like reuniting on Five Island Cove.

It had been a while since Robin had put something together for the five of them, and she closed her eyes and put one hand on the back of her neck. She felt too hot; nothing was how she'd imagined it would be.

"He was your coach," she finally said.

"Yeah, so who do you think knew him better? Me or you?"

Robin honestly could not handle any more revelations right now. But she had to ask. "What are you saying?"

"Nothing," AJ said. "I'm saying nothing. But I honestly don't know if I'll be able to make it."

Robin swallowed, not above begging. "Please try. Even if it's just for a day."

"Five Island Cove is a pain to get to," AJ said.

"And yet, thousands of tourists do it every year," Robin shot back.

AJ burst out laughing, and Robin smiled despite herself. When she quieted, she said, "I'll see what I can do. The sports world doesn't stop for funerals."

"No, but maybe we should," Robin said. A few seconds passed, and she gazed up at the clear, blue sky, wondering how many more secrets she'd uncover that day. "AJ, what happened...I mean...did something happen between you and Joel?"

"I'm sure it's all documented in that office of his," AJ said. "Have you started cleaning that out yet?"

"No," Robin said, her mouth suddenly dry. "You think...he wrote it down?"

"The man wrote *everything* down," AJ said. "Literally everything. And Robin, if I come to this, you have to know it will be the single hardest thing I've done in my life. And I've lost babies and never been married."

"I—AJ." Robin's heart bled for the girl she'd once known so well. "Why?"

"I left Five Island Cove because of Joel Shields, and I don't really mourn his death."

The words landed like bombs in Robin's ears. "I don't understand," she managed to say.

An alarm sounded on AJ's end of the line, and she said, "I have to go. I'll let you know if I'm coming or not." The line went dead, and Robin let her hand fall back to her side.

AJ didn't mourn his death. Unbelievable. Inconceivable.

What had he done?

Robin pictured the frail form of Joel Shields as he laid in bed in the very house she'd just been in. She'd brought him lobster bisque and garlic bread when he could stomach food. She'd sat with Kristen while she wept. She'd never suspected anything about Joel.

AJ might not even come to his funeral, because of what he'd done. Robin's imagination churned, and she turned back to the house, suddenly anxious to go through it. At the same time, she thought she'd rather light a match and toss it into the pile of papers and books and folders than find out any more unsavory details about Joel's life.

Sighing, she rolled her neck, trying to find a way to get AJ there. She wasn't sure why it was so important, only that it was.

She lifted her phone again and tapped to Kelli's name. "Get your game on," she muttered to herself. "Get them all here. Find all the rotten roots and rip them out." It was a lesson Robin had learned from her mother, though neither of them were very good at it—at least not with each other.

She dialed Kelli anyway, ready to plead, beg, and turn tables if she had to. They just all had to get here.

CHAPTER SIX

K elli Thompson eyed the phone like it could grow spiky needles and stab her. Robin would not give up, Kelli knew that. She'd worked with the girl on a school dance once, and when the gym flooded, it was Robin who'd called an emergency meeting and figured out a new plan. Everyone had loved Robin, and she'd led effortlessly.

The phone stopped ringing, and relief flowed through Kelli. She had a new aerobics routine to choreograph, and she should definitely get out to the garden today to make sure Julian could take Parker out there on the weekend and get something planted for the edible neighborhood they participated in with the other people on the block.

Kelli didn't possess a green thumb, and most plants died when she simply looked at them. She chalked it up to the sea water she carried in her blood, though she hadn't been back to Bell Island in Five Island Cove since Parker was a baby.

Not even for her father's own funeral.

The phone rang again, and Kelli figured she better just talk to Robin. Get it over with. "Hello?" she asked, as if she didn't know who would be on the other end of the line.

"Kelli," Robin said brightly. "You never called back." The woman had guts, that was for sure.

"Sorry, my son needed me," she said. She couldn't exactly remember what had happened the other day when Robin had called. She'd left the phone in the kitchen and stumbled down the hall to her bedroom, where she closed the door and collapsed onto the bed. The panic that washed over her didn't allow her to know how much time passed or what she'd been thinking or anything.

Parker had found her there, asked if he could have some graham crackers, and left her alone again.

Even now, talking to Robin again, her skin broke out in a clammy sweat.

"I know you don't want to come to Joel's funeral," Robin said. "But Kristen just found something really damaging, and she needs us. She needs *you*."

Kelli sighed, because while she knew Robin wouldn't give up, she hadn't expected her to play dirty. "When's the funeral?" she asked.

"Next Saturday," she said. "You're in Jersey, right? It's

an in and out trip. Here and back. You could fly in that morning and leave on Sunday morning. It would be enough. Kristen just wants to see you."

Kelli could picture Kristen perfectly in her mind. She had dark auburn hair that had likely gone gray by now, as it had started to lose its color the last time she'd seen her. But her dark, green-hazel eyes would be the same. She'd look at Kelli and know instantly what she needed, whether that was a hug or a chocolate chip cookie or simply someone to sit with.

She'd been there for Kelli through her parents' divorce, and she'd been there when Kelli's father had lost his business and humiliated the whole family when the allegations of fraud came up.

"I have to talk to my boss," Kelli said, continuing to hedge. She did have to talk to Kevin, but she could get the time off. She was teaching aerobics and yoga at a gym, not teaching anyone how to do brain surgery. She could get another instructor to cover for her with a few texts. "And Julian. Parker's in school, and I take him and pick him up every day."

"So you'll stay longer than the weekend?" The hope in Robin's voice could've filled buckets and buckets.

"I don't know," Kelli said, thinking now of her mother. The last time she'd been home was just after Parker had been born, and the boy was eight years old now and in third grade. Her mother had come to New Jersey a few times, and she sent cards for everyone's birthdays, Christmas, Mother's and Father's Day, all of it.

Guilt pulled against her stomach until Kelli could barely stand under the weight of it. "I have to go," she said, her voice right on the edge of breaking. "I'm teaching aerobics in a few minutes."

"Okay," Robin said. "Please let me know, Kel."

"I will." She hung up quickly and took a deep breath through her nose. She would not panic again. She had techniques to help her through desperate moments like this, and she stared at the notebook in front of her that she'd been using to choreograph. One item. Think about that one thing.

She did, breathing in and out until she felt like she wouldn't fall completely to pieces. Her hand shook slightly as she lifted her pencil again and made another note. She tapped play on her phone, and the music blared out of the Bluetooth speaker. She rewound it and did small movements for the items she'd already put in the dance.

When she finished the new routine, her mind immediately flew right back to Five Island Cove. It seemed that Kelli couldn't ignore the pull to return, and she supposed it was time anyway.

She'd seen the Seafaring Girls a few years ago, and she'd enjoyed that. They'd gathered just across the river and enjoyed a weekend in the city together, and Kelli wished Robin had been calling to ask her availability for another get-together like that.

Cinching everything tight, she dialed her mother to tell her the good news. She'd probably cry, and that would only add to the mountain of guilt Kelli had swallowed and was currently trying to figure out how to live with.

CHAPTER SEVEN

Eloise stepped out of the small airport on Diamond Island and moved out of the stream of people so she could stop and take a breath. For a while there, it had been hard to breathe in Five Island Cove, but now the air went down just like it did in Boston.

She continued to the car she'd rented, in no hurry to get to the ferry and continue her trip. Her mother still lived in the cove, on the island of Sanctuary Island, where Eloise had grown up. She'd met Wesley Daniels in high school, and he'd gone to Boston University a year ahead of her.

They'd married too young, Eloise knew that now. Not only that, but Wesley had not wanted a woman who thought for herself. So he and Eloise always seemed to be on opposite sides of decisions that needed to be made. He had followed her to Harvard, though he wasn't continuing his education past a bachelor's degree.

She remembered how they'd both wanted a child, but she was beyond grateful that she hadn't been able to get pregnant. She couldn't imagine being a single mother, having to deal with Wes all the time to arrange visitation and child support.

As it was, she hadn't heard from him since their divorce was finalized, almost eighteen years ago. She'd dated a man here and there, but nothing had ever taken off and become serious. And at this point, Eloise wasn't looking for anything other than her next good meal and the reality television shows she liked.

She did love the beaches here though, and the ferries ran every twenty minutes from Diamond Island to Sanctuary, the two biggest islands in the cove. She could catch the next one, or the one after that.

She'd arrived a day earlier than she'd told Robin she would, and she towed her carryon behind her with one hand while she carried her two cats in the carrier she'd put under her seat for the short flight to Five Island Cove.

She'd told her mother she'd be staying with Robin after their brief visit, because it would be much easier to get to Kristen's to help if she wasn't on Sanctuary Island. Plus, Eloise could only handle her mother in less-than-twenty-four-hour doses, but she didn't want to tell her that.

After pulling off the main road and into a parking lot,

she got out of the car and shed her sweater. She always traveled with a sweater, as airplanes were usually cold. Eloise was always prepared for anything and everything, right down to the bottle of water she'd purchased in the Boston airport so she'd have something to drink when she got here. After all, she knew herself, and she knew she was always thirsty when she landed.

She locked the car, though there was no one else around, and headed up and over the swells of sand. The cats would be fine for a few minutes.

The water spread before her, and she imagined she could see all the way to Nantucket. When she and the other Seafaring Girls got a few minutes alone on the beach, they'd all tried to see the smudge of land on the horizon. And sometimes, on a very clear day, someone would spot it.

The weather today was a bit angrier, and clouds foamed in the sky above the ocean. Eloise went all the way to where the water kissed the sand, kicking off her shoes so she could feel the surf against her skin. A sense of relaxation came over her that she'd never felt anywhere but in Five Island Cove.

If only she could remember this feeling every time she thought about the place she'd grown up, and not that her father had gotten so drunk one night, he'd beaten her and her mother, then gotten into a bar fight and arrested. Not only that, but after she and Wes had divorced, he'd come back to Sanctuary Island for a couple of years until his death. Eloise had hosted her mother at her brownstone in Boston those years.

She drew in a long, deep breath, listening to the constant roar of the waves. Down the beach a bit, a man ran with his dog, coming her way. Eloise would stay for another moment, and then she'd go. Her footprints would be washed away by the time the man got to the spot where she'd stood, and she wondered if the footprint her life had left on the world would be erased as easily.

Before she knew it, a whistle rent the air, and Eloise looked to her right. The man yelled something too, but he was still too far away for it to be comprehended.

The dog, however, was nearly upon Eloise.

She didn't even have time to yelp before the huge animal was upon her, his thick tail wagging as if they were best friends. He jumped up on her, and while Eloise carried a few extra pounds, she couldn't shoulder the lurch of a dog the size of a small pony.

The man whistled again, yelling, "Prince!" as Eloise went down. She cinched her eyes shut, thinking this was it for her. But the dog hadn't barked once, and all she got was a severe licking with the dog's huge tongue.

"Prince." The man dragged the dog off of Eloise, the sound of his panting almost as loud as the waves now washing against Eloise's body. "Stay. No. Stay." He spoke in a commanding voice, and Prince whined, but listened.

"I'm so sorry," the man said, coming back to Eloise. She'd managed to roll to a sitting position so she wasn't a complete lump on the ground. He extended his hand, and Eloise looked up at him.

He had the body of a runner, with plenty of tan skin and tight muscles. Her dormant female hormones leapt as she put her hand in his, and he pulled her effortlessly to her feet. "He's still a puppy in a lot of ways, and he gets so excited when he sees other people." He sucked at the air again. "There's usually no one here, so I let him off the leash." He held up one hand, palm out, and the dog whined again.

Eloise liked the way his voice slid into her ears and tickled. She cleared her throat and reached up to her hair, finding half of it wet. Pure embarrassment moved through her as she tried to comb some of the foam and sand out of the strands glued to her head.

"Do you need a towel?" he asked. "Or do you live around here?" He cocked his head at her. "I don't think you do, because I swear I know everyone on the island. But you look familiar."

"Do I?" Eloise asked, her first contribution to the conversation.

"Yeah." The man narrowed his eyes, as if squinting at her would jog his memory. "I definitely know you. Maybe a younger version of you. What year did you graduate?"

She gave a light laugh, cutting it off when she realized how flirtatious it sounded. "That's like asking my age."

A smile touched the man's lips. "I'm Aaron Sherman." He extended his hand, but Eloise just stared at him. Of course she'd run into Aaron Sherman. "I'll pay for any cleaning or anything." He pulled his hand back, the moment turning awkward when she didn't shake it. "I'm not hard to find. I'm the Police Chief. Just stop by the department, and someone will know where I am." He gave her that grin again, one Eloise had seen countless times before, usually in her own fantasies.

"All right, Prince," he said, turning as if he'd run away now.

"Aaron," she blurted out, trying to find the professional inside her. "Sorry, I was just so shocked." She touched her own chest as he looked at her, waiting for more of an explanation. "I'm Eloise Hall."

That smile returned, and Aaron snapped his fingers. "Of course." His laughter filled the sky, and he stepped right into her and drew her into a hug. She couldn't help but laugh with him as she patted him awkwardly on his bare back. "Eloise Hall. Look at you." He stepped back and did exactly that, head to toe.

Eloise grew much too warm, her smile seemingly stuck in place.

"You look great. What brings you back to the island?"

"Joel Shields's funeral," she said. "Kristen was my seafaring leader for years."

Aaron cooled almost instantly, nodding. "Yes, the funeral is next weekend."

"Yeah," she said. "I'll be here until at least then. Maybe a bit longer." She didn't have another class until

September, and she could stay in the cove until then. And for some strange reason, she wanted to.

He brought the smile back. "We should get dinner or something," he said. "Catch up on old times."

"Okay, yeah," she said, not quite sure if he'd just asked her out or not. "Sounds good."

"Is AJ coming?" he asked, and Eloise's fantasies and hopes came crashing back to reality. Of course he'd be interested in AJ. Everyone in high school had been, and she'd had more boyfriends than the other four of them put together.

"You know, I haven't heard," Eloise said. "I know Robin was trying to get her to come, but I'm not sure."

Prince barked then, and Aaron's attention diverted to him. "Seriously, stop by the department if there's anything I need to replace." He gestured to the dog. "Come on, boy. Right here." He took off down the beach again, and Eloise stood in the sand, watching him until he disappeared from her sight.

Then she remembered she was half-wet and losing daylight, not to mention the pair of felines waiting for her in the rental car. "Get a grip, El," she muttered to herself as she went back to the parking lot. Forty-five-year-old women didn't have island flings, or summer romances, or whatever it was that had gotten her heart thumping so hard at the sight of Aaron Sherman.

CHAPTER EIGHT

R obin wiped the kitchen counter, already late to get over to Kristen's. Duke had come home last night after a few days at sea, and Robin did love welcoming him back to their home, their family, their bed.

He'd bustled off with the kids to get them to school, and Robin didn't have to clean up after breakfast. But her habits hadn't died yet, and she couldn't stand to leave the kitchen a mess. Then she'd have to come back to dirty dishes and pots and pans she couldn't use to make dinner.

She hadn't been doing a whole lot of that either, though. As Mandie and Jamie entered their teen years, they only got busier and busier with friends, activities at school, and homework. And they were becoming more mature, independent girls, and Robin couldn't force them to sit at the dining room table until they'd eaten all of their vegetables anymore. They had their own tastes, their own likes and dislikes, and Robin had learned through several painful meals that her daughters weren't her.

It was an eye-opening thing for a parent—at least for Robin—to realize their offspring were actual people. Human beings, with their own ideas about the world. She'd worked hard to realize this, as she was fairly certain her mother still didn't know that Robin was her own person.

If Robin texted Mandie when school got out, her oldest daughter would probably make dinner. The fifteen-year-old had recently discovered she liked reading recipes and trying new things. It had been Duke who'd suggested they get one of those meal kit boxes for her to try, and Mandie's skills had started out rough but accelerated quickly.

Robin's chest pinched slightly, her emotions so close to the surface these days. Normally, she'd think of the fun-loving girl, straight-A student, she'd gotten in Mandie and feel a flash of pride. She'd smile as she wiped up toast crumbs and make everything smell like disinfectant.

But she wouldn't cry.

Now, she cried.

She sniffled, pulling back on the tears. She couldn't be broken when she showed up at the lighthouse this morning. She'd stayed yesterday as late as she'd dared, and then she'd come home just in time to kiss Duke when he walked in the house, smelling like salt, grease, and the slippery fish he caught for a living.

They'd showered together, and Robin loved the touch of her husband's heated hands on her skin. She loved that he was still excited to see her when he got home after several days at sea, and that she still held enough sexuality to arouse him just by slipping her hand around to the back of his neck.

After making love, Robin had left Duke to sleep while she'd snuck into the office and onto the computer. She needed to know everything she could about Joel Shields, and she'd printed numerous newspaper articles, some as old as forty years ago, when he and Kristen had first taken over as caretakers of the lighthouse, after her parents had turned it over to them.

In the few hours she'd researched and read, she did not find one single thing to indicate he was anything but the upstanding, kind-hearted, generous man she'd known. So he'd written one letter and pushed AJ too hard during her training. Everyone made mistakes, and Joel did write down more than the average person.

Not only that, but he'd probably just wanted the best for AJ. Robin remembered once when AJ had come back after her first year of college. She'd laid on the beach with Robin and told her how incredibly hard collegiate coaches were. How hard they pushed their athletes.

"They just want us to be the best we can be," AJ said. "We're not like normal people."

Robin distinctly remembered being annoyed by the comment, but simply agreeing. That was how she dealt with AJ and how everyone fawned over her. She just agreed. She told AJ her hair was the curliest and the highest—the fashion for the time. She told AJ she had every right to sleep with as many boys as she wanted, that her mother was stupid for being worried about things like sexually transmitted diseases and pregnancy.

Now, as a mother of teen girls, STDs and pregnancies were the stuff of Robin's nightmares. They'd been as a teenager too, and Robin hadn't entered into a sexual relationship until she'd met Duke and they'd decided to get married.

Her doorbell rang, and Robin pulled herself out of her thoughts. She tossed the rag into the sink and smoothed down her shirt. Before she could get to the door, it opened, and Alice walked in. "Good morning." She scanned Robin. "Don't you look perky?" She wore a smile as she came toward Robin, who still wore her running clothes from that morning.

After all of her research, she still couldn't sleep. So she laid in Duke's arms for a few hours and then slipped away to get her exercise in. Running was something she could control. Something that never changed. Something that produced the exact same results every time, and Robin didn't want to know how many pills she'd be on if she didn't run every morning.

"You look classy," she said to Alice as the woman reached her and kissed both of her cheeks. She wore a pair of skinny black slacks and a short-sleeved sweater with a sailboat on it. The kind of thing Robin saw trophy wives wear in fancy magazines about the homes and gardens in the Hamptons.

"I'm not sure I'm ready for today," Alice said.

"What are the kids doing today?"

"They've got the boat packed up for a few days at sea. My dad says the weather is 'superb' this week, and Charlie would literally be *throwing* daggers by ten a.m. if I brought him to clean out a house."

"I understand," Robin said, smiling at her friend. "Let me grab my purse, and we'll go."

"Is AJ really coming?" Alice asked.

"She said she'd try," Robin said. "Kelli said she'd be here. So I did the best I could."

"Eloise got in last night."

"Did she?" Robin grabbed her purse from the built-in desk in the kitchen and went back around the corner. "How do you know? She was supposed to stay with me after she gets here tonight."

"She only posts on social media when she travels," Alice said, holding up her phone. "And she posted last night. A picture of the beach—the one on the north side, so I know she was headed to the ferry to get over to Sanctuary."

"I hope she's okay," Robin said, her worry instant and unbidden. Worrying was one of Robin's superpowers, and she'd given up trying to stop doing it. "She probably just wanted to see her mother for one night." She thought of the two cats and how she hadn't exactly told Duke about their three houseguests coming that night.

"Why wouldn't she be okay?" Alice pinned Robin with a curious look, and Robin kicked herself for saying anything.

"Coming home isn't easy for her either," she said. In fact, Robin was surprised Eloise would fly in early to return to Sanctuary Island and see her mother.

"You two have secrets." Alice grinned like it was such a cute thing that Robin had other friends.

"All of us have secrets," Robin said, rolling her eyes. "Just like I'm the only one that knows you used to sneak over to Billy Bridge's cabin after lights out."

Alice blinked, shock traveling across her face for a moment, before she burst out laughing. "I forgot all about Billy Bridge." She leaned against the wall and fanned herself. "But wow, that was the best summer camp ever."

"I'll bet," Robin said.

Alice's smile stretched so much bigger now than it had only a minute ago. "Oh, come on. I wasn't AJ."

"No one is AJ," Robin said, opening the door to the garage and going out as she hit the button to lift the big door.

"I wonder what Billy is doing now," Alice mused as they got in Robin's SUV.

"He owns the ferry system," Robin said. "All of it. Every ferry from every island."

"Really?"

"Really, really," Alice said. "His uncle owned it while we were growing up, and he bought it, oh, I don't know. Five years ago or so? He's made a lot of improvements too." She backed out of her driveway. "Hey, what time do you get up?"

"Oh, not until seven," she said. "It was great to sleep in. When Frank's home—" She cut off. "I'm usually up early," she amended, keeping her gaze solidly out the passenger window.

Robin wanted to explore that further, but before she could find a tactful way to ask, her phone rang. Duke's number came up on the screen in her car, and she tapped the green phone icon. "Hey," she said.

"Hey, hot stuff," he said. "Are you gone already?"

"Yeah, just left," she said. She had not told him Alice was coming to the house this morning, because she knew she'd be gone before he got back, and Duke wasn't Alice's biggest fan.

He was an easy-going man, but he found Alice downright fake, and that was one thing he couldn't abide.

Wonder what he'd think if he knew who Joel really was. The thought popped into her head, and she hated that it was so clear and rang with so much truth.

"Dang," Duke said, a smile in his voice. "I was hoping we could sneak back to bed. I want—"

"Duke," Robin yelled over him, her whole face burning with bright heat. "Alice is in the car with me."

"Hi, Duke," Alice said, her smile even bigger now.

Duke swore, and that only caused Alice to laugh. She covered her mouth and kept it silent though, and pure mortification moved through Robin. She couldn't look at her friend and gripped the steering wheel instead.

"Listen," he said, clearing his throat. "I wanted to talk to you about Alaska again."

Robin practically stabbed at the screen, trying to get the Bluetooth to disconnect. Really? He was going to bring up Alaska with Alice in the car? No wonder he wanted to sneak back to bed after dropping the girls off at school.

She finally got her finger on the right button and the call transferred back to her phone. She picked it up from the console and held it to her ear. "Can we talk about this later?"

"Yeah," he said. "That's why I mentioned it. I want you to be thinking about it today."

"I don't see how it's going to be different than the last time we talked about it." She flicked her eyes left and right and pulled through the intersection.

"Bryan says they're desperate," he said. "The signing bonus is fifty thousand."

"Oh." Well, that did change things, didn't it? Robin and Duke had money, but just enough to pay for the suburban life on the island. When she had to admit it, she put things on a credit card sometimes, and they lived in her mother's old house, because she owned it and they paid her a nominal amount in rent.

Fifty thousand dollars was a very big incentive, especially for Duke to do the same thing in Alaska that he did here.

But for Robin...Alaska might as well have been the moon. It *was* the moon—a completely foreign landscape on a completely foreign planet.

"Think about it, baby," he said. "And if you're done early, come home. I'm lonely."

Robin's female parts burned, because it was so nice to be wanted. "Okay," she said, and that was all. She did not think she'd get done early—certainly not before the girls got out of school. "And Duke? I told Eloise she could stay with us while she's here. It's just a few nights."

"Okay," he said, easier than she'd thought he would.

"She has cats."

"Really, Robin?"

"Two," Robin said, glancing at Alice, who still looked one breath away from bursting into giggles. "I couldn't get her to come otherwise."

"Well, those felines are going to make me sneeze for days," he said, and Robin shook her head, eternally glad he wasn't still shouting through the speakers.

"I love you, Duke," she said. "I'll call you later."

"Okay," he said with resignation in his voice. The call ended, and Robin replaced the phone in the cup holder. "Sorry about that."

"Don't be sorry for me," Alice said. "That's the most action I've had in months."

Robin looked at her. "Really? You and Frank...?"

"Frank has women in the city," Alice said, immediately clapping one hand over her mouth. "Oh, my goodness. Did I say that out loud?"

"Yes," Robin said, her heart pricking for Alice. "He does, Alice? He cheats on you?"

"All the time," Alice said. "I've known for years. We agreed that he won't touch me when he's home, and I won't divorce him."

Robin could not comprehend a marriage like that. Was the money worth it? The house in the Hamptons? The prestige? Robin would rather have her debts and her bills and her hot husband dying for her to come home as quickly as she could. She'd never not known what to say to Alice, and Robin felt like she'd just stumbled off a merry-go-round, dizzy and disoriented.

"Alice—"

"I don't want to talk about this," Alice said, folding her arms. And Robin knew she wouldn't. Once she decided she wasn't going to talk, Alice was like a vault the President of the United States could put his deepest, darkest secrets in and trust they'd never come out.

"Sometimes Duke's gone a long time too," Robin said, her throat drying up. "It's hard. I'm so sorry."

Alice looked at her, her eyes wide. After a few seconds, she lowered her eyes. "I think this is quite a bit different than your husband going fishing for a few days and then coming home and showering you with love."

Robin couldn't even swallow. Of course it was. Her first

instinct urged her to make her point. She could make Alice see her point of view.

She bit back on that instinct. She was not her mother.

"You're right," she said instead, the words nearly tripping over her tongue. "It's not the same at all."

Alice tucked her hair as if she stood in front of the mirror and practiced it for situations exactly like this. "I'm not sure I've ever heard you tell me I'm right," she said.

Robin looked at her, a healthy amount of surprise moving through her, and then burst out laughing. Thankfully, Alice did too, and all the tension between them broke. A few minutes later, she pulled into the parking lot at the lighthouse, and the weight of the world returned to her shoulders.

"Okay," she said, sighing as she got out of the SUV. "Let's get through this day."

Alice didn't respond, and Robin looked at her to find her staring at the lighthouse. Robin followed her gaze and found Eloise stomping toward them. Her normally passive features twisted with rage or anguish, Robin couldn't tell which.

"He doctored my test scores," she said, waving a fistful of papers. Robin moved toward her, trying to make sense of what she'd said.

Tears ran down the woman's face, and Robin had never seen Eloise react like this, not even when her father had been led away by the police. "Eloise," she said. "Explain it to me."

"He fixed my test scores," she said again, the tears flowing down her face. The calm, studious, professional woman Robin knew Eloise to be crumbled right in front of her. "I shouldn't have even gotten in BU, let alone Harvard."

She opened her fingers and let the papers drift away, tipping her head back as she whispered, "Who am I now? My whole life has been a lie." She closed her eyes while Alice scrambled around to keep the papers from blowing away in the wind.

All Robin could hear was Eloise whispering into the sky, "Who am I now? Who am I now?" over and over again.

CHAPTER NINE

Kristen stared in disgust at the four-drawer filing cabinet. What else would she find inside those drawers? They felt like vaults, like somewhere only the devil himself would file his most important contracts.

First, the letter she'd had to deal with. After a long day of going through things in the living room, Alice and Robin had left her alone to the cottage she'd shared with Joel for the last few years. His scent still rested on the sheets, on every blanket, in the very air.

All Kristen could think as the sun had sunk behind the lighthouse was *Who was she? When did this happen? And the worst question of all: Why didn't I know?*

She'd never even suspected Joel of cheating on her. The man had worked long evening hours at the light-house, and sure, he went into town sometimes for a drink with friends. But town was only ten minutes from the shore, and he wasn't jetting off to other cities to meet women.

Kristen hadn't been able to go get the milk she needed for her coffee that morning. Every woman she saw could be Joel's mistress, and she didn't trust anyone's tears anymore. The clerk at the post office who'd shed a tear or two with her when she'd gone on Monday could have been shacking up with her husband.

She could've been anyone on the island, and Kristen knew everyone who lived here permanently. Maybe not from every island, but definitely Diamond Island. She wanted to rush down to Aaron Sherman at the police station and demand a list of every resident. She could eliminate women under, say, fifty. There couldn't be that many people left.

She'd find them, and she'd—

Kristen cut off the thoughts, realizing how tightly she'd started to clench her fingers. Knowing who the woman was wouldn't do any good; she knew that. Intellectually, she knew that.

Not only that, but the island had been hosting tourists for a solid fifteen years, and Joel could've had a fling with anyone coming in and out of the cove.

She turned when Robin said, "Kristen?"

Thank the heavens that Robin was here. She stepped over a huge pile of paper—what she and Eloise had started on—and over to the blonde woman. She hugged her tight, wishing such an embrace could keep everything inside.

If hugs could re-bury secrets, Kristen would hug every person she saw from now until the day she died.

"What's going on?" Robin asked. "Eloise is ranting about test scores, and Alice is trying to calm her down."

"I don't know," Kristen said. "She found something, and she said, 'oh, these are my SATs' and she sat and looked at them for a minute. When I realized how quiet she'd gotten, I asked her what was wrong." Kristen stepped away and swiped at her eyes. "I think I'm done for today."

Robin frowned around at the mess, but Kristen didn't care about it. She'd been living with piles and papers and a packed house for decades. "Should I make tea?'

"Finish the story," Robin said. "I'll make it." She stepped around the end tables, the bins with magazines, the floor lamp, and moved into the kitchen. When Kristen still didn't start talking, Robin gave her a pointed look.

"She held up a bunch of papers and said, 'these are not mine. But they have my name on them.' I didn't know what she was talking about. That's when she started jabbing at her phone, muttering to herself. A few minutes later, she jumped to her feet and said, 'he changed my test scores,' and ran out of the house." Kristen had lost track of time after that. Lost her train of thought as they started to derail in her mind.

Robin put a cup of brewed tea in front of her, and

Kristen realized she'd done it again. "You haven't heard a word I've said, have you?" Robin asked.

Kristen wrapped her icy fingers around the warm mug and shook her head.

"I said, I think you should let me and the other girls box up every single piece of paper here. Every file. Every single thing and take it back to my house for analyzation. We'll decide what to keep and what to throw away."

"No." Kristen shook her head. "I can't let you do that."

"Why not?"

"Because," she said.

"Because why?"

Annoyance streamed through Kristen, and she glared at Robin. "I'm not your teenage daughter."

"No," Robin said. "But you're stuck with me, and it's nine-thirty in the morning. We can't be done for today. If you're going to be done, we'll take it all back to my house and go through it without you."

"No," Kristen said, panic building in her chest.

"Why not?" Robin demanded again.

"Because," Kristen said. "I might be able to find out who his mistress was if I go through it." Her chest heaved, and she maintained eye contact with Robin until the door opened again.

Alice came in, one hand looped through Eloise's and one gripping a bunch of crinkled papers. "I think I got most of them," she said. She closed the door behind her, and Kristen just looked at the two women. They'd meant so much to her once; they still did. The three of them were the only lifeline Kristen had at the moment. Rueben hadn't been home last night when she'd gone down to the lighthouse, but later, the beam had been on, same as usual.

His wife had not come home, Kristen knew that. He probably hadn't answered the door, because he didn't want to answer Kristen's questions. She didn't want to ask them, but she had to know if Jean was going to be able to come to terms with her life on Diamond Island. And if not, what Rueben was planning to do.

The couple didn't have children yet, and while Kristen didn't want her son to suffer through a divorce, she knew that not all marriages survived.

She'd called Clara last night too, and her daughter hadn't answered. With both of her children dealing with issues of their own, Kristen literally had Robin, Alice, and Eloise.

She didn't want Joel to be the reason they suffered, and Eloise was definitely suffering. Her eyes and her nose held a red tint around the edges. Kristen could not stand the thought of hurting any of them, and instant anger shot to her head that Joel could do this to the people she loved.

To her.

Her insides quaked, and she didn't know how to make them stop.

"I made tea," Robin said, as if tea would fix everything. Kristen distinctly remembered how she'd made tea for the girls when only AJ had been asked to the prom. That night, the four of them had gathered at the lighthouse, and each of them baked a different kind of cookie, and they sat on the deck as the sun went down, eating and drinking and laughing.

The next year, Robin's gymnastics skills paid off, and she joined the cheerleading squad. After that, she had plenty of boys asking her to dances, and the crowd dwindled to Alice, Kelli, and Eloise.

The next year, it was just Eloise, and Kristen remembered going down to the kitchen in the subterranean level of the lighthouse to make cookies, leaving Joel and Eloise on the deck alone. They'd gotten along well, as Eloise loved talking about academic things, and Joel was constantly challenging her to think bigger, think broader.

Eloise had consulted with Joel about what field of science she should study. She'd come to him when she won the Academic Olympiad as a sophomore. She'd come to the lighthouse to show him her SAT scores, her face full of joy and light.

How had he changed them before she'd seen them?

Kristen got up and picked her way across the room, taking Eloise into an embrace that seemed to stitch some of the loose pieces of her heart back together. "I'm so sorry," she whispered. "I don't know what he did, but we will figure it out."

Kristen pulled back and looked at Eloise. "Okay?" She

held her by the shoulders and looked at Alice behind her. "We will. All of us. Together."

Eloise nodded, and pure relief streamed through Kristen. Maybe she wouldn't lose everything. She'd thought she'd lost the world when Joel took his last breath. Looking around, she realized how much more she had—and how much more she could lose—as she met Alice's eyes, Eloise's, and lastly Robin's.

"Come have tea," Robin insisted. "And I'll figure out some breakfast too." She started bumping around in the kitchen, pulling out eggs and bread and setting a pan on the stove. Kristen sat at the tiny table she and Joel had pushed into the corner of the cottage and sipped her tea, trying to find a piece of flat ground to stand on. Alice sat at the bar, pressing the papers down flat and organizing them. The process took a few minutes, and Eloise just stared straight ahead. Kristen wondered where her mind was, and when she'd land on blaming her.

"These are your SAT scores," Alice finally said as the scent of cinnamon and vanilla crisped on the bottoms of the French toast. She turned and looked at Kristen and then Eloise, who didn't even flinch. She looked back at Kristen. "You're saying these aren't the ones you submitted to BU?"

"I didn't submit them," Eloise said, her voice hollow. "Joel did. He helped me with all my college applications, because my father had just been arrested." Her eyelids fluttered, almost like she was replaying the time she'd spent with Joel, researching colleges and putting together the application fees.

Joel had come to Kristen one day, asking if they could afford to help Eloise apply to Boston University. "It's where she really wants to go," he'd said, and Kristen could still hear the echo of his voice in her ears.

She'd been told that the voice would be one of the first things she forgot about Joel. Right now, she was fine with that.

"I'm sorry," Kristen said again, angry that Joel wasn't there to say it himself. "But Eloise, you went to Boston University, and you did well. So well, you got into Harvard." She spoke with as much kindness as she could.

Eloise blinked again, this time her eyes landing on Kristen's. She nodded and even dared to reach out and pat her hand. "*You* did well at BU. *You* got into Harvard."

"Yeah," Robin said, grabbing onto the end of that rope and running. She set a plate of French toast on the table, along with a smaller plate of butter. "You've been teaching there forever, and you're good. So who cares about some test scores from literally thirty years ago?" She turned back to the kitchen and went to get the syrup from the microwave. "Now, let's eat, and we'll decide on what we want to do to go through all of this as quickly as possible."

Kristen took a piece of French toast and put it on one of the paper plates Robin had found somewhere. "I have to meet with the funeral director at three," she said.

"That's right," Robin said. "Is Clara coming?"

Kristen shook her head. She wasn't even sure where Clara was at the moment. She'd come back to the island the day before Joel's death, so she'd been there when he died. But she'd dissolved into a sobbing mess soon afterward, and she'd run out of the house without a word.

Something seethed in Kristen's stomach, and she only managed a few bites of breakfast. She noticed neither Alice nor Robin took any French toast at all, and Eloise ate one piece, seemingly without realizing she'd even done so.

"What's going on with Clara?" Robin asked. "And you don't have to say, but...I feel like there's something going on."

"There is," Kristen said. "She didn't get along with her father, and they fought about everything, every time they were in the same room together. Sometimes more than that." The Internet and texting made prolonging arguments easier than ever. She made a half-hearted attempt to cut another bite of toast. "I thought when he died...I don't know. She'd find a measure of forgiveness."

Alice sucked in a big breath and blew it out. "Well, maybe there's more to what they fought about than we know." She faced the living room, where the pile of paper remained. Joel's bookshelves, and cubbies, and that blasted filing cabinet.

"Maybe we should set the whole thing on fire." Kristen stared at the living room she used to describe as cozy, which was really just a nice way of saying small and cramped. She switched her gaze to Eloise next. She looked like she was seriously considering finding a book of matches.

"Nope," Robin said. "We're going to clean it up, clean it out." She took a deep breath, and Kristen wondered if she knew what she was saying. They could clean out the papers, the journals, the books, the files. But in so doing, she feared they'd have to open the closets of their lives and sweep those clear as well.

"Now." Robin stepped in front of them all. "Can I get volunteers, or am I going to have to assign each of you a job?"

CHAPTER TEN

Alice took another sip of tea, telling herself it contained enough calories to sustain her until lunch. Eloise had just said she was hungry, and she and Robin had left to go pick something up in town.

After Robin had given them all something to do—wisely pairing herself with both Eloise and Kristen—they'd worked mostly in silence. Robin would ask a question every now and then, and Kristen would answer it. The recycle bin kept getting fuller and fuller, while the box Kristen had brought out from one of the back bedrooms only had a few papers and journals in it.

Alice had been shredding receipts for a couple of hours now, and while it wasn't terribly exciting work, she enjoyed doing it. She imagined each faded, almost blue piece of paper was a piece of her life she wanted to let go of, and she relished watching it sliver into thin strands that curled along the ends.

She finished one drawer of files and tossed the now-empty file folders in the recycling bin. A sigh came out of her mouth, and she had the serious urge to eat the door off the refrigerator just to get to whatever food was inside.

Kristen looked up from the book she held in her hand. "You okay, dear?"

Alice smiled at her, and it didn't feel fake against her lips. The scent of dust hung in the air, and while this wasn't the house where Alice had hung out during some of the best times of her life and some of the worst, the woman was the same.

Kristen had been the mother Alice had lost at a pivotal point of her life. She'd told her everything would be okay when Alice didn't understand the world without her mother in it. She'd made seafood scampi with plenty of butter and cream, and Alice hadn't even thought twice about eating it.

As time had passed, the pain had lessened. Alice had stopped hearing her mother's voice telling her to get up and get ready for school or she'd be late. Her father had come back to the land of the living, and Alice had wondered if Jennifer Golden had ever said anything to him about taking care of his teenagers.

Things changed. Alice had changed.

But Kristen had not. Kristen had always been steady in her faith in Alice, and she feared that if Kristen knew the truth about her life, she'd be so upset. Alice was living that life, and she was upset about it sometimes.

Kristen always had a smile for Alice, along with a warm hug, and the exact right thing to say. This visit had been a bit stilted, but Alice understood in a way no one else could.

She hadn't answered Kristen's question, because she didn't know if she was okay. She hugged the older woman, glad when Kristen seemed to need Alice's strength as much as Alice needed hers.

No words came from her mouth. None were needed. Kristen was there, and that had always been all Alice needed. She should've known she'd never survive a marriage where her husband spent the week in another city, leaving her home alone to raise head-strong twins.

"We're back," Robin said, and Alice retreated into the kitchen, keeping her back to the new hustle and bustle as Eloise and Robin came into the cottage, bringing the scent of freshly baked bread with them.

Her stomach absolutely roared, and Alice decided right then and there to eat whatever had come on that bread. She lifted her teacup to her lips and sipped, taking a quick second to make sure her emotions had not leaked out of her eyes. She wanted to be strong for Kristen, though she knew it was impossible to be as strong as Robin.

"Alice," Eloise said, and she turned toward her. "Meatball sub." She put a paper-wrapped sandwich on the counter, and Alice stared at it.

"I haven't had one of these in years," she said, a smile curving her lips. She met Eloise's eyes, and so much was said though not a word was spoken. Alice had lost the art of hugging in the Hamptons, but she easily stepped into Eloise's arms. "Thank you."

"I remembered how much you liked them," Eloise whispered. She stepped back and busied herself with getting out the rest of the sandwiches. She had the most beautiful dark hair that had a natural wave she'd permed into the tightest curls as a child of the eighties. Now, it hung in long curls which framed her pale face.

"Did you get the seafood medley?" They'd frequented Carlos's Deli countless times together, and Alice wasn't surprised that Eloise would choose the establishment for her first lunch on the island.

"You bet I did." Eloise smiled and set the other two sandwiches on the table. "Come sit by me."

Alice didn't need to be invited twice. She took her warm meatball sub and joined Eloise on one of the barstools at the bar. "How's college life?"

Eloise shook her head. "You know what? It's kind of boring."

"Well," Robin said as she entered the small kitchen and started making coffee. "Anything would be boring compared to that man we ran into at the deli." She looked at Eloise with pure suggestion on her face.

Alice looked from her to Eloise, noticing the flush that flooded Eloise's face. She giggled even as she stilled with surprise. "Eloise," she said, nudging the studious, academic woman. Alice had done fine in school, but Eloise knew things Alice didn't even know she needed to know.

"What?" Eloise said, her voice dark. She bit into her sandwich. "It was nothing."

"It was not nothing," Robin said, scoffing. "He was flirting with you, Eloise."

"So you've said," Eloise said dryly. She rolled her eyes and took another bite. "Mm, their garlic shrimp is so good."

"You're not distracting me with garlic shrimp," Alice said. "Who was it?"

"No one," Eloise said at the same time Robin said, "Aaron Sherman."

Alice's attention flew back to Eloise, her eyes widening though she told herself not to react. Even a couple of days away from Frank had broken her concentration, because her mouth hung open too.

Eloise's eyes begged her not to say anything, and Alice clamped her mouth shut. She ripped off the sticker on her sandwich, trying to think of something to say.

"The Police Chief?" Kristen asked.

"That's right," Robin said. "Single, handsome, quite well off."

"How is a police chief well off?" Alice asked, hoping to throw Eloise a bone. She and Eloise were the only ones who'd snuck over to Pearl Island for a beach party, where none other than Aaron Sherman had demonstrated his chivalry and athletic prowess all in one spectacular move.

After that, Eloise had entertained a mad crush on the boy, but Aaron had only friendly smiles for her. Then she'd met Wes, and that had become a whole basket of snakes that didn't end until they'd divorced. She never should've married Wes at all, and everyone knew it.

In that moment, Alice felt the world narrow and slow and stop. Did people think that about her? That she never should've married Frank?

"He's the chief," Robin said. "They make good money."

"He has two cute girls too," Kristen said, and that got Alice's mind off her own problems.

"Really? Married and divorced?"

"Yes," Robin said, something guarded in her tone.

"Who did he marry?"

"Not someone from here," Robin said, moving around the counter to sit at the table with Kristen. "So don't worry, Eloise."

"Why would she be worried?" Alice asked.

"I'm just saying, it wasn't anyone we went to high school with."

"That is a relief," Eloise said, cutting a look at Alice.

"So, did he ask you out?" Kristen asked.

Eloise laughed as she shook her head. "No, he didn't."

"He practically did," Robin said, almost protesting.

"No, he didn't," Eloise said, twisting on her barstool

and glaring at Robin. "He was just buying sandwiches for his guys. He's friendly. That's how he always is." On her way back to facing forward, she met Alice's eye.

A huge wave of sympathy rolled over Alice. Aaron had been friendly in high school too. That was the perfect word for the man, and it didn't seem like he'd changed all that much. And poor Eloise knew that *friendly* from Aaron Sherman meant nothing. She'd read into it once before, and she obviously wasn't going to do it again.

Alice's heart beat a little too fast as she thought about preserving her friend's feelings. She wanted to save Eloise from another fiasco with Aaron Sherman, even though the last one had been Eloise's private suffering.

Alice was well-acquainted with private suffering, and she focused back on her meatball sub, ready to devour the whole thing. Around her, Robin talked, because Robin was very good at filling silence with meaningless chatter. Alice actually liked it, and she wished one of her strengths was talking about absolutely nothing in a way that made everyone feel welcome.

Lunch ended, and Alice went back to the office where she'd been getting files to shred. She'd finished the filing cabinet before lunch though, and she opened a drawer in the desk that looked like portfolios Eloise would keep for her students.

Alice frowned down at the brown hanging file folders with the individual manila folders inside, wondering what Joel would've possibly put in this drawer that had needed to be kept for all these years. He and Kristen must have moved this stuff when they'd left the lighthouse, and Alice couldn't fathom holding on to all of this for so long.

She didn't even like keeping the same living room furniture for longer than five years. Get rid of the old, make way for the new, that was her motto.

Her phone vibrated, and she took a moment to pull it out to see who had texted. She should probably alert Frank to the fact that he'd be coming home to an empty house in a couple of days, but she wasn't sure she cared that much.

If she didn't, though, he'd call her, and she'd have to talk to him.

The text she'd received had come from Charlie, and Alice smiled as she read it. *The sailing is fun, Mom. Thanks for bringing us to the cove.*

Her heart warmed, and she pressed her eyes closed as she took a moment to bask in motherhood. There were so many opportunities to feel like a complete failure as a mother, and Alice had nearly drowned in those for the first few years of the twins' life. Even now, she had no idea what she was doing, and she had absolutely no support. She'd learned early in Frank's career that he did not want to be texted during the week with family problems at home. He claimed it was because it made him feel bad he wasn't there, but really Alice knew it was because he didn't like feeling like a failure either.

From time to time, Alice had a flash of what it was like

to feel like a good parent, and this text had just brought her that joy.

I'm glad, she sent back to Charlie. *How is Ginny handling the waves?*

Good, Charlie said. *Della had pills, and she hasn't thrown up once.*

Alice smiled again, though this time, sadness inched her lips back into a straight line fairly quickly. Her children had never met her mother, and while Alice liked Della, and she was glad her father had found someone to love in his later years, a measure of longing clung to Alice no matter what she did.

She wished her mother could know her kids, because that seasickness that Ginny suffered with had come from Alice's mother. She wanted to share who her mother was with the kids, and she used to tell them about her. She hadn't in a while, though, and Alice made a vow to herself to make a more conscious effort to include her mother in her children's lives again.

The truth was, Alice had been beaten down the past few years. This trip to Five Island Cove felt like a whole bucket of fresh air, as she realized that she didn't have to live this life alone. She could call Robin when she needed to vent about Frank, or text Eloise when she had no idea how to do high school chemistry.

Why hadn't she?

Alice knew the answer to that question instantly. No one had reached out to her, because they had fuller lives than hers. And she figured if she reached out to them, they'd be bothered. But maybe they were just as lonely as she was. Maybe they needed a listening ear too. Maybe Alice could start the conversation instead of merely continuing it.

"Not only that," she muttered, tucking her phone in her back pocket and facing the file drawer again. "But you'd have to reveal all your half-truths for the lies they are."

She reached into the drawer and pulled out as many files as she could hold in her two hands. A couple of folders tried to come too, and they flapped halfway in and halfway out. Alice hefted the folders onto the top of the desk, coughing with the scent of stale paper and old cloth and something else she couldn't identify.

Alice didn't normally concern herself with anything old, unless it was an antique from the high-end shop near the pier. Then, she loved poking through vintage chairs and ancient vases to find the just-right thing to put on her front table that would impress any and all who came to the house.

Not that anyone came to her house just to visit.

She looked down at the folders still in the drawer, the one hanging there, half in and half out, and read the name Denise Williams.

It took her a breath in and out to realize that was her mother's name.

Her mother.

Without telling herself to, Alice reached for the folder. It felt foreign in her hands, almost like she'd never picked up a piece of paper before. She existed somewhere outside her body, her heartbeat reverberating through her whole skull.

Behind her, Robin shrieked, and Alice whipped her attention over her shoulder. Laughter came from the other room, and someone called, "Alice, come here."

Acting quickly now, she opened the folder and found a single sheet of paper. She didn't want anyone else to see this, and she folded it in half, then thirds, mashing it into a tight square. Into her back pocket it went, and she picked up the now-empty folder and tucked it inside another one.

She didn't care what she found out in the living room. She was shredding that folder with her mother's name on it before anyone else saw it.

"Alice!" Robin called, and annoyance sang through Alice's system.

She left the office and went down the short hall, saying, "What?"

There was so much crap in Kristen's house that Eloise had to shift around an outdoor bench that Kristen used for a coffee table for Alice to see who had arrived.

Her breath caught somewhere behind her lungs. "Kelli," she said, already moving toward the strawberry blonde that had showed kindness to Alice precisely when she'd needed it. She laughed as she hugged the fourth part of their group that had arrived on the island. She laughed as she clung to her, glad that Kelli held her so tightly too.

And in her joy, she almost forgot about the folded lump in her back pocket.

Almost.

CHAPTER ELEVEN

Now that Kelli had arrived on Diamond Island, some of her anxiety had ebbed into the ocean waves that flowed forward and pulled back. Flowed forward and pulled back, ebbing back into the giant body of water, where they were swallowed up.

She wanted her anxiety to be like that too, and she'd taken an extra anti-anxiety pill that morning before boarding the plane. Leaving Parker with Julian had been hard, as Kelli hadn't left her son overnight ever. She hadn't started at the gym until Parker had gone to kindergarten, and she only worked while he was at school. She wanted to be there for him any time he needed her, and after she'd talked to Julian, they'd decided she should come to help Kristen and stay for the funeral.

In all, she'd be in Five Island Cove for eleven days, and

she wasn't even sure how to survive the next eleven minutes.

"Does your mom know you're here?" Alice asked, stepping back to beam down at Kelli. Growing up, she'd hated being the shortest girl in their class. She'd complained about it more than anything else, but her mom told her that, at five-foot-one, she could carry a baby. Get married. Live a good life.

Kelli didn't care about living a good life when she was fifteen. She wanted to have all the boys admire her the way they had AJ, who had legs as long as Kelli was tall. She knew now that the things her teenage self had wanted bordered on ridiculous, and yet, some of those feelings she'd had as a teenager had formed who she was, the decisions she'd made following high school and in adulthood, and had almost kept her from coming for this funeral.

"Not yet," she said to Alice as she reached up to tuck her hair behind her ear. She didn't need to hide from Alice. In fact, she *wanted* Alice to see her, and she looked at the woman in front of her, hardly recognizing her.

But when Alice smiled, the girl she'd been emerged, and that girl had been fun, kind, and an absolute anchor in Kelli's life when she'd been floundering.

"Are you going to tell her?" Alice asked, her light brown eyes growing serious.

Kelli shrugged and looked around the tiny house where Robin had directed her. Kelli had been to the lighthouse, of course. Not for years, but the memories had swelled to the back of her throat the moment she'd seen the iconic landmark through the tiny window on the airplane.

"Well, maybe the ferry between here and Bell is broken down," Alice said, draping her arm around Kelli and turning back to the others. A twinge of nervousness flowed through her, because in her house, everything had a place, and there was a place for everything.

The room looked like a bomb filled with paper had gone off, spewing slips of various sizes and colors everywhere. And then someone had plunked down a couch and called it a living room.

"It's a little chaotic right now," Robin said, stepping around the shredded and giving Kelli another hug. "I'm so happy you're here." When she stepped back, tears shone in her eyes. She shook her head and waved her hands like she was being silly. "Someone take over and fill her in."

"Can't we wait until we have a lot of carbs in front of us?" Eloise asked. She'd hugged Kelli too, and she'd definitely felt something strange from the dark-haired beauty Kelli had envied in high school.

"Fill me in on what?" Kelli's skin itched just thinking about touching anything in the room.

"We're going through Joel's things," Alice said. "He wrote a lot of stuff down, and some of it is gibberish that only meant something to him. We're recycling that." She indicated the bin blocking the entrance to the kitchen.

"I've been shredding anything with financial information or personal information. Kristen wants to look at the journals to see if she wants to keep them."

The world spun strangely, and Kelli felt underdressed though that was ridiculous. Anyone would feel underdressed beside Alice, who wore a pair of gray linen slacks with a purple blouse with thick straps that ran over her shoulders.

Eloise sighed and pushed her hair off her forehead. She wore a simple pair of jeans and a T-shirt with a giant square with some letters in it, like an element symbol, but Kelli didn't know which one. Robin wore leggings, which accentuated her trim legs, and Kristen wore what Kelli had always seen her wear: a simple blouse with either flowers or stripes or some other pattern with a pair of plain pants.

On Sundays, she wore sweats, and she had special Sunday sweat suits in a variety of colors. Kelli had sometimes come to the lighthouse on Sundays just to see which color Kristen would be wearing.

Then she'd bake filled raisin cookies, and they'd go up to the deck, and Kelli could just breathe.

"Do you want to come work with me in the office?" Alice asked, and Kelli nodded. She followed the friend who had shown Kelli how to be strong into the office, shocked there was more to go through in here.

"Holy cow," Kelli said. "I didn't realize Joel had all of this." She gazed around, the walls pressing in on her, getting closer, ever closer. She took a deep breath and commanded them to stay where they were. If there wasn't a bookcase lining three of the walls, filled from top to bottom and front to back with books and who knew what else, the room would feel huge.

"Are you still teaching aerobics?" Alice asked, drawing Kelli to where she stood at the desk, flipping open folders.

"Yes," Kelli said, taking another deep breath. "A few days each week. They want me to do more, but I'm okay with just a few days a week."

Alice glanced up. "Yeah? Julian's doing okay?"

"Yeah," Kelli said, aware her voice had pitched up. "The courier business is going well, and he even said he'd take Parker so I could come here."

Alice didn't stop in her examination of the documents in the folders. Kelli marveled at that, because her mother would've paused and said it wasn't normal for Kelli to be so attached to her son.

But her mother hadn't had a problem getting pregnant, and her mother had never been told she'd never have another child. Parker was all Kelli would ever get, and it wasn't wrong for a mother to be devoted to her child.

"That's great," Alice said. "They must like you at the gym."

"Oh, my routines aren't anything fancy," Kelli said. "But the ladies like me, because I'm overweight."

Alice scoffed and twisted toward her. "Kel, you are not."

"I'm not model tall and thin," she said. "They like that."

"I'm sure you're a rock star."

Kelli burst out laughing. "Okay, never say that again, Alice."

Alice giggled and reached into the drawer to extract more files. "Right. I'm too old for that." She grinned at her and added, "My teens are always telling me what not to say."

"I can't wait for that," she said, finally taking a step into the office. "All right. Put me to work."

KELLI BASKED IN THE ENERGY OF THE DOWNTOWN AREA ON the island of Diamond Island. It wasn't full summer season yet, when the island would really be hopping, but many of the seasonal shops had opened already.

"There's a farmer's market on Wednesdays in the fall," Robin said. Tonight, the square where the market would be sat empty, but Kelli still loved the older buildings, the cobbled crosswalks, and the charming, narrow streets.

The women had parked in a paid lot a couple of blocks away, and Robin had been narrating all of the changes that had taken place in the downtown area as if Kelli and the others hadn't ever been here before.

For Kelli, she hadn't been down these streets in many long years, and she didn't mind the audio tour in Robin's voice. No one else said anything about it either, but Alice and Eloise both just burst out with the things they saw, with stories of things they'd done together at the crystal shop, where they sold an array of essential oils as well, or the drug store where AJ had once stolen an entire box of gum that she'd hid in Kelli's backpack for a few days before showing it to anyone.

"Look at that dog boutique," Eloise said. "Can we go in?" She wore excitement in her eyes, the hope filling the air around them.

"You have cats," Robin said.

"They'll have cat stuff."

"No, I don't think they do," Alice said. "It's called The Dog Spot." She trilled out a laugh which caused Kelli to smile.

"That seems unfair," Eloise said, deflating slightly. "Do they have a Cat Spot?"

"Not that I've seen," Kelli said. "Honestly, Eloise, people don't really dress up their cats."

"Well, they should," she said.

"Do you?" Kelli asked. "Put little BU sweaters on your cats?"

Eloise met her eye, surprise in her expression, and then they laughed together. Kelli nudged Eloise with her hip, and they giggled together as they continued down the street. "I'm going to take that as a no," Kelli said, feeling so...free. She wasn't sure why she hadn't felt this way before, or why she'd had so many reservations about returning to this island.

She shouldn't have been worried, not with these people here, waiting to welcome her home with such open arms.

"Here we are," Robin announced, and she opened the door to the crab shack and held it for everyone else to walk through.

Kelli followed Alice inside, the scent of butter and salt calling to her soul. The music was just as she remembered, as were the red-and-white checkered tablecloths and the giant crab-shaped clock on the wall.

"Four, ladies?" a man asked, already getting the menus.

"Yes," Alice said, and they followed him to a table against the wall. Kelli didn't need the menu, as it hadn't changed in years, and the moment they sat down, a huge group came into the restaurant. Relief hit Kelli for a reason she couldn't name. It wasn't like Mort's would run out of crabs.

"Okay, dinner at Mort's," Eloise said. "New Truth."

"No," Alice said, waving her hands. "No, we're not doing New Truth."

"Come on, Alice," Eloise said at the same time Robin said, "I don't have a New Truth."

"I'm sure you can think of something," Kelli said, finding her place in the group. For some reason, she'd thought she wouldn't be safe here, and she'd never been more wrong. "I'll go first." She scooted closer to the table and sat up straighter. "New Truth: I'm scared that while I'm here, something will happen to Parker."

"Kelli—"

"Rules," she said, glaring at Robin. There were no reassurances during the New Truth game.

"Fine, I'll go next," Alice said. She ran her hand through her hair and looked at each woman at the table. "I might need to think more seriously about a divorce."

Shock moved through Kelli, and her first instinct was to reach out and take Alice's hand in hers. Her eyes burned with an intensity she'd seen before when another girl in their class had told Alice she was such a bad singer she'd never make it into the musical.

Alice had practiced and practiced, and when she'd auditioned for the school musical, she not only made it, but she'd been cast in a leading role. Kelli had seen this same strength and determination in Alice's eyes then as she did now.

"I'm up," Eloise said. "After finding out about the test scores, I'm considering a career change."

"Okay, forget the rules," Robin said. "Eloise, no. That's just crazy talking right there. I'm sorry, you know I love you, but no. You're an amazing professor, and what happened thirty years ago does not matter." She clapped one hand flat against the table and looked at Alice. "You do what you think is right, Alice, but there will literally be a place at my house if you find you need it. I don't know everything about you and Frank, but from what I've heard in just the last couple of days, I would support a divorce." She leaned toward Kelli, her blue eyes blazing with hot heat. "And I understand where you're coming from Kelli. I do. I wish I could take that feeling from you, but I know I can't. But I do know you can text any of us, and we'll help you however we can."

Kelli nodded. "Fair enough. But you can't break the rule of sharing. So think of something."

Robin shook her head. "I really have nothing."

"Oh, come on," Alice said. "Would you like me to share about what I heard on the phone this morning with Duke?"

Robin looked like she'd been hit with a hammer. "You wouldn't dare."

"New Truth," Eloise said, starting a slow slap on the table. "New Truth."

Kelli joined in, laughing between the words.

Robin finally rolled her eyes, but Kelli could see the New Truth was causing her some difficulty. "Fine, fine," she said, and the chanting stopped. She glared at Alice, and Kelli wouldn't want to be on the receiving end of that look.

"Duke wants to leave Five Island Cove and move to Alaska."

"Alaska?" Eloise asked, her voice mostly a gasp. "You'll die up there, Robin."

"Yeah, well." She shrugged and looked up as a waiter arrived. They put in their orders for the soft-shelled crabs and lobster they shared every time they came to Mort's. Once the waiter was gone, Kelli looked at the other women.

"Do we have enough carbs for you guys to fill me in?" She looked at Eloise. "You said something about test scores."

"Robin," Eloise said, and Robin once again acted as the voice to tell the story about the secrets they'd been uncovering since Joel's death.

"He *cheated* on Kristen?" Kelli could not believe that. "For real?"

"I mean, the sentence was erased on the letter," Robin said. "But it was visible."

Kelli could not imagine finding out her husband had cheated on her. An intense betrayal burned through her on Kristen's behalf, and she couldn't shake it away.

Their seafood arrived, and Kelli tucked into a lobster claw while Robin explained about Eloise's test scores.

"Unbelievable," Kelli said. "What else?"

"Nothing so far," Robin said. "Thank goodness."

"Actually," Alice said, putting down her fork. She hadn't put a bib on to eat either, and yet she didn't have a drop of butter on her blouse. Everything about Alice was prim and proper and put in precisely the right place.

"Actually?" Robin asked, practically shrieking.

Alice took her time, as she'd always had a bit of a flair

for the dramatic, to reach into her pocket and pull out a folded piece of paper. "I found this today, in Joel's office." She started to unfold it. "It was in a folder with my mother's name on it."

"Your mother?" Robin said, all food forgotten now. She leaned across the table, toward Alice, who wore a mask of stone. Kelli wasn't sure how she caged all the emotions behind such passivity.

Kelli's heart beat against her ribs, because she wasn't sure she wanted to know what was on that paper, not after hearing the amazing stories about Eloise's test scores and Kristen's letter. How many secrets did Joel have?

The music fell away until only Alice and that single sheet of paper remained. "I think I know who Joel cheated with," she said. "And I know why my mother went out into the storm that killed her."

"Why?" Eloise asked.

Alice finished smoothing the paper on the table in front of her and nodded to it. She was still cold, emotionless, and Kelli couldn't believe it. "She died on a Wednesday night—the day of the week Kristen worked at the community center with us girls."

She drew in a breath, the first visible sign that Alice had true feelings. "She was going to meet Joel. She was his mistress."

CHAPTER TWELVE

How do I tell Kristen?

The question echoed in Robin's mind for hours after she'd returned home, set up beds for Eloise, Kelli, and Alice, who she'd refused to let go back to the hotel room alone. Alice could put on a brave face, but she should *not* be alone after what she'd learned tonight. Thankfully, Robin had enough sway to convince Alice to come to her house. Or perhaps Alice hurt more than Robin could comprehend.

Should I tell Kristen?

She turned again, and Duke's deep, even breathing quieted for a moment. She hadn't told him anything other than Alice had decided to stay with them. Duke shouldn't care; they had the space. She didn't know how to put her thoughts into words, even for him.

Joel Shields was definitely not the man Robin had thought he was. Her mind tried to find new pathways for the man, but they wandered, meandered, went to nowhere. Life was often like that, Robin knew. She hadn't realized it until about ten years ago, but planning for this and that, expecting life to be linear, didn't work for most people. It was this linear longing that brought unhappiness, and as soon as Robin let the path go where it needed to go—whether that was up, down, around, or through—she'd been able to let go of some of the things she'd thought she should have and embrace what she already did.

Alaska? ran through her mind now, which made no sense. There wasn't room for a huge life change in her brain right now, and yet, because humans were so complex and so nuanced and so smart, the idea lingered there, even in her completely overwhelmed state.

Duke had put on a happy face when Robin walked in with all of her friends, and he hadn't brought up Alaska. Though she'd been tired and stressed, she'd still made love with him, and then the tossing and turning had begun.

She needed to know more about the night that Alice's mother had died. They did have Seafaring Girls activities on Wednesday nights, but they wouldn't have had it on a night with a storm. That didn't make sense, because the ferries shut down and anyone who hadn't made it home took refuge in the storm shelters that every island had in the town centers.

She tossed again, everything feeling like she needed to scratch it.

"Babe," Duke murmured. "What's the matter?"

"Nothing," she whispered, reaching over and putting her hand on his bare chest, where his pulse ba-bumped under her palm. He was real, and steady, and Robin needed that solid foundation in her life. "I'm sorry I'm keeping you awake. I'll go into the office." She started to get up, but his hand covered hers.

"Stay," he whispered, lacing his fingers through hers. "Try to go to sleep, babe. I know you were up a lot last night too."

She never had been able to fool him, and a whisper of a smile touched her mouth. "Will you hold me?"

He rolled onto his side and opened his arms, and Robin slid into them effortlessly. Part of her felt guilty she had Duke to curl up with while Alice's husband cheated on her in another city. She thought of Eloise and Aaron, who had been flirting mightily in the deli, no matter what Eloise said. Her mind landed on Kelli, who'd come without texting Robin. She'd been nervous and jittery until dinnertime, when she'd finally relaxed into the sweet and thoughtful girl Robin had known growing up.

Finally, she let herself think of Kristen. The mother hen in Robin wanted to bring her to the house too, because she probably shouldn't be alone in that cottage, with all that paper, either. Cooped up with all those secrets lurking around every corner, beneath every journal cover.

How do I tell her?

The thought revolved in her mind for several minutes, but within the safety of Duke's arms, the steady thumping of his pulse in her ear, she finally let go of solving everyone's problems that night.

Duke's lips touched the back of her neck, and Robin reactively pressed against his kiss. "Mm," he hummed, his hand sliding across her stomach.

"Duke," she whispered.

He didn't answer, because he'd started kissing her neck again. Robin felt like she couldn't keep up with his sex drive, but she did like that she ignited something in him that hadn't seemed to have gone out yet.

"Duke," she tried again. "We didn't talk about Alaska." She turned toward him and met his mouth with hers.

"We don't need to talk about it right now," he murmured, moving his lips to her ear. "I know you don't want to go."

No, she didn't want to go, but she loved this man with her whole heart and soul, and as he rested his forehead against hers, Robin placed both of her hands on either side of his face. "I don't want to go," she whispered. "But Duke, I'm helplessly in love with you, and if *you* want to go, and think it's the best thing for our family, I'd go with you." She kept her eyes closed and breathed with him, both of them letting some silence accompany them. "We'd all go with you."

"I know," he said, touching his lips to hers in a sweet kiss. "I know." He shifted, and Robin rolled over again, nestling back into his chest and letting the man she loved hold her, and hold her tight, until she finally fell asleep.

THE FOLLOWING MORNING FOUND ROBIN IN THE KITCHEN, beating egg whites to make chocolate chip pancakes. She felt like today was a hinge, with the situation flapping wildly in the wind, able to go in any direction. Would Alice say something to Kristen? She had plenty of confidence, but even Alice had shut down last night after revealing the letter she'd found in Joel's office.

Robin didn't know how to wrap her head around the man she knew and this alternate version of him that was emerging from the scraps of his life he'd left behind. She wondered why he hadn't thrown them all away years ago. When he'd first been diagnosed with cancer. Anytime, really, would've been better than after he was gone and couldn't explain.

A slip of anger moved through her that he'd done this to Kristen. To Alice. To Eloise. Only a coward would leave the evidence of his indiscretions without any explanation for them. Without the chance to grovel for forgiveness. So why should Robin forgive him? He wasn't even there to defend himself.

The recipe provided the structure Robin needed. An order to things that made sense to accomplish a goal. Her brain buzzed with the next step, and then the next one, and she moved around the kitchen, flipping bacon in one moment and plugging in the griddle in the next. She put the syrup in the microwave and got out plates.

Doing things soothed Robin, calming her mind enough that she could sometimes see through the confusion and misdirection to exactly what she should do next.

"Wow, Mom," Mandie said, coming into the kitchen. "You're really going all out today."

Robin grinned at her oldest. A sense of desperation swept over her, and she abandoned the fruit she'd started to cut up and engulfed her daughter in a hug. "I love you," she whispered, glad that Mandie wasn't too old to accept an embrace from her crazy, emotional mother.

"I love you, too, Mom." Mandie watched her as Robin stepped back and swiped at her eyes. She shook her head as her voice stayed clogged down deep in her chest.

"I'm okay." Her daughter had seen Robin cry before; this was nothing new. What she didn't know was how close she was to leaving the house. Robin could suddenly see the next five years, then the next ten. Mandie was smart, and strong, and there wasn't a man on Earth good enough for her. But she'd graduate, and go to college, get married, have babies.

Robin stepped back to the griddle, smiling through the tears in her eyes, the vision in her mind's eye glorious and beautiful. She'd raised Mandie to leave the house, go out and make her way in the world, and she wanted that for her so badly.

"Remember, I'm going to Brady's after school," Mandie said as Robin poured perfectly level scoops of batter onto the hot surface. "He's, uh, well, I'm—we're sort of dating."

Robin froze, her hand in mid-air as pancake batter dripped onto the griddle. Her eyes locked onto Mandie's and her heart thumped and pumped and stuttered in her chest. "Sort of dating?" she managed to push out of her throat.

Don't make a big deal out of this, she told herself sternly. That got her to move again, scooping up another dollop of batter and pouring it into the last space on the griddle.

Mandie looked over her shoulder, her face growing redder by the moment. "I mean, we talked about it yesterday, and he didn't friend-zone me."

"Is that what you do now?" Robin asked. "Talk about it?"

"Yeah," Mandie said. "You know, DTR."

No, Robin did not know, so she put down the scoop

and picked up the spatula, waiting for her daughter to explain further.

"Define the relationship," Mandie said.

"Ah." Robin wiggled the tip of the spatula under the first pancake she'd poured, knowing it wasn't anywhere near ready. She couldn't help feeling the same way about Mandie and having a boyfriend. She blinked, and life changed again.

Looking up, she smiled at her daughter. "You've been friends with Brady for a while."

"Yeah." Mandie smiled. "I do really like him, Mom. He's a nice guy. He's not a pervert, and he said he's never kissed a girl."

"Oh, wow." Robin giggled with her daughter. "So... does that include you?"

Mandie nodded, her eyes growing serious again. She fiddled with her fingers, the ten of them clam-shelling together and then pulling apart again. Robin hated this nervousness in her daughter, but more relief than she'd ever known accompanied the feeling. Mandie hadn't lied to her about Brady and "their relationship." She was talking to her, and as the floorboards above them squeaked, Robin looked up.

"But you want to kiss him, right?" she asked Mandie.

"I mean—yes?"

Robin smiled again and checked the pancakes. Most of them had crisped along the bottom edges, and little bubbles had started to pop on the surface. "Mandie, kissing is pretty fun. And if you like him, and he likes you." Robin shrugged as she flipped one pancake. "The key is not to get your hopes up too high." She grinned as Mandie stepped fully into the kitchen, almost like she was now ready to fully engage in the conversation as well.

She opened the microwave and got out the syrup. "What do you mean?"

"Well," Robin said, her voice a bit high. "If he's never kissed anyone, he might not be very good at it." She glanced at Mandie. "So don't be upset if it's not great—at first. He'll get better at it."

Mandie shook her head and smiled. "Okay, Mom."

Robin flipped all the pancakes and then pointed the spatula at Mandie. "And just kissing, do you hear me?"

Mandie actually looked scared, as if Robin would sneak into her room in the middle of the night and stab her with the spatula. "I'm afraid to even kiss him, Mom. What if that makes everything weird?"

"Like what?"

"Like, I don't know." Mandie glanced down at the plate she held in anticipation of having a hot pancake.

"Well," Robin said, very aware that she'd started a lot of sentences that way. "Kissing does change things."

"See? *I* should've friend-zoned *him*."

"No." Robin slid two pancakes onto Mandie's plate. "Change isn't always bad, dear. Some changes are really good."

Mandie looked at her, her eyes wide and open and so

trusting. She wanted to believe Robin so badly, so Robin nodded and removed the rest of the pancakes from the griddle. "Just try it. If it's too weird, then go for the friend zone, because Brady's been a good friend."

Robin pictured the tall, lean boy that had been around the house many times over the past few years. He was a cute kid, with a lot of dark hair. His limbs had grown too long for his body, but he was slowly catching up, and he played for the freshman basketball team now, putting that long reach to good use.

Robin should've seen this coming, as Mandie had been going to all the basketball games this past winter and spring.

"Thanks, Mom," Mandie said at the same time Duke entered the kitchen with the loud, booming word, "Pancakes." He growled as he wrapped Robin in a hug from behind, the tip of his tongue sliding down the curve of her ear.

She laughed and swatted at him with the spatula. He laughed too, released her, and opened the fridge. "Juice? Milk? Hot chocolate?" He looked at Mandie, who asked for milk.

"These are hot," Robin said. "Eat up." She glanced toward the hallway, expecting to see Jamie arrive at any moment. She loved the way she could cook in the morning with the sunshine coming in through the windows lining the back of the house. And with Duke laughing with Mandie about something, and the genuine talk she'd just had with her daughter, Robin wondered if her life had been taken from the pages of a magazine.

Of course, it wouldn't be one of those pristine ones that Alice surely got delivered to her mansion in the Hamptons. But one labeled Real Life, where all the pictures would feature dirty dishes in the kitchen sink, and damp towels lying in heaps on teenager's bathroom floors. They'd have a man wearing an undershirt with a pair of gym shorts, though he knew his wife's friends would be down for breakfast at any moment, and a kitchen table covered with various items that hadn't found their way to their permanent homes yet.

Sure, the cabinets had been painted a modern white, covering the old oak finish that was so nineties. The back door could be cracked to let in the salty breeze and the call of seabirds as they said good morning to one another. The couch had more pillows on it than anyone needed, and the plants always got watered. Meals got made on stainless steel appliances, and the man and wife both drove a nice car.

But it wasn't those features of the Real Life house that would be printed. There'd be a feature on how to keep a messy office, and an article on how to deal with grief, and a right column commentary on how to disagree about moving across the globe for a new job only one half of the partnership wanted.

Footsteps sounded on the stairs, and Robin flipped

another batch of pancakes as her friends came into the kitchen.

"She really did make them."

"I told you she would."

"I could smell them upstairs."

Robin smiled at her friends and indicated the stack of plates, the butter dish, and the syrup. "Eat. I have a feeling we're all going to need the sugar and carbs today." She looked at Duke, who seemed at ease with the additional three women who had invaded his home. "Baby," she said. "Would you go check on Jamie? She should be out by now."

"Yep." He picked up his plate and took it with him as he walked through the kitchen to the hallway.

Robin caught all three of her friends looking at her, but she returned her attention to the griddle. Familiar guilt crowded into her throat, and she worked against it. She shouldn't feel guilty because she had Duke. That was ridiculous.

"Robin?" His voice came down the hall, tinged with something that made Robin pause and quietly panic.

"Alice, will you take over here?" She handed Alice the spatula as she left, despite Alice's protests.

"I've never made pancakes," she said dumbly as Robin left the room.

"You're kidding," Kelli said. "Oh, my word, Alice. Give that to me. It's not hard."

Down the hall and into Jamie's room, Robin found Duke standing in the doorway. "What's going on?"

"I don't know how to deal with this," he hissed as Robin pressed in beside him.

Jamie sat on the bed, apparently ready for school. She was dressed, with her backpack hitched over both shoulders.

And crying.

"Sweetie," Robin said gently, slipping past Duke. "What's wrong?" Jaime had just turned twelve over Christmas, and she'd become emotional lately, almost like she was reverting to age five, when literally everything had brought the girl to tears.

"Tara's cat died," Jamie said, looking at Robin with big, fat tears clinging to her eyelashes.

Robin's irritation flashed inside her, but she pushed against it. Patience. That was what she needed in this situation. "Oh, I'm sorry," she said, thinking it was about time the cat had died. "Wasn't it blind in both eyes?" She looked at Duke, who still stood in the doorway with his plate of pancakes in his hand.

Their eyes met, and Robin wasn't sure who laughed first —her or him. No matter what, Jamie didn't think Robin's question was funny, and she leapt off the bed. "Mom."

"What?" Robin asked, still a little giggly. Jamie rolled her eyes and stomped past Duke, who had the good sense to get out of the way. She stepped over to her husband, still grinning, and patted his arm. "You could've done that."

"Yeah," he said, grinning too. "That was masterful."

Robin snorted as she started laughing again. They went down the hallway to the kitchen together, and Duke joined the girls at the table, the six of them all eating pancakes and bacon, even Alice.

A sigh filled Robin's soul, and while she'd never planned for breakfast to go this way this morning, with all the conversations and crying, she was still here, in this moment. And it was beautiful.

"Come eat, babe," Duke called. "I saved you some bacon from these savages."

So Robin did just that.

LATER, AFTER DUKE HAD TAKEN THE GIRLS TO SCHOOL AND then gone to the docks to work on his boat, after Kelli and Eloise had helped Robin clean up breakfast, after Alice had claimed she was going to get some cats of her own, the four of them sat down in the living room with sugared and creamed coffee.

"So," Eloise said. "What are we going to do?"

Kelli said nothing, and Alice just kept stroking the pure black cat Eloise had brought with her from Boston. Robin looked at Eloise, and the two of them had an entire conversation without vocalizing anything. She couldn't believe she'd let five long years go by without having these women in her daily life. She loved them so much, and they knew her so well. Knew her in a way no one else did.

"I think," Eloise said slowly. "We shouldn't tell Kristen. She's dealing with enough right now."

Robin nodded as she took a sip of her coffee. But she wasn't going to say anything; she and Eloise had just agreed that Eloise would lead this conversation. Heaven knew that Robin led enough of the others.

"Do you know who you are today?" Alice asked softly, still not looking away from the feline.

Eloise shifted on the couch and lifted her own mug to her lips for a drink. She cleared her throat. "Not entirely," she finally admitted. "But all I can do is take things one day at a time." She looked at Robin and then Kelli. "Thanks to you guys, I know I can't make any big decisions while I'm in the middle of the crisis."

"Smart," Robin murmured.

"You always were the smartest," Kelli said, smiling. "I don't think we should tell Kristen either."

Alice finally tore her attention from the cat. She met Robin's eye and lifted her eyebrows. "What do you think?"

"I'm going last," Robin said. "You're up."

Alice sighed, anger flashing in those eyes. Robin had seen Alice angry plenty of times, but a flicker of worry still flamed through her. An angry Alice wasn't pleasant.

"I think I'm living enough lies," she said. She pressed her teeth together, making her jawbone stick out on the left side. She needed another plate of pancakes, though Robin knew the carbs would only add the body fat Alice lacked, not soothe the pain.

"And I'm not sure I can go work at that cottage today," she added.

Oh, did Robin feel that down in her bones, and it had only been a couple of days. She still said nothing, because she didn't want to dictate what the group did. If Alice couldn't go, she couldn't go.

"I can go today," Kelli said.

"Me too," Eloise said.

"It's fine if you don't want to," Robin said. "I can go today too. Maybe you'd like to go to the beach or something, Alice."

She shook her head, resignation crossing her face. "No, I'll go today too." She drew in a deep breath, her chest rising and rising, before she blew the air out slowly. "But if any of us find anything, can we just wait until tomorrow to talk about it?"

"Deal," Robin said, the others affirming as well. "And I don't think we should tell Kristen about your mother right now either. There's a time and place, and perhaps this is neither of those."

Alice pressed her lips together and nodded. "I'm going to go finish getting ready." She got up and left the cat on the couch as she walked away.

"Finish getting ready?" Kelli asked after she was out of

earshot, also watching Alice as she turned and started up the steps that sat right inside the front door of Robin's house. "Did you see what she's wearing? How is she not ready?"

Robin still wore her yoga pants and a T-shirt she gardened in. And while she'd change before they went over to the lighthouse, it wouldn't be into a designer pair of slacks the color of eggshells or a bright blue, sleeveless blouse that had cost more than her house.

Eloise giggled, which sent Kelli laughing too. "That's Alice," Eloise said.

Robin sipped her coffee, smiling on the outside but wondering on the inside. Was it Alice? Perhaps she felt trapped inside the wardrobe she owned, powerless to change it as easily as everyone thought she should be able to.

Robin had been there before, feeling small and insignificant inside a situation that felt so big and wide and all-encompassing. She knew she just needed to work and wait, and things would settle down. They'd shrink back to their real size, and she wouldn't feel like the sky was about to crack and crash, crushing her and everything she loved.

So she breathed. She changed her clothes. She brushed her teeth and her hair, pulling the latter up into a ponytail. She hugged Alice, and Kelli, and Eloise, and the four of them huddled up together in Robin's foyer.

"Okay," she said, taking control again. "We can do this,

ladies. We're strong, and capable, and confident. No matter what happens."

"No matter what happens," the others echoed, and together, they left the house for another day of going through a stash of secrets that should've been burned a long time ago.

CHAPTER THIRTEEN

Eloise heard her phone go off again, and she couldn't believe she had someone texting her in the middle of the night. She didn't even have students right now, and she fumbled for her phone, determined to silence it without even looking at it.

Number one, her eyes felt like someone had smashed sand in them, and she wasn't sure she could even open them. Number two, it was *the middle of the night.*

"I'm going to go shower," Kelli said, and Eloise sat straight up in bed, remembering that she wasn't at home, in her beautiful brownstone, in Boston.

"I'm sorry," Eloise said.

"It's fine," Kelli said. "It's after seven."

"It is?" Eloise glanced around the bedroom she shared with Kelli. Robin had closed the blackout curtains when she'd set up the beds, and not even a trickle of light came into the room.

Eloise reached for her phone as it chimed yet again, wondering who on Earth was doing all this texting, especially so early in the morning. Her mother didn't know how to use a cellphone, and apparently, Eloise didn't either, as hers slipped from her fingers and fell between the bed and the nightstand.

Of course. If there was a way for something to go wrong, for Eloise, it did. She tried to banish the negative thoughts, because she knew they weren't true. She'd just dropped her phone; the world wasn't conspiring against her.

She had a few friends back in Boston that could be texting, but she'd notified them of her trip to Five Island Cove. So it was either important, or—

"Holy biomes," Eloise said, using her biology swear words. "It's Aaron Sherman." Fear moved through her, and she jerked her head up as if Robin would be standing right there, her eyes flashing with triumph.

She'd squeal and enter the room saying, "I knew it! I *knew* he was flirting with you."

Of course Aaron had been flirting with Eloise at the deli a couple of days ago. She'd known he had been. What she didn't know was *why*.

And she didn't need to deal with squealing and explanations. She was forty-five-years-old, and he wouldn't be her first boyfriend. She reminded herself of this as she tapped on the screen.

She'd done so too gingerly, and the text didn't open. Another try, and his messages filled the screen.

Morning Eloise. It's Aaron Sherman.

I was wondering if you might stop by the station later today. I have something I want to talk to you about.

I realize it's early. Sorry. Just text me back when you can.

"Something he wants to talk to me about?" Eloise wondered aloud. "What could that possibly be?" She let her phone drop to her lap and looked up, thinking through the last two interactions she'd had with the man.

She did not need him to pay her cleaning bill, something he'd mentioned both times. Her jaw clenched. She didn't want to go down to the police station and tell him that again. She'd had to do a little explaining to her mother about why she was wet when she'd shown up at the house on Sanctuary Island, but that had been easy. The ferries sometimes had big waves come over the side, and her mother hadn't questioned her.

Her mother likely hadn't been off the island in years, though, so she certainly couldn't argue either.

Okay, she texted Aaron back. *Can I ask what it's about?*

Nothing big, he said, but that didn't soothe the nerves attacking her stomach. *I'll be quick. I just have a question about Sanctuary Island.*

Eloise frowned at her phone as if it were responsible for giving her these cryptic, confusing texts.

Okay, that was a lie. Aaron sent another smiley face. *I just want to—can I call you?*

Eloise's stomach swooped then, and she pressed her eyes closed.

"You okay?"

Her eyes flew open and toward Kelli, who came in and closed the door behind her, a towel wrapped around her body and one turbaning her hair. She flipped on the light, which only activated the lamps, sending soft, yellow light chasing the shadows up the walls.

"I need some advice," Eloise said, pressing her phone to her chest. "But you have to promise not to tell Robin."

Kelli's whole face curved into a smile. "I love keeping secrets from Robin."

"And Alice."

"And Alice," Kelli said, joining Eloise on the bed. "Show me."

Eloise did, her heartbeat picking up speed with every second Kelli read the text conversation and didn't say anything.

She looked at the side of Kelli's face, noting the wide eyes, the shocked expression. "Tell him yes."

"Yes?" Eloise couldn't comprehend the word for some reason.

"Yes," Kelli said. "Tell him to call. I'll take my clothes into the bathroom to get dressed."

"No, I'll go," Eloise said, standing up. She needed

some fresh air and a room that wasn't one shade away from midnight.

"Your voice will echo in the bathroom," Kelli said, and Eloise paused.

Kelli giggled, gathered her clothes, and left the room again. Before Eloise responded to Aaron, she walked over to the curtains and yanked them apart. The sunshine assaulted her eyes then, and she bathed in it, using it to calm her heart and quiet her mind.

She was Eloise Hall, and she could talk to a man on the phone.

She was Eloise Hall, and she had a bachelor's degree in biology from Boston University.

She was Eloise Hall, and she had a master's degree in science education and biology research from Harvard.

She was *Dr.* Eloise Hall, and she held a doctorate from Harvard in Biological Sciences in Public Health.

Joel may have gotten her through a door she couldn't have stepped through without his help, but he had not earned a single credit of those degrees. He had not paid even a penny for her education.

Eloise knew she was different today than she'd been yesterday, and for sure different than she'd been when she'd first run into Aaron on the beach, though that was only two days ago.

She tapped out the three letters—*yes*—to let him know he could call, and only a moment later, her phone rang. "Hey," she said, making her voice as bright and carefree as she knew how.

"Hey, Eloise," he said, and a smile touched her heart as his deep voice said her name. She pictured him in her mind, and he was a handsome man. A very handsome man.

He chuckled, and Eloise would categorize the sound as nervous. "Sorry about those texts," he said. "I'd sleep a lot better if I knew you were going to delete that whole thing." Another chuckle.

"All right," Eloise said, determined not to giggle. It seemed unfair that men could giggle and it got categorized as a chuckle, something sexy and throaty and desirable. But if women did it, they were flirty schoolgirls. And Eloise was definitely not one of those.

"All right," Aaron said. "Phew. Listen, I wanted you to come to the station, because well, I wanted to see you."

"You wanted to see me?"

"Again," he blurted out. "I wanted to see you again, and I was hoping to ask you about dinner tonight."

"Dinner tonight." Eloise pressed her eyes closed again, commanding her brain to start working. "I think I'm going to eat dinner tonight."

Aaron chuckled again, and Eloise let her lips relax into a smile. "Would you consider eating it with me? I mean, I know you're here for Kristen and with your friends, but well, I thought we could...go to dinner together."

Eloise's fingertips buzzed as pure warmth moved over her. "I'd like to go to dinner together," she said.

"Great," Aaron said, and his relief came through the line like a palpable being. "Should I come pick you up, or do you want to meet me somewhere?"

Eloise glanced at the closed bedroom door, sure Kelli had finished getting dressed by now. "I better meet you," she said. "I have a rental, and that way I won't have to explain anything to the ladies."

"I think you mean Robin," Aaron said, his voice full of teasing now.

"I definitely mean Robin," Eloise said, giving in to the laughter inside her throat. But it was not a giggle, and Aaron's throaty laugh definitely wasn't either.

"What do you like?" he asked.

"Oh, I like food," Eloise said. "You pick somewhere, and I'll be there."

"How about going to a different island?"

"I know how to ride a ferry."

"Great." Aaron wore a smile in his tone. "Let's meet at the south ferry station. There's a great seaside restaurant on Pearl Island. I'll get us a reservation."

"Seven?" Eloise asked.

"See you at seven."

The call ended after Eloise and Aaron said their good-byes, and Eloise simply stared straight ahead. She couldn't believe what had just happened, or that she'd agreed to it.

A light knock sounded on the door—definitely Kelli. Eloise strode over to the door and pulled it open.

"Well?" Kelli asked as Eloise ushered her back inside the bedroom.

"He asked me to dinner," Eloise said, feeling wild and completely out of control. "Tonight. Seven. I'm meeting him at the south ferry station, and we're going to Pearl Island."

"That's great, Eloise," Kelli said, grinning like she really meant it.

But a scream had started in the bottom of Eloise's soul, and it grew louder and louder. She couldn't go to Pearl Island. What had she been thinking?

You weren't thinking, she admonished herself. She'd let the man's sexy voice fuzz her senses, blur the lines between fantasy and reality. Maybe she could just say she didn't want to leave Diamond Island. She'd need a reason for that, though, and she didn't want to lie to Aaron. Eloise tried to tell the truth as much as possible, because it made the secrets she kept easier to keep track of.

She smiled at Kelli, showered, and joined everyone downstairs, where she found Robin had sent Duke for breakfast sandwiches that morning. Eloise liked Duke Grover a whole lot, and it was obvious the man worshiped the ground Robin walked on.

Eloise realized in the moment Duke leaned down and kissed Robin that she wanted a man like him. She wanted someone to wake up with and text throughout the day, someone who was anxious for her to walk through the door when she got off work—and not just because they wanted another can of the wet cat food and a bowl of fresh water.

Duke waved to the ladies and left, off to work on his boat for another day.

"He'll be gone until Sunday or Monday," Robin said. "Should we throw a party tonight?"

Kelli's gaze immediately flew to Eloise, and Robin didn't have to be Sherlock Holmes to see that. She acted like she didn't though, and that was one of the best things about Robin. Eloise loved her powerfully in that second of time, and she cleared her throat.

"I have a date with Aaron Sherman tonight."

Eloise had never been in an emergency situation. Or a tornado. Or a hurricane. Or nearby when a bomb went off.

But the silence streaming through the room, rendering every woman in the vicinity absolutely mute, felt like the calm before the storm. The way the air would rush out of the tornado zone. The eye of the hurricane. The silence before the screaming.

"I'm sorry, what?" Alice asked at the same time Robin launched herself off the couch, that trademark squeal filling the air.

"I knew it," she said, engulfing Eloise in a hug. "Didn't I tell you he was flirting with you?"

"You told me," Eloise said, smiling despite her best efforts to the contrary.

"Flirting *shamelessly*," Robin said, straightening again. "Oh, can I do your hair, please?"

Eloise looked at Alice. "Only if Alice will use her professional makeup on me."

Surprise crossed Alice's face, and her polished, perfect demeanor cracked for a moment. "Please, Eloise," she said with a crisp bite to her voice. "You don't *need* my makeup. You're beautiful without it."

Eloise watched her, wondering if she knew she was beautiful at all. Perhaps she thought she had to hide behind the expensive makeup and high thread count of her clothing. Today, she wore a pair of black shorts that went down to her knee—prim and proper for a woman her age. She had a killer figure, and her legs had always been a source of jealousy for Eloise. Kelli too, she knew. The shorts were amazing, but they paled in comparison to the silver blouse Alice had paired them with. This one had sleeves that went to her elbows, hugging tight around her arms, and she looked like a model for middle-aged women in every way.

"I still want you to help me with it," she said. "Remember when you did that for my first date with Harry Eames?"

"Oh, Harry Eames," Alice said, smiling as she lifted her coffee mug to her lips. "That was a disaster, wasn't it?"

"Only a little bit," Eloise said, though that date had

definitely been a disaster and a half. Maybe two disasters. "But my makeup was flawless, and I kind of want to feel flawless right now."

"Oh, honey," Robin said. "You're already flawless."

"Yeah," Eloise said, because agreeing with Robin was sometimes the easiest thing to do. "But I want to *feel* like it." She surveyed the three women looking at her. "Don't you ever just want to feel like something you aren't? Even for just an evening."

"All the time," Kelli admitted, glancing at the other two.

Alice nodded, and Eloise saw the carefully hidden pain she carried everywhere with her. "I'll do your makeup tonight," she said.

So it was that hours later, after they'd survived another day of sorting and shredding and soft sniffling, the four of them returned to Robin's house, where her eldest daughter, Mandie had made dinner and had it baking in the oven, which the others would eat once Eloise left for her date.

The six of them then got to work on Eloise, all giving their opinions on her hair, her shoes, her jeans—even the twelve-year-old Jamie said Eloise should "for sure wear her hair half-up and half-down."

Eloise couldn't remember the last time she'd had this much fun, and she hadn't even left for the ferry station yet.

When she arrived at the ferry station, she promptly

wanted to leave again. She had no idea what kind of car Aaron drove, and she hadn't heard from him since that morning. She parked, paid at the booth for parking and a ferry ticket to Pearl, and looked around.

The ferry to Pearl left every twenty minutes, on the nines. If Aaron didn't show up soon, they'd be waiting here until seven-thirty.

In the distance, a siren blared. Eloise thought a car had been dispatched to arrest her for loitering, but such a thing was ridiculous.

The crowd swelled, as everyone seemed to be heading to Pearl Island this Thursday night. Eloise kept the smile on her face, recognizing some of the faces, though they'd aged. She hoped none of them had recognized her.

Desperation built in her chest, and she started wondering if she'd hallucinated the texts and phone call that morning. Her phone waited in her purse, but she did not pull it out to check it. It did not buzz or ring or chime.

The ferry horn sounded, and Eloise turned toward it. Perhaps she'd misunderstood. Perhaps he'd already gone to Pearl, and she was supposed to meet him over there.

But if so, wouldn't he have called by now? After all, she was late if they were to meet on Pearl at seven. She lifted her hand to her lips, her natural instinct to bite her nails. She'd tried for most of her life to overcome it, and most of the time, she won out. But in times of stress, or when she was really nervous, the old habit returned.

This is why you shouldn't blame your father, she thought,

that door in her mind creeping open again. She shoved against it, realizing that the siren was coming toward her, and fast. There was nowhere else to go, and she knew the police would be arriving at the ferry station at any moment.

Perhaps she could ask them to page Aaron. He'd said she could come to the station anytime, ask for him, and someone would find him. She wasn't sure she was comfortable with that, as Eloise liked to hang out in the back of lectures and turn in her professor ratings at the last minute, even if they'd been completed for weeks. If there was no one watching her, she didn't have to be perfect all the time.

The car screeched around the corner and into the lot, actual smoke coming from the tires as the driver skidded. Then it came right toward her.

Eloise scooted out of the way, but the car came to a jarring and complete stop, siren wailing, lights flashing, at the curb right in front of her.

Aaron got out of the driver's seat and jogged around the car, high-fiving the man who'd gotten out of the passenger side door. He grinned like he'd just won the Indy 500 with that cornering move, and easily slipped one arm around Eloise's waist as he said, "Hey, I'm so sorry I'm late." He looked at the ferry. "I think they'll still let us on. Come on."

She had no idea what was happening, but she went with Aaron, because he had his hand in hers. He was holding her hand. Holding it. Eloise enjoyed the rough, warm sensation of his skin against hers, and she couldn't help smiling as they hurried over to the attendant.

"Walk's still down," Aaron said.

"Tickets," the man standing there said. Eloise produced hers, but she hadn't bought one for Aaron.

"Sorry," she said. "I—"

"It's fine," he said smoothly. "I know Gilbert here, and he knows I'm going to buy a full fare ticket on the other side." With that, he stepped through the turnstile, clapped Gilbert on the shoulder, and led her up the ramp to the ferry.

Everyone—positively everyone—looked at them, and Aaron let go of her hand to shake several others, say hello and grin around as if he personally knew everyone on the boat. He probably did, Eloise realized, about the same time she realized the small-island gossip mill had already started turning.

Aaron led her to the back of the ferry and found a somewhat private spot along the rail. "Is this okay?"

"Hm." She nodded, because she'd also just realized he still wore his police uniform, and the man was downright lethal to her pulse wearing black from head to toe.

"You must've had a busy day," she said a few moments later, when she'd gathered all of her hormones and stuffed them inside a jar.

"Yeah," he said. "It was a little crazy." He glanced at her, those dark eyes drinking her right up. And Eloise wanted him to take more. "Really, I went home around four, and I lost track of time as I tried to figure out how to multiply fractions. So that meant dinner for the girls was late, and then my babysitter canceled right when it was time for me to leave."

"Oh, no," Eloise said, her heart skipping at the thought of "the girls." She hadn't heard from him about them, but Robin had mentioned he had two, and the mother didn't grow up here and hadn't been back in years. "You could've canceled with me."

"No," he said, shaking his head. "Do you know how hard it was for me to ask you out in the first place?" He chuckled and ducked his head now, his dark hair showing no signs of gray. Too bad, in Eloise's opinion, because there was nothing sexier than a man with silver hair salted among the darker parts.

Eloise had no idea what to say.

"No," Aaron said, taking another step closer to her, his eyes shining and dazzling. "I called in my backup, and we got here on time."

"Are you telling me the man who just left with the siren still on is watching your girls tonight?"

"Yeah," Aaron said. "That was Paul Leyhe. Best deputy in the cove." He slipped his arm around her waist again, and Eloise had never been happier for Kelli's body shaper. "And the girls were in the back seat."

Eloise pulled in a tight breath, whether from what

he'd said or the very masculine touch of him, she had no idea. "Tell me you're lying."

He laughed, tipping his head back and filling the sky with joy. "I'm not," he said chuckling. He bent closer to her. "I just couldn't miss my date with you." His eyes drifted closed, and for some reason, Eloise's did too.

And then Aaron Sherman kissed her.

CHAPTER FOURTEEN

Alice waited on the bottom step at Robin's house, her phone her only companion. This felt so much like her life at home—sitting, waiting for someone to come home, hoping they'd had the time of their lives.

If there was anyone on this planet who deserved an amazing first date, it was Eloise Hall. Behind her and down the hall in the living room, Robin snored softly. She wanted to hear all about the date too. Kelli had gone to bed at least an hour ago, but she wanted to be awakened when Eloise finally returned.

The clock had just ticked to midnight when the motion light on the front porch burst to life. Alice looked up from her phone, where she'd been entertaining herself with a game. She heard voices, one low and one Eloise's. She wanted to jump to her feet, rush to the window only five feet away, and pull back the curtains to see what was happening. Alice forced herself to stay. She'd had plenty of practice in staying put when she wanted to flee, and her will now remained as strong as ever.

Aaron and Eloise had fallen silent, and Alice wondered what they could be doing. Perhaps they'd just lowered their voices, so as to not wake anyone in the house. But if Eloise thought she could sneak in with her shoes pinched between her fingers, she wasn't as smart as Alice knew she was.

Several more seconds passed, and finally the doorknob creaked and the door opened a couple of inches. "...okay," Eloise said. "See you tomorrow." She entered, her smile made of pure gold and filling her face with light.

She closed the door and looked at Alice as she leaned against it, a sigh coming from her mouth. Alice knew instantly that she'd kissed Aaron Sherman, and her own heart started beating too fast. "Well?"

Eloise just shook her head slowly and closed her eyes. "If he asked me to marry him tomorrow, I'd say yes."

Alice appreciated the dreamy quality of her voice, and she took the couple of steps and embraced Eloise. "Oh, I'm so glad. He's nice? You like him? You had a good time?" She stepped back, feeling so protective of Eloise that night. She'd been the only one of them never to go to a school dance, because no one had ever asked her.

She told Alice once that she felt invisible, but Alice

had assured her she wasn't. It sure had seemed that way, though, and now that Alice knew what it felt like to be passed over by someone she desperately wanted to see her, her heart ached for Eloise.

Her heart ached for herself.

She'd texted Frank that night about being in Five Island Cove, and he'd responded with five words.

Great. I won't come home.

Great?

Alice had no idea what was so great about not coming home, or her being gone, or the fact that she'd pulled the children from school to come to a funeral.

"He's amazing," Eloise said, obviously still on a high. "Dinner was amazing. Kissing him is amazing."

"Eloise," Alice admonished, pure surprise moving through her. "You kissed him on the first date?"

Eloise looked at Robin, so much hope in her face. "He kissed me, if we're going to be technical. And I'm going out with him again tomorrow night." She took Alice's hand and squeezed it. "Thank you so much for helping me with the makeup." Her hazel eyes sparkled with a new kind of life that Alice had forgotten existed. She hadn't felt this excited about anything in far too long. "I felt beautiful, and he told me I was."

Alice squeezed her hand back. "Remember the beach party, El."

She nodded, some of her happiness diminishing. "I

remember. I'm not going to do anything stupid." She started for the stairs at the same time Robin cried out in her sleep. "Did she wait up?"

"She tried," Alice said. "You better go talk to her. She'll never forgive you if you don't."

Eloise detoured around the steps leading to the second floor and walked toward Robin. Alice stayed next to the banister and watched as Eloise woke Robin. She sat straight up and hugged Eloise, already asking her a question. The two of them sat side-by-side on the couch, and Alice found the scene before her utterly serene.

Safety lived in this house in a way Alice had never experienced in hers. Growing up, her father was always late, or her mother was always mad. Then her mom had passed away, and a drape of sadness had covered the Williams house twenty-four hours each day.

The only time she'd felt like she could breathe was at the lighthouse, with Joel and Kristen. Now one of them had become the reason her mother had died and the other would be devastated once she knew. Alice had stewed all day about pulling Kristen aside for just a few minutes. She wouldn't even have to speak; she'd just unfold the letter and show it to her. Kristen was smart. She'd put all the pieces together by the third line, the same way Alice had.

She blinked, her mind conjuring up the image of her in Kristen's tiny bathroom, sitting on the toilet, the letter shaking in her hands as she read it. She'd given herself a huge amount of credit when she'd come out five minutes later, and not a single person—not even Robin—had seen or sensed her distress.

Of course, she'd been living with Frank for eighteen years, and Alice had learned to cover everything with enough makeup, enough gold veneer, enough laughter, and no one even wanted to know what was underneath.

She smiled, because she loved the safety in this house, the same way she had at the lighthouse. Then she started up the steps to her bedroom, where she curled into the bed Robin had provided for her, and cried.

"HEY, GUYS," SHE SAID THE NEXT DAY, RUNNING DOWN THE ramp as she exited the ferry. Ginny opened her arms for a hug, and Alice swept right into her, holding her tight. "Oh, it's good to see you." Alice had always had Very Important Things To Do, but she'd made sure her children knew she loved them.

"Charlie," she said, stepping over to him. "Looks like you got too much sun." She hugged him tight, glad when he returned the favor.

"A little," he said. "But I'm fine."

Alice stepped back and looked at her father. "Thanks for taking them, Dad."

"They had fun," her dad said, smiling at the twins. He took Alice into a hug too, and she nearly came undone.

She'd let the others go to the lighthouse without her that morning, and she'd borrowed Eloise's rental car to get to the ferry station. Then onto a boat, and then twenty minutes later, this reunion.

She'd come, because she needed clarity. She'd come, because she needed answers. She'd come, because she needed to find herself, and she knew the last place she'd been herself was right there on Rocky Ridge.

"Della didn't come?" she asked, glancing around for her step-mother.

"She's in the car," her dad said. "She doesn't like the wind."

"So she didn't go sailing." Alice shouldered her purse and stepped, the others going with her.

"Oh, no," her father said. "She doesn't even like boats."

Alice had no idea what to say. She'd come to Della's and Dad's wedding, and they'd certainly seemed like they loved each other. But her mother had been born on Rocky Ridge, and she'd earned her US Coast Guard commercial boat operator's license before Dad had. In fact, Alice's mother had been the one to get her husband to complete the training, and they'd run the rescue operation from here to the Massachusetts coast, and over to Nantucket and then to Martha's Vineyard too.

Her mother had loved Five Island Cove, and she'd explored every trail and path on all five islands. Not only that, but she'd gone off-road too, and Alice's questions about her death kept piling up on top of each other.

She couldn't ask in front of the twins, and a part of her clung to the idea of letting this conversation stay in the silence. That part sent tremors of terror through Alice, and she just wanted to enjoy lunch with her kids and her father and even Della.

"Hello, dear," Della said, getting out of the car to greet Alice.

She smiled at the aging woman, who was fighting every step of the way. Alice knew she'd be expected to do the same, and she instantly bucked against the idea. She didn't want to have the fake black-from-a-bottle hair Della had, or the false eyelashes, the tucked skin along her mouth and forehead.

Elderly people should look elderly. Wise. Weathered. Like her father, who wore his wrinkles proudly. Alice waited while the twins got in the back seat, and then she slid in beside them.

"How is—how are things at the lighthouse?" Dad asked, and Alice might've thought the question innocent had she never found the letter.

"It's a huge mess," she said honestly. A sigh simply came from her mouth as she thought of the cottage up the cliff from the lighthouse. "We're almost done though, at least with the house. Then we apparently have to tackle the lighthouse."

"Wow," her dad said, his hands on the steering wheel perfectly loose. He didn't seem to mind talking about the lighthouse or Kristen, and Alice's mind raced.

She was very good at compartmentalizing things until they needed to be dealt with. So she enjoyed lunch, asked her children about their studies, and measured and scooped powder into water to make lemonade. She settled on the back porch of the home where she'd grown up with her father and Della, all of them with tall glasses of lemonade nearby.

"Getting hotter," Dad said, and Della hummed in response.

Alice checked to make sure the twins had stayed inside, both of them on their computers, catching up with the week's lessons. The private school they attended put all assignments online, and they could access them twenty-four-seven through a portal. No reasons for missing school were necessary. One email, and done, the twins could finish the entire year online if they needed to.

Alice honestly wasn't sure what she'd do, if she'd stay in the cove past the funeral.

Great. I won't come home.

Neither Ginny nor Charlie had asked about their father, and Alice hadn't expected them to. The three of them were used to living their lives without him, and Alice let her thoughts go to a situation where she filed for divorce and left Frank to his women in the city.

She'd have to leave the Hamptons, but Alice didn't care about that. She'd been in Five Island Cove for five days, and not one friend from the Hamptons had called or texted to see how things were going.

She'd have to find a new house. Alice lifted her lemonade to her lips, sure she could find a home suitable for a single woman and two children.

Where? she asked herself, and Alice thought of her favorite cities. Paris. London. Seattle. Halifax. Any of them would do, though she couldn't take the children from their school, or their friends.

She thought of the vacation home she and Frank owned on Rocky Ridge. She and the twins could easily live there. "But that would require a serious move for the children," she murmured.

She'd get money from Frank, as she'd supported him through the last two years of law school, while she worked at a family law firm so Frank could earn the same degree Alice already had.

She'd loved her job, and she'd started to help the people who needed it just before the twins were born.

Inside the house, Charlie laughed, and Alice remembered why she hadn't left Frank. The kids. They had three years of high school to finish, and then they'd hopefully be out on their own, making amazing lives for themselves.

And Alice would be all alone in that house, the roof growing heavier each day.

Three years. She could probably hang on for three more years—if she had Robin, Eloise, and Kelli with her.

And AJ, she reminded herself. She'd heard Robin talking about AJ with Duke that morning, and her husband had actually participated in the conversation like he hoped AJ would come to the funeral too. No, Duke likely didn't wear the same worry in his eyes that Robin did, but he listened, and he supported, and he'd let Robin talk as long as she wanted about it.

She'd only stopped when Alice had entered the kitchen. Then she'd hung up the phone real fast, her eyes searching and worried.

"I'm okay," Alice had told her, because she was.

Or at least she hoped to be.

"Dad," she said, clearing her throat. "I wanted to ask you some questions about Mom."

"Alice?"

She heard the fear in his voice, and Alice wished with everything in her that she didn't have to hurt him to get the answers her soul needed.

"It's okay, Connor," Della said, gently patting his knee. "Let the woman ask her questions."

"Was she..." The words had been right there, stuck in the back of Alice's throat for so long. Now she couldn't get them out. She took a drink, swallowing as if through a straw. "Did she cheat on you?" She swung her head toward her father, needing to see his reaction.

The color had drained from his face, and he ground his teeth together. "Yes," he said through them.

"With Joel Shields," Alice said, noting that it wasn't a question.

"Yes," he said.

"You knew?" Alice asked.

"Yes," he said again, and she wondered if that was all he'd say. "I knew. I found out when—" His voice muted, and guilt gutted Alice. Still, she waited, because she'd come for the story. The truth. Her need for it seethed beneath her skin, and it would not go away, no matter what she'd tried to tell herself.

"I found out when I found a pregnancy test in the trash can," he said. "She'd tried to hide it from me, of course." His voice took on a monotone quality. "But I went on her boat regularly, and I found it there. We hadn't—I wasn't able to be a father again by that point. You were fifteen, and Scott was twelve."

Alice nodded, because she knew the precise day her mother had died. In many ways, she felt trapped in that time, unable to move on. The world had stopped that day, yet only for her. She continued aging, but she'd been living her life from behind glass ever since. Just watching through a window as things happened to her. As she made impossible choices, as she tried to figure out how to be a mother when hers had been taken from her far too early.

"So I confronted her about it," Dad said, turning away from Alice. "It was a terrible night. So much thunder, heavy rain, such strong wind." He fell silent for a moment, then a minute. He looked into the distance, as if the scene was replaying on the clouds in the distance, reminding him of the storm that had swallowed his wife whole.

Finally, he said, "She admitted she was pregnant with

his baby, and I told her I wanted a divorce." He cleared his throat and swallowed once. Then again. And again. "I told her she couldn't stay in my house, not with another man's baby inside her. I told her she could go stay with him in the lighthouse."

Alice's face felt wet, and she reached up to find tears there. Her father swiped at his eyes too, finishing with, "She left on the boat. That was the last time anyone saw her alive."

"Dad," Alice said, but her voice broke. Everything broke. Absolutely everything. And Alice Kelton did not break. She bent, sure. She swayed. She slid to the floor and wondered how her life had come to whatever cross-roads she found herself at.

She sobbed as she got up and knelt in front of her father. "I'm sorry. I'm so sorry."

He looked at her, and the sky that Alice had been holding up by sheer will fell, and the fall thereof was great, and horrible, and so terribly loud inside Alice's soul.

THE NEXT MORNING, ALICE STOOD ON THE SAND, HER TOES just out of reach of the surf. The day had dawned several minutes ago, and the breeze coming off the water mean-dered around her bare shoulders. She shivered, but she hadn't brought a jacket with her.

She relished the cold, because it reminded her that

she could still feel something. The water washing ashore left behind patches of seaweed, broken shells, and the stench of something half decayed.

Alice loved the smell of the beach, the memories here such good ones.

Her father's house sat up on the cliff above the beach, the black sand here the stuff of luxury resorts and private beaches. But here at Rocky Ridge, it was untouched by most, unknown to all except the residents of Five Island Cove, and absolutely Alice's very favorite place on Earth.

The last time she'd seen herself, she'd stood on this beach, the night before she'd left for college. Three years, seven months, and thirteen days after her mother's death.

Then, Robin had come to the black sand beach on Rocky Ridge. Eloise had come. Kelli had come. AJ had come.

They'd made a pact—the summer sand pact—to congregate here every summer, no matter what. Alice had come for a few years. Then she'd met Frank, and their lives had become so busy.

To Alice's recollection, Robin had asked about the pact once or twice, and then her life had been one of studies, and a husband, learning to make dinner for two, then four.

Alice hadn't known herself since standing on this beach, and she reached out toward the horizon, sure she could bring back the young woman she'd been then. Grasp onto some strand of herself that had been lacking lately; the exact strand she needed to know how to deal with the new information she'd learned about her mother, what to say to Kristen, and how to unravel the knotted mess her life had become.

She closed her fingers into a fist and shut her eyes, imagining she could feel some thread of her soul. She pulled, pushing all the air out of her lungs as she seized onto the very core of herself, and sucked in a new breath.

When she opened her eyes, the ocean was still the ocean. Unrelenting and constantly moving—like she needed to be. The sky was still the sky—and it had not fallen. The sand was still the sand—and she knew she needed to get all of them to this patch of black sand again.

Soon.

She pulled out her phone, shivering in the wind again, and dialed Robin.

"Alice," she said after only half a ring. "You didn't come home last night."

Home.

Alice smiled at the concern in her friend's voice. Robin had been as close as a sister once, and Alice wanted her to be again. "I need AJ's number," she said. "Can you text it to me?"

"Sure," Robin said, surprise replacing the concern in her voice. "Are you okay?"

"Yes," Alice said. "I slept in my old bed last night, and my back aches, but I'm okay. I'll be back later today."

"Okay," Robin said. "I'll send you AJ's number."

"Thanks." Alice lowered the phone and let Robin end the call. A moment later, her phone buzzed, and Alice studied the clouds moving in the distance. They were still clouds.

She lifted the phone and called AJ.

CHAPTER FIFTEEN

AJ already had the phone arcing toward her ear before she checked the ID of the caller. She didn't have the contact saved in her phone, and AJ hesitated.

"Can't be Robin," she murmured, but it also wasn't Trevor, the assistant coach she'd been conversing with for the past twenty-five minutes. He'd promised her an exclusive quote from one of the top recruits coming to play baseball at the University of Miami, and AJ was not leaving the sports complex without it.

She'd been there for two hours already, and she'd learned to wait through hunger, heat, and hurting feet for the interview, the quote, or the picture.

The call went to voicemail while AJ wrestled with the decision to answer it. *Just as well*, she thought as she tossed her long, shiny, straight hair over her shoulder. She couldn't be on the phone when Trevor did call back.

Part of her wanted to get the quote and get back to the office. She was replaceable on the local sports show she did during the nine and ten PM news, and she hadn't been on the air for a week now.

AJ loved being in front of the camera, and she loved seeing herself on the screen. She loved reading comments about how pretty she was, but also how competent in the world of sports. She'd grown up an athlete, and she'd searched for a way to stay in the world as she neared the beginning of her senior year.

She'd been a good swimmer and soccer player, but she knew she wasn't one of the elite.

Joel Shields had taught her that.

She shook the man out of her head once again, hating that he'd snuck back in. At the same time, every time someone said her name, she could be reminded of him. He'd been the one to suggest the change from AvaJane to AJ.

"It's more masculine," he'd said, his voice as clear to her now as it had been twenty-eight years ago.

Twenty-eight years. Why couldn't she let go of that? She'd slept around well into her thirties, and she could let those men and the things they did go right down the drain. She hadn't been able to commit to anyone, and she'd never been in love.

Until now.

But AJ wasn't dwelling on Nathan right now either.

Never mind that he'd barely called in the six days she'd been in Miami. Her chest tightened, one inch at a time as if someone had a vice and was twisting the screw one revolution at a time to make breathing more difficult for her.

Her phone rang again, and the shrill tone of it drove everyone and everything she didn't want to think about out of her mind.

Finally.

The same unknown number. Annoyance made her ears ring, and she decided to simply answer and get it over with. Perhaps it would be Dante Matthews, the young man expected to sign with Miami next week.

"AJ Proctor," she said, completely business-like.

"AJ," a woman said. "It's Alice."

AJ silently pulled in a breath and spun away from the doors leading to the locker room, which she'd been watching almost without blinking.

Alice said nothing else, and she'd always made AJ feel like filling the silence. *Not this time*, AJ told herself. Alice had called her. She could say what she wanted.

"How are you?" Alice finally asked.

"Busy," AJ said, trying to drive home the point. The truth was, as soon as she got this quote, she'd be free to work on the story. She could go to Five Island Cove, but she guarded that secret well, and she'd had no contact with any of the four women who had been her whole world once upon a time.

But once upon a time was a fairy tale, and AJ didn't believe in those. Not anymore.

"I'm sure," Alice said, her voice so proper. "Listen," she said smoothly, and AJ had a feeling she'd had a lot of practice talking to people who didn't want to talk to her. "I know there's something keeping you from coming back to the islands. I understand that, probably more than you know."

Something like static or scratching came through the line, and only a moment passed before AJ identified the sound. The beach. Waves coming ashore. Alice was standing on the beach somewhere, and AJ could almost feel the sea breeze on her own face.

"Why don't you want to come back to Five Island Cove?"

"I told Robin this already." AJ heaved a great sigh. "I don't mourn Joel Shields."

"Yes, I know that," Alice said. "And it's also not what I asked. I didn't ask why you didn't want to come to the funeral. I asked why you don't want to come back to Five Island Cove."

"I—" AJ's mouth hung open, her mind racing through possibly answers. Surely she had one that would appease Alice.

"I know you come back to see your dad," Alice said. "You've even brought your boyfriend to see him. Or are you married to Nathan Cooke now?"

AJ's smile was not made of happiness, but utter disbelief. "You know I didn't get married."

"Yes, of course I know that," Alice said. "Because I
would've gotten an invitation, and I would've been here
on the island to celebrate with you."

"What makes you think I'd get married on the island?"

"Because you've always wanted a beach wedding, on
the beach that your father owns. Altar on the dock, right?"
Alice gave a blissful sigh, the way she'd had when they
were sixteen and talking about their dream weddings as
they looked up into the night sky and counted the stars.

AJ could practically feel the slight wobble from the
trampoline as Alice lifted her arm and said, "Right there,
AJ. That's the star you want."

AJ could hear her laugh, and that had made the trampoline move even more. Robin hadn't been able to come
that night, because she'd been fighting with her mother
something fierce about the length of the cheerleading skirt
she was required to wear for the new squad she'd just made.

Jennifer Golden had a lot of opinions and a very loud
bark. But in the end, Robin got her way. She'd worn the
short skirt—up on top of the pyramid too, where all the
boys could look right up the length of her legs.

"You think I want a star to stand guard over my
marriage?"

Alice had turned her head and looked right into AJ's
eyes. "You don't?"

"I guess." She'd looked up at the stars again, the idea of having a soul mate written in the stars very romantic and appealing to AJ. Her experience with men up to that point had been that they liked sleeping with her and not much else.

Her father had brought home plenty of women over the years, and AJ had witnessed him not committing, not caring, not calling back afterward. He hadn't liked her going around with boys, but he'd never taught her to respect herself. He'd taught her that women were for his pleasure, and AJ had liked the way she turned heads and got the boys to say how much they liked her.

Her mother wasn't in the picture, and AJ still didn't know where she was. She'd thought her mother would reach out to her when AJ left Five Island Cove, but it was a phone call she was still waiting to receive.

"AJ?" Alice asked in the present moment, and AJ pulled herself out of the past. Sometimes she preferred to live back then, when things were simpler. When she didn't have to wonder why her own mother had abandoned her, and she didn't have to wonder why Nathan couldn't commit to her, and she didn't have to wonder why she was never, ever good enough.

At sixteen, she was good enough, because the boys she slept with told her so—over and over.

At fifteen, she was good enough, because Robin and Alice told her so—every time they chose to spend time with her, despite her stealing all the boys from them.

At fourteen, she was good enough, because Kristen made her feel like a queen for learning to tie knots and sail a boat.

She'd been good enough for a few years, and then she'd started training with Joel.

"AJ?" Alice said again. "Did I lose you?"

"No," she blurted out. "No, I'm still here."

"We're all here," Alice said. "And I don't blame you for not wanting to go to the funeral. I'm standing on the black sand beach on Rocky Ridge, and I wish you were here with me."

Tears pricked AJ's eyes, and she felt her face scrunch with emotion. "I wish that too, Alice."

"Then come," Alice said, and it sounded so simple.

AJ tilted her head back and looked up into the brilliant, blue sky above Miami. She didn't want to admit it, but life was simpler in Five Island Cove too. At least hers had been. At least before Joel had started filling her head with lies about what kind of athlete she was and what her life could be if she just "applied herself."

"I have something to tie up," AJ said. "And then I'll see where I am." Her phone buzzed against her palm, and she checked it to see she had another call coming in, this one from Trevor. "I have another call, Alice. I'm sorry."

She swiped over to Trevor's call, stuffing her emotions as deep as she could. "Talk to me, Trevor," she said.

"Five minutes," he said, nearly under his breath. "West door."

AJ swore and started moving. "You told me south."

"We changed it twenty seconds ago," he said, his voice filled with annoyance. "Why do you think I'm calling you?"

"Okay," she started, but he'd already hung up. And AJ knew why he was calling her—the man owed her a favor, and this would bring them even. The agent didn't like to be in anyone's debt, and AJ didn't blame him. She wouldn't want someone to be able to call in a favor from her anytime they wanted. But she *had* helped him out of a sticky situation with his boss, and he had slept with her afterward. He hadn't had to do that; they could've just disappeared into the hotel room so his boss wouldn't think she could.

She broke into a run as she neared the corner of the building, because she couldn't have this day be a waste. All the others had been, and AJ was tired of Miami.

She was tired of a lot of things, and she had the fleeting thought of abandoning her quest to get this quote, quit her job, and quickly return to the island where she'd been raised. She could find something to do there with her journalism degree. Or she could wait tables and make a killing during the summer months. Joel wasn't there anymore, and she didn't have to rush from the airport on Diamond Island to the ferry that would take her to Pearl so she wouldn't run into him.

She'd just arrived at the west door into the building when it opened, and she hurried down the sidewalk, wishing she just had one moment to run her fingers through her hair and put on some more lipstick.

"Dante," she said. "AJ Proctor from Southern Sports News. Have you signed with the University of Miami?"

He looked at Nathan, and Nathan gave one single nod. Then Dante put a smile on his face and stepped forward. "Nice to meet you AJ."

Her skin crawled, because she knew what that smile meant, and this eighteen-year-old would be sorely disappointed when she walked away with her quote, and he didn't get anything in return.

I'M GOING TO FIVE ISLAND COVE TO SEE MY FRIENDS.

AJ had expected Nathan to call after he received that text. She'd gone from the college to the airport, and she hadn't booked a flight back to Atlanta and Nathan Cooke, her long-time, live-in boyfriend. He played football with the pro team there, and somehow she managed to call and text him when he was on the road. Once, she'd had a case of his favorite protein bars sent to his hotel in Los Angeles during one of his long road trips when he'd off-handedly texted that he couldn't find the brand on the West coast.

She looked up from her phone, not wanting to see his response. She'd waited through security, through the hour outside the gate, through boarding before he'd finally responded.

She didn't know for sure, but it felt like Nathan had waited to respond so she'd be in the air and wouldn't get it until she landed in Five Island Cove.

Great, have fun.

No miss you, AJ.

Come home, AJ.

Do you have to go, AJ?

"Do you want a drink, ma'am?"

She glanced up at the flight attendant and nodded. "Red wine, please." She did enjoy the benefits of flying first class, and she definitely needed alcohol in order to face her friends and apologizing for not being on the first plane out of Miami the moment she'd heard they were all there, waiting for her.

CHAPTER SIXTEEN

Kristen carried the plate of blueberry muffins up the path and over the slight rise in the rocks, feeling a bit better that morning. The girls would be arriving a little late today, and Kristen had decided to take the muffins she'd made when she couldn't sleep that morning to her son. That way, Robin wouldn't feel bad for not being there to eat them, and she'd get a chance to talk to Rueben.

Her mother's heart had never been so full of worry, and her hands shook slightly as she crested the rise in the path and started down the other side. The sun shone down on this place where she'd lived for so many years of her life. She could see the milestones etched on the rocks at her feet, each crack and vein of color in them as familiar to Kristen as her own hands.

She could hear Rueben's first word, see him take his

first step, smell the baby soft powder of him when she'd first brought him home from the hospital. A smile accompanied her all the way to the navy blue back door, where she raised her free hand and knocked.

"Coming," her son said from inside, and she heard his footsteps on the stairs immediately inside the door. She knew every one of those too, to the fourth one that was slightly higher than the others, to the last one that got very slippery whenever it rained.

The door opened, and her boy stood there, leaning into the frame and looking from her to the muffins in her hand.

"Have you had breakfast?" she asked.

"No." He stepped down. "Come on in."

"I think you should know I'm going to ask you about Jean. If you don't want to answer, you can take the muffins and go. I'll go sit on the deck." Just inside the door, she could go up or down, and while the stairs were steep, Kristen could still get to the deck in only a couple of minutes.

"It's fine," Rueben said coolly, and he reminded her so much of Joel though he had her pointed chin and her hazel eyes above the shape of his father's long, slanted nose. His hair color sat somewhere between Joel's and Kristen's, and he'd let it grow out enough to have it curl along the ends.

"All right then." She stepped into the lighthouse, the familiar scent of glass cleaner and polish mixing with the coffee Rueben had obviously already started. "I'll give you a head start to think about what you want to tell me."

He took the muffins from her, turned deftly on the stairs—something she never would've been able to do at her age—and started down. Twenty-five steps down, and Kristen could take them in her sleep. Rueben, thankfully, had inherited more of her minimalist personality, and the room the stairs ended in held a single couch with a simple table next to it. They both faced a cabinet with pretty seaglass green doors which bore a TV on the top.

Around the corner, Rueben set the plate of blueberry muffins on the counter and went into the small kitchen to get down a pair of mugs. "I guess you want to know if Jean is going to come back."

"That would be a great place to start," Kristen said, taking one of the two barstools that faced into the kitchen.

"I don't know," Rueben said, lifting his chin as if trying to be brave. She'd seen this hopeful, bright look in her son's eyes before, and Kristen's heart grew and pulsed simultaneously. He'd wanted to be the captain of the chess club too, and he'd worn such a desperate expression then too.

He'd gotten that position, and then he'd wanted to go to college, knowing that Joel and Kristen didn't have a lot of money.

He'd asked—actually asked—if he could go and pay his own way. And he had, working two jobs to put himself through semester after semester until he'd earned a degree in architecture. He'd been working for the citifies up and down the Atlantic Seaboard for the past twenty-seven years, and he'd retired from that job to come keep the lighthouse.

Kristen loved her son with all the energy of her soul, and she couldn't abide his obvious pain.

"When's the last time you spoke with her?" she asked.

"Last night," he said. "We talk every day, Mom. She just hates it here, and she doesn't understand the significance of the lighthouse." Rueben gave a partial shrug, like he and Jean disagreed on where to spend their summer holiday.

Kristen ran her hands along the pale countertop, the same one that had been in the lighthouse when she and Joel had lived here. She saw the red stain she'd never been able to get out, though it was so faded now that it was hardly noticeable. But Kristen could still feel the red-hot anger that had filled her heart when Clara had spilled the permanent dye on the countertop. She'd told her daughter to put down newspaper, but of course, Clara knew better than everyone, about everything, and she'd just rolled her eyes.

"Are you going to stay?" Kristen asked, accepting the cup of coffee her son gave to her.

He set a bowl of sugar and a pint of cream in front of her and leaned into the countertop. "Mom..." He shook his head. "I don't know."

"I need to know," she said, her pulse picking up now

and not just from the second dose of caffeine she was giving it that day.

"I want to stay," Rueben said, staring down into his mug. "But I love my wife too."

Kristen nodded, because she understood the exact place where her son found himself. She'd loved Joel with everything she had. She'd given him everything. Her whole life. Two beautiful children. A life on the island he loved so much. Room to write and breathe when he needed it. All of her earnings, to keep their small family and humble surroundings theirs.

If Rueben couldn't keep the lighthouse... Kristen cut off the thought. Someone had to run the lighthouse, and the house where she lived came with it. If she had to sell, she'd lose everything she'd ever known.

And she'd already lost so much.

Rueben rounded the counter and sat down next to her. "How are you holding up?"

She hadn't told him about any of the secrets she and the girls had unearthed. She hadn't seen the point, and she was still trying to iron them flat in her own mind. Then maybe she could see the kind of man her husband had really been.

Dealing with his physical death was actually the easiest part of the past week. It was the slow, painful uncovering of the truth that painted a different picture of Joel than Kristen had in her memory that had been utterly exhausting.

"I'm okay," she reassured her son, reaching over to pat his hand. "Have you heard from your sister?"

"Nope." He stirred his coffee and took a sip. "She'll come around when she's ready."

Clara always took her sweet time getting ready, though. Kristen wasn't sure how she'd gotten such a dramatic daughter, but Clara had cried every day of fifth grade, and she'd joined the theater company in junior high and high school.

Kristen could ask her a simple question about one of her classes, and Clara would get offended and refuse to return calls for a month. Then, when she finally did speak to Kristen, she'd admit she didn't even know why she'd been upset.

Kristen had been through it all before, and Rueben was right. Clara would come around when she was good and ready, no matter what everyone else wanted or needed.

She sighed before she could pull back on the show of emotion. But her son didn't say anything, and she remembered she didn't have to guard every reaction around him the way she did her Seafaring Girls.

She loved them as much as her own biological children, but she didn't want them worrying over her. They had their own children, families, and problems to deal with. She didn't want to be one of them.

They sat together, mother and son, sipping coffee in the silence of the lighthouse, and Kristen finally found a measure of the peace she'd enjoyed before Joel's cancer diagnosis. When it was time for her to go, she stood and embraced her son, glad he seemed to hold as tightly to her as she was to him.

"You're a good man," she whispered. "You do what you think is right."

He stepped back and looked down at her. "Even if it means leaving the lighthouse?"

"It's just a lighthouse." She tried to smile, but it only stayed put for a moment before falling right off her face. She turned quickly and started for the steps, bypassing the ground-level exit and going all the way up to the deck.

Six flights definitely made her huff and puff, and she leaned into the railing and let the wind push and pull her hair as she sucked at the fresh air. Kristen didn't make it a habit to lie, especially to her children, but she'd just told a bold lie.

This place was so much more than a lighthouse. It symbolized her entire life, and if Rueben walked away from it, it would be like he was walking away from her.

She watched the clouds roll through the sky, seeing so many memories of the past playing on the puffy surfaces. How many times had she stood here, seeking clarity? Seeking answers? Praying for her girls, and her own children?

Many. So, so many.

Below her, the water crashed into the rocks, creating a spectacular white spray that arced into the sky. Kristen smiled at it, because she loved the ocean and its antics. She loved that it was different every single day, and completely unpredictable. She loved that the lighthouse had tamed that unpredictability over and over again, and that she and Joel had led dozens, hundreds, and thousands of boats to safety.

The lighthouse was so much more than a home for her, though if that was all it was, that would be enough. Having a place to call home meant something, and she'd always been safe in the lighthouse.

She took her phone from her pocket and dialed her daughter, seeing Clara's life in the several seconds it took for her phone to connect, ring, and go to voicemail.

"Hello, dear," she said, her neck muscles tightening. Her throat narrowed against the emotions there, and Kristen couldn't say anything else. In such times, every second felt too long, and she finally said, "I love you," in a high-pitched voice that would say everything else she wanted to say to her daughter, and hung up.

She had the sudden, inexplicable urge to hurl her phone over the railing and out into the ocean. But she knew she didn't have the strength in her arm to even get it to the water. She'd tried to throw things off the deck of the lighthouse in the past, and they'd barely reached the edge of the cliffs. Then she'd had to explain the broken, cranberry-colored pieces of pottery Joel had found and brought inside, confusion in his eyes.

She half-laughed, half-cried at the memory of that pot.

When she'd told Joel that she'd found it in Clara's room, with a Mother's Day note attached that said cruel things, he'd held her tight and tried to reassure her that they should be grateful they had a daughter who could think for herself.

"I still didn't want that pot," Kristen had said, and he'd quietly cleaned it up. That was what Joel had done his whole life—live quietly.

"A little too quietly," she muttered, thinking of the things she and the girls had found in his personal and business papers. He hadn't seemed to put a divide between them, and that only made the chore of going through his things that much harder. If she knew she was going to open a folder of receipts, perhaps her chest wouldn't constrict with every beat of her heart. As it was, she teetered on the edge of a complete breakdown with every movement of paper, every file that got flipped open.

She stayed on the deck for another minute, and then she held tightly to both handrails in the stairwell and pushed open the door to the first subterranean level in the lighthouse.

The door had just closed behind her when Rueben opened it again. "What are you doing?"

"I'm going to get started," she said.

"You're not going to wait for your girls?" The concern on his face sparked joy in Kristen's heart.

"I'm okay," she said. "Where are you going?" He wore hiking boots now, along with a hat with a wide, oval brim.

"I'm going up to the electric box," he said. "Make sure the path is clear. Bring back some supplies."

She saw the straps of the duffel bag on his back then, and she smiled. "Okay. I'm just going to be in the spare bedroom. I won't touch your things."

He nodded and backed out the door. Kristen faced this space, which was like the second level of their home. Three bedrooms, one bathroom. She stood on a small, circular landing with doors leading off of it every so often.

The lighthouse had only had room for a washing machine, and that was downstairs in the kitchen. She'd hung their clothes outside to dry, and April had been the perfect month for that. She held back a sob as she remembered how many times she'd hear rain hitting the lighthouse and shout for Joel and the children to come help her gather the clothes from the line before they got too wet.

She pushed through the first door on her right and entered the spare bedroom where Joel had left some of his papers. After the children had grown and moved out, he'd slowly started to take over their rooms. This one still had all the glow-in-the-dark stars and constellations Clara had stuck to the ceiling, and Kristen let the door close behind her. She didn't turn on the light, and she waited for her eyes to adjust to the pure blackness in the room.

Since they'd lived underground, and her kids were like other kids and afraid of thunder and the dark, Kristen had found little ways to bring light to their world. It had actually been a friend of hers that had shown her the glow-in-the-dark stars, and Kristen had ordered them instantly.

Clara had loved them, and Kristen wished she'd held onto her ten-year-old daughter for longer instead of being annoyed by her constant questions and eagerness to help with things she was too little to help with.

She flipped on the light, and all the magic of the stars fled. It took her several moments to find where they'd stopped working yesterday, and she pulled up a chair and opened a folder.

Annual report from 1989. Trash.

Another folder. Another report. Trash.

Another, another, another. Kristen worked steadily, keeping her mind busy by examining the documents. Gradually, they began to change, and she sorted through budget analyses, the bills Joel had paid to keep the land, the cottage, and the lighthouse.

She finally opened a folder that held the deed to the lighthouse, and she pulled in a breath. "Oh, Joel," she whispered, lifting the paper with one shaking hand while the other went to cover her mouth.

A blue sticky note had been placed in the top right corner, and it read, *It's ours!*

She remembered the day he'd paid the last mortgage payment for the place where they'd labored and loved for so long. They'd both cried then, and Joel had gone to town for lobster. They'd feasted that night, and Kristen allowed some of that memory to brighten her heart now too.

She set the deed to the left, the only thing she'd be keeping so far today. In the folder, another deed sat, and confusion furrowed her brows as Kristen reached for it.

They didn't own anything else—at least to her knowledge.

Her heart thumped in her chest, the vibrations landing in her ribs, her arms, and the back of her throat.

She couldn't read fast enough.

When she realized what she held, she gasped, her fingers releasing the paper so that it floated neatly back into the folder.

"It can't be," she whispered. She closed her eyes as if not being able to see the deed to Guy's Glassworks would make it not exist.

She saw Kelli standing on the stoop, tears falling down her face. The memories played in stilted images, as if the videotape of it had been cut and spliced back together, one scene per second.

Kristen making cookies.

Kelli explaining about the divorce.

Advance time a year.

Kristen making more cookies.

Kelli crying.

Sitting on the deck, looking at the water while Kelli says her father has lost his business.

Kristen hugging her, saying that she'll help anyway she can though she and Joel don't have much money either.

Going to the grocery store and seeing Paula Watkins there, working now that her husband's art studio and custom glassworks is out of business.

Kelli in her hand-me-down clothes and shoes.

Guy Watkins getting questioned by authorities about fraud.

The rumors Kristen had heard then...

She screamed, effectively making the wicked film stop jumping through her mind. Her fingers crunched over the paper, crushing it into a ball and throwing it across the room.

Just as quickly as her emotions had exploded out of her, they calmed again. She drew in a breath, her mind trying to find a way through the misty maze she'd just entered.

That deed was for Guy's Glassworks, and it had her name on it, right beside Joel's.

Her name.

She felt damned.

"Kristen," someone called, and she jumped to her feet faster than a woman her age should be able to. Robin could not see that paper. Worse, Kelli could never know.

Kristen rushed to where the crumpled ball waited, and she picked it up, flattened it, folded it, and shoved it in her pocket.

"There you are," Robin said with a smile in her voice.

Kristen didn't bother to brush the tears from her eyes.

She wouldn't have to explain them, and she'd rather not lie to Robin.

"Guess who I found?" Robin asked. She stepped to the side, and AJ stood there, tears already pouring down her face too.

The air left Kristen's lungs, and all she could say was, "Oh," before she opened her arms and AJ rushed into them.

CHAPTER SEVENTEEN

Robin was too old to sit on the ground, even leaning her back against the wall. But Kristen had only been able to find four deck chairs, and one of them couldn't bear any weight.

Alice had taken it in her bony hands, her tight muscles straining as she lifted it over the nearly chest-high railing on the upper deck of the lighthouse, and a primal yell ripping from her throat as she'd heaved it over the edge.

As the plastic chair shattered against the stones below, Robin cheered with everyone else, all six of them dissolving into laughter a few moments later.

They didn't have cookies or lemonade. No sweet tea or even water. None of that mattered. Somehow, Alice had worked a miracle, and she'd gotten AJ on a plane out of Miami yesterday. When Robin had asked her how she'd done it, all Alice would say was, "Luck."

Robin knew it was more than that. It had to be. She'd decided she didn't care, because AJ was there, and they still had an entire week until the funeral.

Kristen took one of the chairs, and the rest of them stood there, looking at the remaining two. "I'll take one," Alice finally said. "I feel weak from lifting that other one." She giggled like the young woman Robin had once known, and she was so happy to see that person back on Diamond Island.

"My back is sore," Eloise said. "Can I have the other one?"

"Is it because of the bed?" Robin asked, instantly worried. "I told Duke we needed new guest beds." But they hadn't bought them, because no one came to stay with them all that often, and they didn't have thousands of dollars lying around for things they didn't need.

"The bed is fine," Eloise said, rubbing her back.

"It's because of Aaron," Kelli said suggestively, and Eloise smiled and shook her head.

"No, it's not," she said.

"Maybe he has a bad bed," Alice said in a complete deadpan, and a beat of silence passed before they all burst out laughing again, Eloise included.

"I didn't miss the date update, did I?" Kristen asked.

"No," Robin said as she slid down the wall and came to a rest on the hard cement of the deck. As a teen, she'd sat up here like this many times. But her joints and hips had been much younger then, and they didn't ache when they came in contact with hard things. "She's refused to say a word about it." She threw Eloise a dirty look—at least what she hoped was a dirty look.

"I didn't want to repeat myself," Eloise said. "Thursday night and Friday were brutal."

"Yeah, going out with a hot cop is probably torture," Alice said dryly, though she wore a smile on her face.

"Someone catch me up on who Aaron is," AJ said as she sat on the ground too. She hadn't lost her long legs or her trim waist, and she folded her legs under her as she settled down.

"Aaron Sherman," Kelli said. "Surely you remember him."

"Of course she does," Eloise said. "And AJ, I love you, but if you go *near* him while you're here, and I'll bury your body where no one will find it." She pealed out a string of laughter after that, and Robin giggled with her.

"I'm not interested in Aaron Sherman," AJ said.

"Seems like your interest in a boy didn't matter," Kristen said, immediately clapping her hand over her mouth. Her eyes widened, and Robin watched AJ, sure the woman would get to her feet, stare them all down, and walk out.

"I'm sorry," Kristen said. "I'm so sorry, AJ. Heaven knows a person can change after almost thirty years."

AJ nodded. "It took me a long time to learn that I didn't have to sleep with everything with a Y chromosome."

Robin was interested in that story, but she really did want to hear Eloise's first. And there was something going on with Kristen. The woman she knew would've never said such an unkind thing to AJ, even if it was true. She'd dealt with all of their idiosyncrasies, during the worst years of their lives, and always handled them with firm, loving gloves.

She kept her eyes on Kristen as Eloise started to detail her second date with Aaron, and sure enough, Kristen seemed distracted. Robin switched her gaze just before Kristen looked at her, hitching a smile on her face as Eloise said, "I've always wanted to go to one of those Friday night sand bakes, you know?"

Robin loved them too, with the scent of salt in the air, and cooked shrimp, and all those clams buried in the sand, cooking and roasting until they were just right. The fruity drinks weren't bad either, and the fruit salad.

"And we ate and talked and laughed." Eloise looked like she'd died and gone to heaven. "And then there was the dancing."

"No wonder your back hurts," Alice said. "Dancing on sand without shoes shouldn't be done by a woman our age."

Robin had to agree, as she bought expensive running shoes with a high arch support. If she didn't, she couldn't even make it a mile before she experienced crippling pain.

"Is he a good dancer?" Kelli wanted to know, and Eloise confirmed he was.

"When are you going to meet his kids?" Robin asked, and Eloise's eyes flew to hers.

"I—we haven't talked about that."

The mood sobered, and Robin cursed herself for saying anything about Aaron's daughters. She was happy for Eloise; she was. She just didn't understand the end game. She lived in Boston, with a prominent position at the university. He lived here, raising his girls alone as the Police Chief. Both of them seemed rooted where they were.

"Do you think this will be a...fling?" she asked, and Alice shot her a glare. "What?" Robin asked. "Someone has to ask these questions. She has a plane ticket back to Boston next Sunday."

"No, you're right," Eloise said, nodding. "I suppose there's technology, and weekend trips, and video chats."

"So you're going to do the long-distance thing?" AJ asked. Robin couldn't quite get a read on her. Alice had returned from Rocky Ridge with AJ in tow, and Robin had burst into tears the moment she'd seen the leggy blonde.

But she couldn't tell if she was happy to be here, putting up with them, or something else entirely.

"I can't even do the close-distance thing," AJ said, turning to look through the rails.

Everyone fell silent again, and Robin met Alice's eye. The other woman shook her head, but Robin opened her mouth anyway. "Tell us about that," she said, looking at AJ.

Before she could say anything, Kelli's phone rang, and she said, "It's Julian. I'll be back." She got up quickly and hurried over to the door, answering her husband's call as she left the deck.

"I'm not telling it twice," AJ said.

"We'll catch her up," Eloise promised.

Robin wanted to press a button and freeze time for just this one moment. She could see a situation exactly like this one in her past, where the five of them had sat on the deck without Kelli, discussing how they could help her. Her parents had been divorced for a year or so, and her father had lost his glassblowing company due to another investor coming in and buying it out from under him. He hadn't even known what he was signing.

The way Robin knew the story, Guy Watkins had thought this private investor was giving him money to expand his studio and grow the business, but that hadn't been the case at all. He'd bought the business right out from under Guy, who then came under scrutiny for fraud, and proceeded to lose everything.

Kelli had not come home for his funeral, though Robin had tried to persuade her to please come. There could be so much forgiveness at a funeral, and Robin would be lying if she said that wasn't one of the reasons she wanted AJ there.

"I've been dating Nathan Locke for eight years," AJ said. "Every time I bring up marriage, we'll talk about it for a few days, and then it's like I never said anything."

She shrugged one shoulder and studied her hands. "I don't know. Feels like...stale, you know? We live together, and either I'm traveling or he is, and I just—maybe I'm not cut out for a real, lasting relationship."

She looked up then, the vulnerability in her eyes too much for Robin. AJ held people like a deck of cards. Sometimes, when it didn't matter, she'd show anyone everything. Other times, with very important things, she kept everyone close to the vest. Right up against her chest. Inside her heart.

"Of course you are," Eloise said. "If that description fits anyone, it's me."

"Just because you had two years of a bad marriage doesn't mean you can't have a real, lasting relationship," Alice said.

"I fear I've let too many years go by," Eloise said. "I mean, you guys, we're almost fifty years old. Marriage at this point is simply about companionship."

"That's not true," Alice argued. "Look at you and Aaron. No." She held up her hand as Eloise tried to talk over her. "I know you and Aaron aren't going to have any kids of your own, but he has two girls, Eloise. Young ones too, I think." She looked at Robin for confirmation, and she nodded.

Alice focused back on Eloise. "That's a family, Eloise. And families are about more than just companionship."

Robin smiled, because her own definition of family had definitely changed over the years. "You guys are part of my family," she said, and while she'd never been shy in the spotlight, their eyes did weigh on her. "I'm so glad you came, AJ."

AJ nodded, her face seemingly placid—until the muscle in her jaw jumped. "So what do you think?" she asked, bringing the topic back to her.

Robin basked in this conversation, which flipped and meandered, just like it always had. As teenagers, they'd done it because they'd all been so selfish, and every conversation had to be about them.

"Do I give him an ultimatum, or just be happy we're still together?" AJ looked around at the others, and Robin would not be the first to give any advice in this situation. Alice had likewise clammed up, and Eloise studied the horizon like it held the secret to lasting happiness with Aaron Sherman.

"I find," Kristen finally said. "That ultimatums rarely work the way we hope they will." She smiled kindly at AJ. "If you want to marry him, ask him to marry you. If he says no, there's your answer. If he says yes, start planning a wedding."

"That's the problem, though," AJ said, clearly frustrated. "It's not a yes or no question anymore."

"It's not?" Kristen asked.

Robin shook her head. "I mean, kind of." She watched AJ, hoping she was about to get this right. She felt like a fraud talking, as she'd been married for twenty years. "My guess is that Nathan says 'not right now,' or 'the time isn't right. I have a game in Seattle.'" She spoke in a low-pitched, bad male imitation voice.

Alice burst out laughing. "I'm sure he doesn't sound like Elmer the Fudd," she said through her giggles.

"You know what I mean," Robin said.

"That's exactly what he says," AJ confirmed. "But the game was actually in Texas." She smiled at Robin, and all at once, the path between them was clear.

"Ah, I see," Kristen said. She got to her feet. "Well, then, I have no solutions. And you know what that means?"

"Cookies," the four of them said together, and Robin could fall into the laughter that followed and swim around in it until it flowed through her whole body.

"Jamie, get the mayo out please." Robin took in the huge mess on her kitchen island. She wasn't sure how they were going to pack all of this to the beach, which is why she hardly ever went. She got her fill of sand and surf and sun by running five miles along the water's edge every morning.

"Mandie, did you get the sunscreen?"

"In the beach bag."

"Do we have enough towels for everyone?" With four visitors taking showers—well, only three, as AJ had insisted on staying at a hotel so she could escape and get some work done during the week—Robin had been throwing a load of towels into the washing machine every night.

"Yes," Duke said from somewhere. "I'm going to start loading up, babe."

"Okay," she called to him. She hadn't seen hide nor hair of any of the women sleeping upstairs, and she wondered if she needed to get the broomstick out and start banging on the ceiling to wake them up.

They'd been out late last night, taking in the island nightlife as it never seemed to die, even during non-tourist season. The karaoke machine had been heavily utilized last night, and Robin had never seen so many appetizers in her life. She hadn't eaten fried food in such mass quantities, and her stomach swooped as she said, "Chairs. Do we have enough chairs for everyone?"

"We have four," Mandie said.

That was enough for their family, and Robin started worrying the inside of her cheek with her teeth. She reached for her phone and dialed Aaron Sherman before giving anything a second thought.

"Robin Grover," he said. "What can I do for you?"

"Hey, Aaron. Sorry to call so early. Do you have any beach chairs you can bring today?"

"Bring where?"

Robin paused, her mouth open. "To the beach," she said stupidly.

"You want to borrow some? I have a couple. Maybe three or four."

"Didn't Eloise invite you?" she asked. They'd talked about a beach day over dinner, and Robin had told Eloise to invite Aaron.

"No," he said slowly. "This is the first I've heard of going to the beach today."

Horror filled Robin's already sick stomach. "Oh, my goodness," She said. "I'm so sorry. I'm going to hang up now, and you're going to pretend like I never called."

Aaron started to chuckle, but Robin ended the call and practically threw her phone on the counter, where she couldn't do any more damage with it.

"Mom," Mandie said, and she jerked her attention toward her.

"What?"

"Dad's asking about the life jackets."

"We don't have enough of those either."

"Doesn't matter," Alice said breezily. "I won't be going in the water, so I don't need one." She stepped over to the coffee pot, something gauzy and light flowing around her limbs as she moved. Was she really going to wear that to the beach? It looked like it was made of cobwebs, and Robin could see her swimming suit beneath it.

"And we don't expect you to stock beach chairs and life jackets for us," Alice said, giving Robin a warm hug. "Let's stop at the store on our way."

Easy for her to say, but Robin nodded like that was a

fantastic idea. Commotion broke out as Eloise and Kelli came downstairs arguing about something that Robin couldn't quite catch as Duke poked his head in from the garage and yelled for Robin to come talk to him.

Because her husband had been so great about having her girlfriends stay with them for an extended period of time, she excused herself and went. She helped him find the life jackets, and everyone proceeded to get loaded up.

She found Eloise on the front steps, tapping madly on her phone, a disgruntled expression on her face. "There you are. Are you coming?"

"Is there room in your van?"

"Yes." Robin sat beside her, the need to confess about her phone call to Aaron Sherman nearly desperate. "I may have mentioned we were going to the beach to Aaron."

"I know." Eloise looked at her, no smile in sight. "He texted me, and that was when Kelli told me I needed to loosen up."

"She said that?"

"Can I help it if I'm not a summer fling type of woman? And it's not even summer. It's *April*." Eloise shook her head. "So I didn't invite him. It's not the end of the world."

Robin put her arm around Eloise, regret cutting her to the core. "I'm sorry I asked you all those questions yesterday. I didn't mean to burst your little April fling bubble."

Eloise scoffed. Then snorted. Then giggled. By that

time, they both let out a laugh. When they quieted, Eloise said, "So what should I do?"

"What do you want to do?"

"I want to see Aaron."

"Then invite him."

Duke called her again, and Robin rolled her eyes. "I swear, that man wouldn't be able to find his head if it wasn't attached to his body."

"But I want to spend the day with you guys, too," Eloise said. "And I feel like if Aaron comes, I'll have to entertain him. I won't really be able to relax. And I'll ignore you guys or miss out on a conversation I don't want to miss out on."

"Ah, I see. There's a root to this non-invitation."

"Yes, a big root." Eloise sighed. "And you don't get it, because you're married to Duke. You can relax with him around. He can get his own dang sandwich."

Robin laughed again, squeezing Eloise to her side. "Honey, I guarantee you that Aaron does not need to be entertained. He can get his own sandwich too."

"I know." Eloise held up her phone and shook it. "He's bringing them for everyone." She sounded so miserable about it too.

"Well," Robin said. "Had I known that, I wouldn't gotten up at seven a.m. to start packing lunch for everyone." She gave Eloise a small smile. "It's going to be okay. Aaron's a grown man. He doesn't need you to entertain him."

"Robin," Eloise said. "Some of us don't run five miles every morning."

Robin blinked at her for a moment, sudden understanding washing over her. "Eloise, you're not fifteen anymore. You're a strong, smart, *sexy* woman, no matter what size you are." She stood up and pulled Eloise to her feet too. "Now, come on. It's our beach day, and we're not going to let anything ruin it." She nodded like that was that, like the mighty Robin had the power to make everyone get along, and Eloise to relax, and AJ to have fun.

She didn't, but she sure could pretend like she did.

CHAPTER EIGHTEEN

Eloise basked in the late April sunshine, the rush of the waves crashing against the shore, and the pull of the tide going back out. Robin had always been an excellent party planner, and she directed Duke and her girls to put the two coolers where she wanted them, set up the chairs, put up the shades and umbrellas.

Alice had turned into everyone's rich aunt at the store, buying beach chairs, umbrellas, life jackets, floaties, sunscreen, and anything anyone wanted to put in the cart. She'd gotten a football, a Frisbee, sand toys, the whole nine yards.

"Charlie will want this," Alice had said at least three items, and Eloise wasn't sure if she'd been telling the truth or not. Her kids hadn't arrived yet, and Alice had set her chair facing the parking lot instead of the water so she'd see them when they did.

Eloise felt like doing the same thing, because Aaron hadn't arrived yet either. He'd called to ask if he should bring the girls or get a sitter, and Eloise had told him to make that decision himself. She was fine to meet them, she'd said.

But now, her nerves boiled in her stomach and chest, but she absolutely refused to watch the parking lot.

Eloise watched a lot of other things, and she knew Alice had something festering just beneath the surface. She knew Robin was tired and stressed and determined not to show it. Just the way she collapsed into her beach chair with a sigh as loud as the ocean waves said that. Eloise wondered if Duke heard it, if he knew how hard Robin worked to make sure his home was a place he wanted to spend time. The long hours she dedicated to his children, to being his wife, to supporting him—and everyone around her. She wondered if Duke knew what a treasure he'd gotten in Robin, and Eloise sure hoped so.

Because she saw it all.

She'd observed a change in Kelli after she'd scurried inside the lighthouse to talk to her husband, but Eloise didn't quite know what to say to her. She sat in the chair next to Robin, always just one step away from the epicenter of what was happening. Eloise knew exactly how that felt, because she'd done the same thing for a lot of years of her life.

"They're here," Alice said, launching herself out of her chair. "Hello," she called, waving as if her father and children wouldn't be able to find them. They weren't the only group at the beach that day, but they were the biggest.

Eloise turned and watched as Alice hugged two teenagers, the sight something Eloise hadn't been able to imagine. At least not with the Alice she'd spent the last several days with. But she turned and led her family toward their group, and Eloise got out of her chair for the introductions.

"My twins," Alice said. "Charlie is six minutes older than Ginny. And you guys remember my father. He married Della about ten years ago." She beamed at them like she was just so, so happy about the marriage.

Eloise saw it all. She smiled, though, and she shook Connor Williams's hand, as well as his wife, Della's. She grinned at the kids while Robin called her girls over from where they'd started to build sand sculptures.

"How old are you two?" she asked, but Eloise suspected she already knew.

"Fourteen," Ginny said.

"We'll be fifteen on Wednesday," Charlie added.

"That's right," Alice said brightly. "We're having a party."

"Where?" Robin asked.

Alice looked at her, and then Eloise, but Eloise didn't know how to answer the question either. "Probably Rocky Ridge." She glanced at her dad. "Could we have it at your place, Dad?"

"Sure," he said.

Jamie and Mandie arrived, and Robin put her arm around her oldest. "These are my girls," she said. "Mandie is fifteen, and Jamie is twelve. These are Alice's twins. Charlie and Ginny."

To Robin's credit, she didn't suggest they play together or anything, and Alice turned her chair around to face the water. Her twins took a moment to pick a chair, drape the new towels Alice had bought over them, and face the water.

Jamie and Mandie walked back toward their sand castles, giggling. Eloise was sure those giggles belonged to Charlie, who was a cute fourteen-year-old boy. Almost fifteen. He pulled his shirt over his head and jogged down the sand toward the girls, and they made room for him near their sand city.

Alice settled into a conversation with her family on the other side of Eloise. Kelli and Robin chatted, while Duke floated out in the water on a boogie board. Eloise felt like an island, surrounded by beautiful things; the same beautiful things that wore her down, eroding her strength one particle at a time.

Not that Alice or Robin eroded Eloise. If anything, they built her up, made her feel like she was the same Eloise Hall that had boarded a plane in Boston, the same Professor Hall who knew her material inside and out, the same friend they'd loved in high school.

"Eloise," Robin said, and she blinked away from the glinting blue water to look at her.

"What?"

"Aaron's here with his kids." She jerked her head back toward the parking lot, and Eloise twisted and looked. "Do not jump up," Robin hissed, her voice barely louder than the wind and surf. "What did he tell his kids?"

"I have no idea," Eloise said, turning back to face forward.

"So play it cool. He might not introduce you as his girlfriend."

Eloise sucked in a breath. How did she want him to introduce her? She was leaving in a week, and she and Aaron hadn't talked about what happened after that. Not even once.

"Aaron, hey," Robin said as she stood up. "Let us help you with that. Eloise, could you come help?"

"I'm going to kill her," Eloise said under her breath. Foolishness heated her face, and she stubbornly stayed in her seat. She looked at Kelli and AJ, both of whom were watching her. She shook her head, and they both dissolved into giggles.

"I can help," Kelli said, standing up. She took a few steps while Eloise stared straight ahead, her nerves morphing into beads of anger that shot through her body like pellets. A chair landed in the sand next to her, and Kelli set it up.

Aaron came around to the front of it, and Eloise looked up at him. He wore a smile on his face, and with his hair lit up by the sun, he seemed made of silver and gold. Eloise couldn't help the way her heart turned to marshmallow, and Aaron looked away.

"Girls," he said. "These are daddy's friends. Robin, Kelli, AJ, and Eloise." The two girls came to stand next to him. "Alice is down there with her dad and Della." He turned his head and looked at the teenagers down the beach a bit. "And look, Robin brought her kids. Billie, you'd probably like to go see what they're doing."

The taller of the two girls looked up at him. "Can I?"

"Sure," Aaron said easily. "You can too, Grace, if you'd like."

Billie and Grace. Eloise took them in, seeing pieces of Aaron in the shape of Grace's nose, and the dark color of Billie's hair.

"We'll go together," Billie said, taking Grace's hand. The two of them went down to the spot where the water sometimes ran up on the sand when a big wave crashed into shore.

Aaron exhaled as he sat in the chair next to Eloise's, and she felt more like a zoo exhibit now than ever before. Six pairs of eyes watched her and Aaron, and if he felt it, he didn't show it.

Eloise had no idea what to say, and exactly what she'd feared—having to babysit him and entertain him—bloomed to life. Finally, Alice said something to her father, and AJ got up to dig the football out of one of the shopping bags.

"You want to throw it back and forth?" she asked, and

Eloise sent her a special kind of glare. She'd warned AJ not to even look at Aaron, and she was definitely looking at him right now.

"I will," Alice's dad said, and Duke came jogging up the beach, dripping wet.

"Are you playing?" he asked, tossing the boogie board on the sand several feet in front of them. "I'll do it."

The three of them walked away from the group, and Eloise relaxed. Alice's conversation had halted though, and Robin had fallen silent too.

"Do you want to go for a walk?" Eloise asked, and Aaron practically shot to his feet.

"Sure." He extended his hand toward Eloise, and she let him pull her out of her chair. She left her sandals next to her seat, and she settled her sunglasses into place. Aaron turned to Robin and asked, "Can you keep an eye on them?"

"Of course, go," Robin said, smiling. "They'll be fine."

Aaron flashed her a smile before facing Eloise. He didn't try to take her hand, and they didn't speak until Eloise couldn't hear anything but the breeze.

"Sorry that was so awkward," she said. "It's just that...I didn't know what was going to happen, and..." Eloise stopped walking and faced Aaron. "We need to talk about what happens next Monday."

Aaron blinked at her and then nodded. "All right. What do you want to have happen next Monday?"

"I don't know. I mean, in a perfect world, you'll call me

to see if I got home okay, and you'll ask me what my plans are for the week, and..." Eloise paused and thought for a moment. "And you'll ask me to look at my calendar and see when I can get back to the island to see you."

Aaron's smile grew and grew and grew until he burst out laughing. He took Eloise's hand in his, all the awkwardness between them gone. They kept walking, and Aaron repeated what she said. "So I'm going to call, and ask if you got home okay, ask what you're doing that week, and if you can maybe sit down and look at your calendar and we'll find a time we can spend some time together."

Eloise smiled at the horizon. "Sounds right."

"And that's your perfect world?"

"Pretty close," she said.

He took several steps in silence before he said, "I'm sorry for the weird introduction. I didn't really know where we were."

"Your girls are cute."

"Thanks. I kinda like them." He carried so much happiness in his voice, and Eloise wanted to have his sunshine in her life all the time. She realized where her thoughts were taking her, and she pulled back on the reins.

She'd felt like this before too, and she'd married Wes after rushing into the I-do. Aaron Sherman had come back into her life six days ago, and Eloise wasn't going to go too fast this time.

"You haven't said anything about your wife. Ex-wife."

She watched him, because while Robin was very good at seeing things, she didn't corner the market on being observant.

"Yeah." He drew in a deep breath and pushed it out, their feet squishing through the sand for another minute before he said, "You know how you sometimes make a mistake, and you know you're making it, but you do it anyway?"

"Like the potato chips I stress-ate while waiting for you to show up?" Eloise grinned, hoping he'd laugh at her attempt to lighten the mood.

He did, and his hand in hers tightened. "Yeah, kind of like that."

"Or running on the beach with an unleashed dog."

"Hey, now," he said, still chuckling. "But yeah. I met Carol, and I fell in love with her like, instantly. We dated for a while, and I knew we didn't really get along. But well, I loved her. I thought maybe that would be enough." He shook his head, and Eloise wished his sunglasses would allow her to see his face. "And you know, life tip, but if there are any maybe's anywhere in your mind about a marriage, you shouldn't say the I-do." He glanced at her, and Eloise looked steadily back.

"That's a good one," she said. "I'll keep that in mind."

"You married Wesley Daniels, didn't you?"

"Yes," Eloise said, a squirrel of shame moving through her. "It only lasted a couple of years. There were plenty of maybe's there too." She nudged him with her hip. "I could've used your life tip twenty years ago."

"You and me both." Aaron smiled. "So I don't know, Eloise. I don't know exactly what happens after next Monday, but I know, right now, I don't have any maybe's about you."

Eloise warmed on the inside, though this stroll through loose sand already had her starting to sweat. "I feel the same, Aaron."

He paused and leaned toward her, and Eloise tipped her head back to kiss him. He kept the kiss sweet, because they were in public, and Eloise wouldn't put it past Robin to use the binoculars she'd brought to bird-watch to spy on Eloise.

She broke the kiss and tucked herself into his chest. "Aaron?"

"Hmm?"

"Before I go, I need to go to Sanctuary Island and do something." She stepped back to put a few inches between them so she could look at him. "It's something I don't really want to do. Would you go with me?"

"What is it?" he asked. "Something with your mother?"

"No," Eloise said. "Though I probably should stop by at least once more before I go back to Boston." She wished she'd brought a water bottle with her, because her throat was suddenly so dry. "It's a building I own. My mother doesn't know about it, actually." She swallowed, trying to work up enough saliva to keep talking. "It's something I bought a long time ago, and I don't know. Maybe it's time to do something with it."

"All right," he said. "Let me look at my schedule for the week, and we'll make a plan."

Eloise nodded, and they continued their walk. She hadn't been to the Cliffside Inn in far too long, and she hoped there wasn't a mold issue or water damage, broken windows or vandalism.

The inn sat near the top of the cliffs on Sanctuary Island, and Eloise had bought it from the bank after they'd repossessed it following her father's death. She'd told no one about it, not her brother; not her mother; not Robin, or Alice, or AJ, or Kelli, or Kristen.

Her heart skipped a beat as she thought about telling Aaron, sharing the space with him, explaining why she'd bought it and what she hoped to do with it someday.

But she'd gone to Pearl Island with him, and that had turned out radically different than the first time she'd tried that. So maybe this would be different too. Maybe *she* was different, and maybe she was ready.

In that moment, she realized how many maybe's she had in her life surrounding the inn. At least they weren't about Aaron, and Eloise made a decision right then to enjoy the rest of the day with him and his girls.

CHAPTER NINETEEN

Alice kept her eye on Charlie and Ginny as they played with Robin's girls. It wasn't Ginny she was worried about, but she knew her son was popular with the girls, and she wasn't so old that she couldn't recognize flirting.

Mandie seemed absolutely smitten by everything Charlie said and did, and knowing him, he knew it. He was his father's son, after all.

With her father off throwing a football with Duke and AJ, Alice was left to her own thoughts. She didn't have much to say to Della, and the woman had laid a towel on the sand and fallen asleep soon after Alice's father had left. She snored softly, and Alice wished sleep would come that easily to her.

Robin's beds did the job, but Alice had found herself

lying there, awake, for at least half the night since finding the letter.

The knowledge of it was slowly eating her alive, and she had to do something about it. She glanced to her left, where Eloise and Aaron had been. She hadn't even noticed them leaving. Another peal of laughter erupted from the sand city several yards away, and Alice watched as Mandie shoved Charlie away.

Then Jamie and one of Aaron's girls started stomping on all the structures they'd spent the last fifteen minutes building. Mandie turned back to it, and then she glared at Charlie. "Look what you did."

"Oh, let's just build it again," he said, grinning. He ran his hand through his hair, and Mandie would probably go to the moon if he asked her to with that trademark Kelton hair swoop.

Alice folded her arms, trying to decide if she was happy about Charlie's playful banter or not. She wanted her children to have fun while they were here, because she had pulled them from their friends and studies and plunked them down with her elderly father and step-mother.

Charlie had texted a lot last night, saying how much fun he'd been having, and that had alleviated some of Alice's worries. But she still wanted to make sure their needs were provided for.

On the other side of the empty chairs, Robin sat under an umbrella, reading something on her phone. Kelli had joined her in the shade, and the two looked to be talking about something. Robin showed Kelli her phone, and they both laughed.

She saw her life from behind that pane of glass again, and she wanted to break right through it. The Alice she'd been when she'd gotten on her private jet and flown here wasn't the same woman who saw herself as part of this group.

Alice got up and went to join them, gathering her billowing cover up around her bony body. "What are you guys doing over here?" she asked, inserting herself into their conversation as if she should've been in it all along.

"Oh, just cat memes," Robin said, smiling at her. "The kids seem to be getting along okay."

Alice watched them for a moment. Charlie raked the sand with one of the plastic toys she'd bought, and then he sat back on his heels. The girls surrounding him started to build, and he didn't take his eyes from Mandie.

"Yeah," she said, sure Robin could see how her daughter and Alice's son flirted with one another. *It's harmless*, Alice told herself, because it was. Charlie didn't live here, and an innocent spring romance *was* harmless, especially between fifteen-year-olds.

"Listen," Alice said, looking from Kelli to Robin and back. "I think I should tell Kristen about my mom."

Robin leaned forward, her eyes suddenly earnest and wide, worried. "You do?"

"Yes." Alice knelt in the sand and picked up a handful

of it. The grains sifted through her fingers, and she couldn't hold onto them no matter how hard she tried. Secrets were the same way. She could clench her fist for a while and keep some of the truth from coming out. But eventually, her fingers would tire, and whatever she'd been hiding would come to light.

She knew, because she'd been holding the lie of her marriage so tight for so long, and Alice was very, very tired.

She looked up from the sand, dusting her hands together to get all the grains off. "If it were me, I'd want to know."

"There's nothing she can do about it now," Kelli said. "I'm not sure it matters."

Alice nodded. "You might be right."

"What are you thinking?" Robin asked.

"I'm thinking I can ask her if she wants to know." Alice's chest vibrated, and she reminded herself that she didn't have to hold back the truth, not with Robin and Kelli. "And I'm thinking that I don't want this secret on my shoulders for very much longer. It's heavy." Her shoulders sank, as if she had just unburdened a heavy load from them.

"I know what that's like," Kelli said, and Alice switched her gaze to her. Kelli had always been slightly quieter than Alice, and definitely less outgoing than Robin. She'd seemed happy in AJ's shadow, and even Eloise had earned academic achievements while Kelli simply lingered in the background.

Alice exchanged a glance with Robin, silently urging her to say something first. After all, she'd been the one to call out Eloise on what she wanted from a relationship with Aaron Sherman.

But Robin leaned back in her chair and frowned.

"Kel," Alice said gingerly. "What's going on?"

She lifted one shoulder in a shrug, wearing her misery on her face plainly now. "I talked to Julian yesterday, and he says he can't keep getting Parker this week. He wanted me to come home."

"You can't go yet," Robin said instantly.

Alice held up her hand, and Robin clamped her mouth shut.

Kelli looked out at the water. "I never leave Parker. I do everything for him and Julian. I thought that was what I wanted, but..." She smiled as the kids laughed again, sighing in such a longing way that Alice felt it down deep in her own soul. Of course she did. She longed for so much more than what her life had become.

She'd once thought that money could buy her whatever she needed. If her husband didn't come home one weekend, that was okay. She could get a new bedroom set. If she was lonely in her own bed, no problem. She could get a new luxury SUV to drive around the Hamptons.

Alice had been carefully bandaging her unhappiness

for two decades, and no amount of money could cure her now.

"But what?" she prompted, because she felt like Kelli was right on the edge of something important for her.

"But being here with you all, and I see how Duke treats Robin. I see Eloise glowing when Aaron shows up— and you know what? He was glowing too. I can't even remember the last time Julian slept in the same bed as me."

Surprise darted through Alice, but she kept it carefully contained behind a stone mask. Robin, however, did not. A scoff came out of her mouth, and she only realized it too late. Kelli looked at her, and Robin just pressed her lips together and waved her hand. She'd gotten really good at taming what came out of her mouth, Alice would give her that. And she loved her for her maturity.

"Where does he sleep?"

"On the couch or in his office." Kelli looked absolutely forlorn, and she swiped at her eyes. "He's going to have his mother take care of Parker so he can keep working."

"Does he ever take days off?" Robin asked gently.

"No," Kelli said. "And it's usually fine. It is. I just guess I'd told myself that we weren't any different than any other couple. But... I mean, even Joel and Kristen were happier than I am. Sure, we're learning now that he was kind of a jerk. Or different." She shook her head, sighing. "I don't know what I'm saying."

"I know what you're saying," Robin said. "You're saying

that we all had an image of what Joel was like, who he was. And we're learning that that image might be a lie."

Alice nodded, and while she'd been struggling a little bit this past week, she knew it wasn't anything like what Robin was going through. She'd also been living with someone who portrayed one image of who he was to the world but was actually something quite different behind closed doors.

She was used to the duplicity in people; Robin wasn't. She took everyone at face value, a trait Alice wished she had.

"I guess I've just realized that Julian and I aren't even connected anymore, and it's my fault. I know it's my fault."

"How so?" Alice asked, not meaning to be challenging, though her voice came out a bit harsh.

"I let my whole world become Parker instead of my husband." She looked at Alice with wide eyes. "That's what he told me yesterday."

"Kelli—" Robin started.

"And he's right," Kelli said, in a rare show of talking over someone. "He's right, guys. He is." She looked away again, studying something in front of her. "He's replaced me with his business, and I replaced him with my son. We barely know each other anymore."

Alice's heart tore for Kelli's plight, because it felt and sounded so familiar. So familiar, Alice could taste the disappointment in the back of her throat that Kelli surely did too.

She pulled in a deep breath and faced Alice again. "I think you should tell Kristen—if you think that's the right thing to do. She should know the truth. Then she'll be able to do something about it."

"You think so?" Alice asked, still oscillating back and forth in her decision.

"We'll support you," Robin said. She looked at Kelli. "And you too, Kel. Tell us what you need, and we'll do whatever we have to in order to make it happen."

"Thanks." Kelli smiled and nodded. "Do you think you could bottle up Duke and let me take the elixir home? Maybe if Julian just had one sip, he'd look at me the way Duke looks at you."

"Oh, well," Robin said, her eyes moving down the beach to where her husband played football.

"If she gets a bottle, I'd need a barrel," Alice said, following that with a laugh. The mood broke, and she got up out of the sand and sat in the chair next to Robin, the echo of their laughter filling her ears as she went right back to thinking about how she could possibly tell Kristen about the letter.

CHAPTER TWENTY

K risten went up the steps slowly, taking care to make sure her foot landed solidly on each stair before committing her weight to it. She carried a box that didn't contain very many items, but she needed some fresh air. The second-floor bedrooms in the lighthouse had been filled with people all day, including Alice's twins.

Kristen smiled just thinking about them. Ginny was a spitting image of her mother, while Charlie had obviously taken some parts from Alice's husband. No matter what, Alice had trained them well, and they'd worked all morning without complaint, their manners impeccable.

AJ had treated everyone to lunch, which they'd taken outside to a picnic area down the hill a little bit. Kristen hadn't been down there for a long time, as she usually only went with Joel and he hadn't been able to traverse the rocks surrounding the lighthouse for some time now.

The wooden picnic table still sat there, proudly overlooking the water that stretched for miles in every direction. At that point on Diamond Island, none of the other islands in the cove could be seen, as they all lay to the west, behind the point.

She pushed open the door and took a deep breath of the island air. She couldn't wait until this week was over. She loved having her girls back in town, and the tender way they attended to her needs reminded her of how much she was loved, even without Joel at her side.

For a day or two there, Kristen had forgotten how to breathe. Every now and again, the feeling returned, and she'd stop whatever she was doing and just stare. Seconds, minutes, or hours later—she didn't know how long— she'd come back to herself and realize the world had kept moving after Joel had taken his last breath.

She needed to keep moving too.

Sighing, she turned and went down the sidewalk that circumvented the lighthouse as well as led down to the parking lot. Only six stalls, the lot hardly ever saw visitors. Maybe a teenage couple or two every so often, as they wanted to come stand in the bright light of the lighthouse as they held hands or shared their first kiss.

The stories around the islands included the lighthouse and kissing under the bright beam as she guided seamen back to safety. Kristen smiled at the memories, at the tales that the kids told to one another and passed down to their children.

She'd first kissed Joel under the beam of the lighthouse, and the rumor went that if one did that, they'd have a lifetime of happiness with the person with whom they'd shared the kiss.

As she lifted the box over the top of the Dumpster and let it fall on top of the other trash she and the girls had been cleaning out of the cottage and the lighthouse, Kristen wondered if she had gotten her lifetime of happiness with Joel.

Until she'd found that blue piece of paper stuck partially under those books, she would've said yes. Even now, her heart beat to a rhythm that only he'd been able to understand. When she thought of that letter, of the deed in the folder now under her mattress in the cottage, of Eloise's test scores, then her heart would stop for a moment. A minute. An hour.

She didn't know how long.

What she knew was that when her heart restarted, it hurt in a way she'd never known before.

As she stood beside the Dumpster, the sun shining overhead, and the distant sound of waves crashing against the cliffs, Kristen tipped her head back and looked into the sky. A brilliant blue laid the perfect background for the puffy clouds moving east, out to sea. The wind chased them, and she caught a couple of birds hitching a ride on the currents.

A smile touched her mouth, and she wasn't even sure why. She normally loved the night sky, with her mistress the moon. She loved thinking of the stars as guarding those out on ships, and when they couldn't provide the way the sailors should go, the lighthouse always could.

The lighthouse had always been able to point Kristen in the right direction too. She turned to face it, admiring the five stories that extended above the ground, the point of it piercing right into the blueness of the sky. Spots of grass grew around it, and as a young mother, Kristen had planted bulbs that came up in the spring to add life to the mostly rocky land. Joel had put in a new rose bush every year for many in a row. Rueben hadn't done anything to change the landscape, so the roses endured, but the tulips and daffodils were long gone.

Kristen felt like so much in her life had gone...just gone. Passed by. Ended.

The sound of a car coming up the road to the parking lot met her ears, and she watched as a truck appeared, the sun gleaming off the dark red paint. Alice's father drove, and he hadn't even fully pulled into a spot before Kristen heard voices behind her.

She found Ginny and Charlie walking down the sidewalk, Alice holding onto the door that led into the lighthouse, a smile on her face. She lifted her hand in a wave to her father, and Ginny and Charlie got in the back seat of the truck.

No one appeared to have noticed her, standing there

beside the Dumpster, and Kristen wondered if that indicated the future she had to look forward to. She knew from personal experience that life went on. People died. She'd had friends whose spouses had passed away, and the whole island had gone into mourning. They'd filled the seats at the funeral, and brought flowers to the ancient graveyard that sat on the rise near the middle of the island.

And after that...gone. Just gone.

She'd have to cling to her cottage, her son, her daughter, the lighthouse, and her girls.

The thought of her girls brought a cleansing breath to her lungs, and as Connor Williams pulled out, he suddenly stopped too. The passenger window rolled down and he said, "How are you holding up, Kristen?"

She blinked, seeing a different version of this man when she'd taken the ferry to Rocky Ridge to implore him to please take care of Alice. She'd seen those light brown eyes that Alice had inherited staring back at her, rimmed with red. His agony had been complete, and Kristen thought she had harder days ahead than she realized.

"I'm doing okay," she said.

"Please call me if you need anything," he said, and she didn't doubt his sincerity.

"I will." She waved at him, Della, and the children, and the red truck left the parking lot. After her visit to Connor, he had sobered up, at least in the evenings. He'd made sure his daughter and son had what they needed for school, and he'd kept his job with the Coast Guard. When he'd retired from that, he'd taken up shrimping with his vast knowledge of boats and the sea.

He'd survived.

Kristen would too.

Armed with this belief, she turned toward the path that led back to the cottage. She didn't want to live the rest of her days with regrets, which she now knew Joel had done. They hadn't been strong enough for him to reveal his secrets while he was alive, and Kristen wanted to be stronger than him.

Stronger than a secret.

Her legs shook as she went down the path, her mind zipping from one thing to another. She wanted to pause against the side of the cottage and throw up, but she continued inside. The living room had been completely cleaned out so all that remained was a single couch, which faced the TV on a single cabinet. Her beloved bench, which she'd had sitting on the east side of the lighthouse so she could sit there without having to climb the flights of stairs to the upper deck, had been put in front of the window.

Gone were the bookshelves, the end tables, the stacks of papers, files, folders, books, and magazines. Gone was the clutter. Gone were the several pairs of shoes always threatening to trip her as she came or went from the house.

The pictures on the wall were yellowed with age, some

going back a couple of generations. They showed the keepers of the lighthouse, and Kristen felt a strong pull toward them, like a planet's need to go toward the sun.

She paused in front of them, seeing her grandmother and grandfather, both Diamond Island residents. They'd bought the lighthouse years and years ago, and it had been in her family for four generations now.

Reaching out, she touched the edge of the frame with Grandmother Rose's picture in it, her eyes wise and knowing, her smile not present. "I'm trying," Kristen said, the thought of losing the lighthouse almost worse than it had been losing Joel.

In that moment, she thought she knew exactly how Guy Watkins had felt when he lost his glassblowing shop. She faced the hallway that led down to the two bedrooms, one completely empty now, save for Joel's desk and chair. But the desk too had been emptied, and Kristen thought she might take it outside and paint it. Next week, after everyone had gone back to their regular lives.

After all, she needed something to go back to as well, and she'd always liked painting furniture. Sprucing it up and making it into something new and different. Maybe she'd help Rueben with the whitewashing of the lighthouse too, at least the lower areas she could reach without having to climb a ladder.

She went down the hall and turned into her bedroom. Her phone chimed, and she knew if she didn't respond to whoever had texted, the girls would come find her.

She didn't want that. She wanted to take them up to the upper deck and give Kelli the folder. Try to explain, if possible. And offer to sign the business back over to her or her mother. She couldn't make it one-hundred percent right, because Guy Watkins had died about the same time Joel had been diagnosed with cancer.

And still, he'd said nothing.

Kristen's anger grew as she bent to retrieve the folder from underneath her mattress. With it securely in her hand, she pulled out her phone to find Robin had texted to ask where she'd gone.

Tucking the folder under her arm, Kristen then used both hands to quickly send a text to all of her girls. *Can we meet on the upper deck? Ten minutes?*

Her throat narrowed, and she told herself this needed to be done. Kelli deserved to know. Besides, what was Kristen going to do with an old, shut-down glassblowing studio? Even if she had use for it, she'd give it back. The Watkins family deserved that.

With all the confirmations in place, Kristen took one more breath and went to meet her girls in the safest place she could think of—the lighthouse.

Huffing and puffing, she paused on the landing just before the door that led outside. It had been left open a couple of inches, and she could hear the five of them talking on the deck. Oh how she loved their voices. She loved that they'd come back to Five Island Cove for her—

for *her*—and that their bond seemed to be as strong as ever.

She stepped out onto the deck, and Robin said, "There she is."

Everyone faced her, and Kristen's chest collapsed in on itself. She couldn't do this. She couldn't cause any more grief for Kelli, who had seemed quieter than usual today.

"What's going on?" Alice asked, standing next to Robin. She folded her arms, and Kristen thought the woman might blow away with a stiff wind coming off the water.

She couldn't speak, so she held out the folder.

"What's that?" Robin asked. No one moved. No one spoke. Pure terror moved through Kristen, and tears gathered in her eyes.

Alice swore softly under her breath and stepped forward, practically ripping the folder from Kristen's fingers. AJ held her gaze for a moment, but everyone else followed the movement of the folder, and then they all gathered around Alice.

Kristen told herself to breathe. That this secret couldn't be buried beneath her mattress until the day she died. She'd seen Robin's face, and Alice's eyes, and Eloise's disbelief when the first secrets were revealed.

She knew that when she died, her girls would come to clean out the cottage. She couldn't do to them what Joel had done to them all, and she wouldn't leave that folder there for them to find after she'd gone.

She blinked, wondering how much time she'd lost standing on the deck. Slowly, Alice looked up from the folder.

Robin's head still bent over it, and Eloise reached toward the paper inside in slow, slow, slow motion.

The silence broke with the words, "Kelli, it's the deed to your dad's glassblowing shop."

The sky she loved so much broke.

Her heart broke.

The siren in Kristen's head sounded, and she let the tears fall down her face.

CHAPTER TWENTY-ONE

Kelli heard Alice, but the words simply bounced off her eardrums. Then Eloise had the paper in her hand, her eyebrows furrowed. She extended the paper toward Kelli, who wasn't sure she should take it. It felt like a snake, ready to strike.

Finally, AJ, who stood the closest to Kelli, took the paper and said, "What do you mean?"

Robin sniffled, and Kelli focused on her, watching the tears flow down her face. Why was she crying?

Numbness moved through Kelli, and she wasn't sure when the world had narrowed to just the upper deck of the lighthouse.

AJ stepped in front of her, blocking her view of the other three women. "Kel," she said gently. "Alice is right. This is the deed to your dad's studio. You know, the one he had to sell when...everything happened?"

Kelli nodded. She knew what had happened. Her dad was a very talented artist. He sold beautiful, hand-made glass pieces to tourists when they came to the island, and he even went to Nantucket, Cape Cod, and some markets on the mainland when the summer season in Five Island Cove dried up.

He'd made a very good living, and she could close her eyes and see the stained glass he'd put in her bedroom for her tenth birthday.

He'd fallen on some hard summers—three in a row—and he brought in an investor. But instead of just funding the business until it could recover, this investor had actually bought the shop out from under her father. He hadn't even known until it was done.

They'd lost everything, including the house with all the custom windows, all the sparkling, colorful light, all the happy memories.

Kelli and her family had moved from Bell Island, where everything and everyone was happy, clipping their grass on Saturday mornings in near unison, and glad to see each other—until something bad happened.

Then they whispered over fences and cast sidelong looks from down the aisles at the grocery store. The kids teased about the length of someone's jeans and how they had to use duct tape to keep the soles of their shoes on.

Kelli could see the house clearly now. Much more clearly than the paper AJ now held up for her to look at.

"Joel bought it." AJ's words fuzzed and blurred in Kelli's ears, and she had to get off this deck.

Off this island.

She snatched the paper, turned, and ran for the door. She didn't care that she knocked into Kristen as she went, and she ignored the calls of her friends for her to come back. She pulled at the air and commanded her feet to move faster.

She'd felt like this before, a couple of times. Once, when she'd first found out they had to sell their home and move to an apartment on Diamond Island. Yes, she'd been closer to Robin's house on the biggest island in the cove, but she longed for the winding paths through the trees on Bell Island, and the swatch of beach where she used to go with her sisters to see the sea lions and whales.

She'd mourned the loss of her stained glass window until her father was arrested, and then she'd decided the less she had to do with her family, the better. She never invited anyone to the apartment. She always went to her friends' houses—or the lighthouse.

The lighthouse had saved her.

And now she knew that Joel Shields had been the one to take everything from her. She expected tears to come, but they didn't. Her eyes stayed extraordinarily dry as she burst out of the navy blue door that had once brought her so much comfort.

She didn't have a car; Robin had picked her up at the airport. She couldn't wait around here for a car.

Frantic, she ran down the sidewalk toward Kristen's house, suddenly so glad for the aerobics classes she taught twice a week. It was odd what her mind landed on in this panicked moment, and that it would be a job back in Jersey she'd never set out to get.

Inside Kristen's house, she snatched the car keys from the peg next to the door, turned, and left again without even closing the front door. She made it to the car as Alice came out of the lighthouse, but Kelli didn't slow down.

She got behind the wheel, and she twisted the key in the ignition, and she put the lighthouse in her rear view mirror as quickly as she could.

Her fingers gripped the steering wheel like it was that poisonous snake she needed to strangle. With her heart racing, she drove to the closest ferry station, which was on the north side due to road construction leading to the south station.

She needed the south station to get to Bell Island, but any ferry would do. Anything to get off this island.

She pulled up to the curb, not caring that it was red and the car would likely get towed, and hurried to the ticket kiosk. Ten minutes later, she boarded a ferry going to Sanctuary Island, huddled on a bench on the inside so she wouldn't have to deal with salty spray and sea air.

From Sanctuary, she continued on to Rocky Ridge, where she ignored everyone trying to get people to come eat from their food trucks, and Kelli bought the long cruise from Rocky Ridge to Bell Harbor.

It would take over an hour, and if any of the women could follow her trail, Kelli would be impressed. She kept her eyes closed on the seventy-five-minute journey from Rocky Ridge to Bell, but she didn't sleep. She just didn't want to decline the food cart or talk to the woman next to her.

Twilight fell, but Kelli didn't need light to navigate to her destination. She knew the way like her own face, and she could make the walk from the west station to the house on Seabreeze Shore in ten minutes. No car needed.

She still had not cried, and her chest and throat felt like someone had pressed her between two slabs of concrete. Somehow, her feet kept moving, the paper still clenched in her fingers flapping with each step.

She turned the corner onto Seabreeze, and the trees thickened. There were no sidewalks here, and only four houses on this lane as it curved out to the very edge of the island before connecting back to the main neighborhood. She'd always been at home in these woods, and she used to cut through the trees and brush on her right to get to the bus stop that would take her to the ferry station, where she'd ferry over to Diamond for school.

The kids on Bell had to get up early to be on time, and Kelli once again marveled that she was thinking about her childhood wake-up time in such a crisis.

The house appeared in front of her, seemingly out of nowhere. It was a great, hulking, black shape against the graying trees. Kelli could suddenly breathe, the concrete slabs being pulled apart so her lungs could expand.

The window above the front door spanned ten feet, and while Kelli stood too far down the street to really see it, she knew precisely what it looked like. The last name *Watkins* had been done in blue glass, her father's favorite color. Surrounding that were all the trees Kelli loved. In this island environment, the trees didn't tower like they did in other places. The trunks were often gnarled and twisted, and she'd had to crawl under the limbs to find shade as a child. Pines had been introduced as wind breaks, and they grew taller. She used to know all the names of them, but her memory had been filled with other things over the years.

She stepped again, feeling calmer now that her destination waited in front of her. The house called to her, welcomed her home after many long years away.

Kelli bypassed the front door, which would be locked. She had the key on her ring in her purse, which currently sat in the bedroom she shared with Eloise at Robin's house. But she kept a spare in a box inside the garage, and as she moved past the dwarfed trees that had once brought her so much companionship, Kelli finally started to cry.

She collected the key while sniffling. Fitted it into the lock while sobbing. And the first wail filled the house the moment she stepped inside and locked the back door behind her. She slid to the ground, utterly spent now that she was in the house on Seabreeze Shore, and let the storm that had been gathering in her soul for hours finally come out.

KELLI HEARD A NOISE SOMEWHERE AROUND HER, AND SHE shot to a sitting position. Sunlight streamed through the stained glass window in her childhood bedroom, throwing pinks, purples, and greens around the room.

Perhaps she'd been dreaming, because she heard nothing now but the pounding of her own heartbeat. She wasn't sure how she'd managed to stumble up the steps to her bedroom, or how long she'd cried by the back door.

Her stomach growled at her for something to eat, but she didn't keep anything in the house.

Guilt, familiar as this house, crept through her. She should've told her parents she'd bought the house. They could've lived here in the last years of her father's life. He could've died with his creations standing guard over him.

But Kelli had made a box for herself over thirty years ago, and breaking out of it had been impossible. That, and her father had said some very hurtful things to her when she'd left the cove. He'd apologized, but Kelli hadn't known how to forgive in her twenties, and she'd let the sore between them fester until it was too late.

Kelli swung her legs over the side of the bed and put her feet on the dusty hardwood floors. She hadn't come to the cove to sign for the house, but she'd asked the real estate agent to send her everything necessary to get the deal done, claiming to be out of the country during the signing period.

And in a lot of ways, New Jersey was a completely different country than Five Island Cove. Sitting on an old bed, which the family who'd lived here when she'd bought the house had left behind because they didn't have a way to take it with them, Kelli felt like she was staring right into the face of unhappiness.

She'd done so many things wrong, and she had no way of fixing them. She couldn't tell her mother about the house now. She'd tried to buy it back, years later, but the house on Seabreeze Shore wasn't for sale anymore. And when it did go on the market, she hadn't been able to afford it.

Kelly had, though.

She'd owned the house for twelve years, having purchased it back when she and Julian hadn't thought they'd be able to have children. She'd told him it would be their baby, and they'd take care of it, come visit the cove in the summertime, when so many other people wanted to do the same. And they'd always have somewhere safe to stay. Somewhere beautiful and serene.

But in reality, Kelli had come to the cove alone for the first few years. She'd cleaned up behind the family that had left the island suddenly, and she didn't talk to any of the neighbors. She hadn't alerted her parents or Robin to her presence.

Then, when Parker had come along, Kelli came less and less. She hadn't been back to the cove or the house on Seabreeze Shore in almost seven years, and she'd never told her father she'd reclaimed it for their family.

The air held a feeling of neglect, and Kelli sniffled as another round of tears threatened to spill from her eyes. She wiped them and left the bedroom just as someone pounded on the front door.

She froze, her heartbeat going right back to that booming pulse that radiated through her shoulders and up her throat. She had heard a noise, and now that she stood in the hallway, she could hear AJ calling her name too.

Without hesitating, she flew down the steps and around the corner to the front door. Her fingers fumbled with the lock, but when AJ heard her, she at least stopped yelling. Kelli got the lock undone, and she paused to take a deep breath.

She did not want to face all four of them. AJ was fine. AJ had been there for Kelli in the lowest moments of her life. The others had tried, but Kelli and AJ had always been the outliers in the group, and they'd bonded over that as much as they had over their mutual love for rainbow sherbet.

Kelli pulled open the door, and thankfully, only AJ

stood on the front porch. Their eyes met, and Kelli leaned into the door for support.

"Kel." AJ swept into her personal space, wrapping her up in a tight, tight hug that Kelli needed so desperately right now. They cried together for several moments, and then Kelli stepped back and said, "Come in, so we're not putting on a show for everyone."

"Everyone who?" AJ asked, giving a half-laugh. She came in, and Kelli closed and re-locked the door. She had no idea what to do now. The air felt stale, so she stepped over to the thermostat midway down the hall that led back into the kitchen and main living room and pushed the button to turn on the fan. In April, she didn't need heat or air conditioning, but it would be nice to get some of the desolation out of the air, some of the dust, some of the desperation.

"How did you know where I'd be?" she asked.

"Please," AJ said as she followed Kelli into the kitchen. "I know the places where you hide."

Kelli turned to face her, half-wishing that weren't true. At the same time, she was eternally grateful it was true.

"I would've been here last night," AJ said. "But the last ferry to Bell left five minutes before I got to the station."

Kelli nodded and looked around the bright, airy kitchen. The whole place needed a thorough cleaning, but the bones of the house were still perfect. "I was okay," she whispered.

"You went silent," AJ said. "And I'm sure you know how that affected Robin."

"I'm sorry," Kelli said, though she didn't have to apologize for not answering her phone, especially to AJ. Robin could be a little too mother hen sometimes, and Kelli was forty-five-years-old.

She did love the mother hen, though, so she probably should at least text the group thread so they wouldn't worry about her.

"You don't have to apologize to me," AJ said. "Or anyone, Kel. I wouldn't even be in the cove right now if I'd learned what you did yesterday."

Kelli nodded and stepped over to the fridge. "There's no food here, but I might have left some bottled water in the fridge." She couldn't remember, because so much had happened since the last time she'd been in this house.

Parker's first words, his first day of preschool and then kindergarten, his discovery of lobster mac and cheese, and his first lost tooth. Kelli loved all of his firsts, and she needed to find a way to preserve the life she had in Jersey and meld it with the one she also wanted to have here.

But she didn't know how to thread them together, because she'd spent so long keeping Five Island Cove at a distance.

"We can call and order something," AJ said. "Did you eat at all last night?"

Kelli shook her head as she opened the fridge. A case of eight water bottles sat there, along with a box of baking soda. She wasn't thirsty, and she closed the fridge aimlessly. She couldn't look at AJ as she asked, "So now what?"

"Now," AJ said. "We order lunch—because it's after noon, Kel. Did you know that?" She cleared her throat. "Anyway, we order lunch, and then we talk about what you're going to do with that deed."

"What can I do?" she asked, desperate for AJ to just tell her what to do. Kelli knew she wasn't the sharpest tool in the shed. She had no idea about contracts, and deeds, and titles.

"Kristen said she'd give it to you," AJ said. "After you left, she said she intended to tell you she'd sign the shop back to you, or your mother. Whoever. She doesn't want it."

Kelli's hopes started to lift, and when she met AJ's eyes, she couldn't help but feel like maybe the shattered pieces of her past could be mended. Somehow.

"And I'm going to call and get that shrimp fried rice we used to eat by the boxful before we do anything else," AJ said. "We can't be making huge decisions without it." She lifted her phone to her ear, a smile stretching across her beautiful face.

Kelli had always admired AJ's confidence. She'd been jealous of her beauty, and she'd wanted all the boys to pay attention to her, until some of them did. Then she'd learned what a great burden AJ carried, managing their expectations and her own life and her athletics simultaneously.

"Yes," she said, leaning in to press her cheek to Kelli's, a gesture they'd established at age thirteen as an alternate form of hugging. "I need two orders of shrimp fried rice... yes, large. Extra-large, if you've got it." She grinned at Kelli, and Kelli couldn't help feeling that now that AJ was here, they'd get everything figured out.

She stepped over to the light blue table that sat in front of a pair of French doors. The deed to Guy's Glassworks lay there, but Kelli didn't remember putting it down. She smoothed the crinkled edges where she'd gripped it during the journey from the lighthouse to the house on Seabreeze Shore.

AJ finished ordering their food and stepped to Kelli's side. She slipped her arm around Kelli, who leaned her head against AJ's shoulder. "It's going to be okay," AJ whispered, and just like she always had, Kelli believed her.

CHAPTER TWENTY-TWO

R obin came out of the bedroom, fully dressed and
ready to get over to Kristen's. But she didn't want
to go, and she should text her friend and say they weren't
going to make it. Maybe by lunch, she'd feel better.

But Kelli hadn't come back to the house last night, and
AJ hadn't checked in.

She'd gone into the bedroom after breakfast while
Duke took the girls to school, and she stopped on the edge
of the rug and looked at Alice and Eloise curled up on the
couch. Neither of them had moved to go change out of
their pajamas.

Alice's were pale blue and made of some kind of fancy
silk that probably came from worms raised in special bins
and earmarked just for women like Alice.

Robin took in a breath as she spiraled out of control,
but the air shook in her lungs. She couldn't break down;

she'd never been able to. Robin was the strong one. The one who already knew what to do, and who never took no for an answer. If something happened that left everyone scratching their heads, Robin had the solution, tucked away in the back of her mind.

But right now, there was nothing tucked away anywhere. No money left in the bank account, and they still had a week to go until the end of the month. No ideas for how to soothe Kristen or get Kelli to text her back. No solutions for Joel's lies that continued to pile on top of each other, drowning her, suffocating her, killing her.

She tried to breathe again, but it got stuck in her throat and sounded very much like a sob. Her hand flew to her mouth, but it was her eyes that betrayed her as they filled with water that spilled down her cheeks.

"Oh, dear," Eloise said, springing to her feet.

"I can't—" Robin said, sucking at the air. Eloise reached her, and Robin allowed her to fold her into her arms. "I don't know what to do." Her voice sounded like she'd inhaled helium, and she clung to Eloise as her shoulders started to shake.

Robin did not break down in front of people. She kept herself composed at all times. Sure, she could be frustrated, and she could cry. But this was so much more than that, and Robin felt like she was falling.

Falling down into a hole she'd never be able to get out of.

"Tell me what to do to help," Eloise begged her. "You take on too much, Robin."

"I know." She stepped back and wiped her face, where every available opening was leaking. "I know I do. It's what I do. It's what I'm good at." She looked at Eloise. "If I'm not good at shouldering the load for everyone, and making eggs and toast for everyone, and knowing precisely what everyone needs, then what am I good at?"

She looked wildly at Alice, who'd stood from the couch but hadn't approached.

"I can't do this," Robin said. "This—this thing with Joel lying about everything and living this completely separate life—I *can't do this*." She turned around, feeling smaller and more insignificant than she ever had in her whole life.

Eloise put a light touch on her back, and Alice moved like a wraith, silently and swiftly, so Robin flinched when her cold hand landed on her shoulder.

"You're the only one who can do this," Alice said. "But I know exactly how you feel, and I think you should start throwing things while you scream about how unfair it all is."

Robin half-laughed, half-choked on another sob. That made her throat hurt, and she shook her head, fresh tears pouring down her face.

"Come on, now," Alice said, turning her into her own body. She wrapped Robin in a hug too. "Cry on me, Robin.

Heaven knows you've let me wet your shoulder with my tears."

And cry Robin did.

Eloise moved away, taking her voice with her as she explained something to someone. Robin wasn't sure who she was talking to, because her entire world had narrowed to this one pinprick of grief and despair.

Robin usually didn't cry for very long, and it felt like no time at all had passed before she stepped back, keeping her head down out of the sheer embarrassment now flooding her. "Okay," she said. But she didn't know what came next.

She looked up too, hopefully, because in the past, when Robin had run out of ideas, her insane suggestions had usually sparked something in Alice or Eloise.

They stood side-by-side, looking at her. "Right," Alice said. "Eloise is going to drop me at Kristen's, and I'll help her today."

Robin looked at Eloise, who nodded at Alice and then faced Robin. "I'm going to go spend the day with Aaron. I need a day off too."

"I can't today," Robin said. "I just...can't."

"And that's fine," Alice said.

"Where do you think Kelli went?" Robin really needed to know that she was okay. She'd seen the horrified, desperate look on the woman's face before she'd snatched the deed and run from the lighthouse.

The rest of them had stayed on the upper deck with

Kristen, who'd composed herself enough to say she'd found the deed in Joel's files on the second floor of the lighthouse, and she was willing to sign the shop right back to Kelli or her mother.

AJ had said, "I'll find her. Don't worry," and she'd left too.

But if Robin was good at making enough scrambled eggs for a houseful of guests, she really excelled at worrying.

"I'm sure AJ will check in soon," Alice said, instead of answering Robin's real question. "Come, Eloise. Let's go get dressed so we can get out of Robin's hair." They left her standing in the living room, the kitchen to her right still filled with the evidence of breakfast.

Normally, Robin wouldn't leave the dishes sitting on the counter or in the sink. She'd scrub everything, set things right, and then retreat to her office to get started on whatever event awaited her attention.

But she stared at the mess that no one else had bothered to think about, and the feeling of overwhelm engulfed her. She turned her back on the dishes and the mess, and she walked down the hall to her office just as Alice and Eloise came back downstairs.

"We're headed out." Alice gripped Robin in a quick hug, stepping back as Eloise did too.

"Okay, you two have a good day. Be safe." Robin watched them go through the front door, and then she turned back to her office.

She'd laid out her clients and tasks associated with them in neat rows on her table, and she hadn't touched them since. Normally, her work grounded her, gave her an anchor to hold onto when she felt one breath away from drowning.

But now, she lunged at the table, knocking into it and sending it skidding closer to the wall. That scream Alice suggested Robin let loose gathered in her gut and rose quickly through her body. It flew from her mouth as she swiped her hand across the table in a wide arc, dismantling her rows and details—all the things she'd relied on for so long.

Cards laid neatly on a table didn't make what Joel had done to Guy Watkins okay. Her carefully organized events didn't make him into the decent person she'd believed him to be. No amount of tears or screams or the signing of deeds to transfer ownership would ever make anything that had happened in the past week bearable.

"Robin."

She spun to find Duke standing behind her, filling the doorway, complete alarm on his face. "What's going on?"

Robin's chest heaved as she faced him. "Nothing," she managed to say. "Get the girls off to school okay?"

"Yeah," he said. "Eloise's car is gone. I'm surprised to still see you here."

"I didn't...feel like going to help today. Alice is going to take care of everything today."

"Great," he said with a grin. "Did you clean up the leftovers yet? I'm still starving." He pushed out of the doorway and headed down the hall, and Robin simply stared after him.

Had she cleaned up the leftovers yet?

She looked down at her feet, where her papers and cards lay littered on the floor. Did Duke not see those?

"Of course he doesn't see them," Robin said. Duke didn't see anything but what he wanted to see. Robin's obsessive cleaning meant nothing to him, and the invisible load she carried to make sure the breakfast dishes were taken care of was only a weight on *her*.

He didn't even consider for a moment that *he* should clean up the leftovers so she could relax, get to work in her office sooner, or go take care of Kristen.

"Babe," he called while she still heard her scream reverberating in the ceilings of the house.

Robin drew a breath and started toward the kitchen as he asked her where the salsa was. "Mandie finished it," she said, and Duke opted for ketchup to pour over his scrambled eggs.

"Listen," Duke said as he settled at the bar for round two of breakfast. "I want to run something by you."

Robin pushed down the lid on the ketchup bottle and turned to put it in the fridge, keeping her back to him as she then turned her attention to the stovetop, which had splashes of dried scrambled egg all around the burner. She'd never been the neatest cook, but it didn't matter, because *she* cleaned up after herself.

"Bryan says they're taking summer fishermen. I think I'd like to go to see how it could really be."

Robin froze, her eyes on the crusty, yellow stain on the stove. "Go where?" she asked, turning around and bracing herself on the stove behind her.

"Alaska." Duke shoveled another bite of eggs into his mouth before he realized she'd gone completely still.

"I thought we were done talking about Alaska," she said, her voice barely made of enough air to make sound.

"It would be from the end of May to September," he said. "Just four months. I'm gone all the time in the summer anyway, and you and the girls wouldn't even know I was gone. You could still have your beach days, and your spa days, and—"

"Four months?" Robin asked, cutting him off. "Where would you live?"

"They put the temporary guys in a cabin on the coast." He spoke evenly, but at least he didn't keep eating.

"How much?"

"A guy was on the call who went last summer, and he said he made as much in four months as he'd made all year down in Louisiana." Duke got up, abandoning his breakfast as the scream started to gather again. "Babe, listen. If I can make as much as I do in four months, we'd be crazy not to do this."

"Crazy," Robin echoed as he rounded the island. He reached for her just as she broke for the second time in an hour. And if he didn't know how to deal with his twelve-year-old daughter while she cried over a cat, he definitely had no idea what to do with his sobbing wife.

Robin knew this, but she couldn't stop herself. She collapsed into his arms, the scream morphing into a wail as it traveled through her throat. Duke had the good sense to hold onto her, though Robin wanted to pound against his chest and ask him how he hadn't even noticed how upset she was.

Was he really that blind?

Perhaps he should go to Alaska for the summer, she managed to think amidst the chaos in her mind. But she didn't want to think what would happen come September, when he returned. Would they grow apart so quickly? She missed him already, and he hadn't even decided to go for sure yet.

Yes, he has, her mind whispered, and Robin had learned to listen to that quiet, internal voice that always spoke the truth.

"I just want to try it," Duke said, rubbing her back.

Robin broke free from his comforting embrace and swiped angrily at her face. "I don't think it's wise for us to live apart," she said. "We've never wanted that."

"I know." Duke wore a helpless look on his face, and Robin usually knew just what to do to erase it. But not this time.

She couldn't control this situation, any more than she could control all that had happened at the lighthouse and in Kristen's cottage.

She couldn't control Joel, or any of the choices he'd made.

She couldn't control Duke, or Alice, or Kelli, or AJ.

She needed to stop thinking she could. She stepped around Duke and picked up a washrag from the sink. She could control the state of her kitchen. She could load the dishes in the dishwasher and start it. She could scrub the ugliness from the stovetop and pretend she could do the same with her life.

"Robin," Duke said again, helplessly this time.

"Go," she said. "If you want to go." She looked up at him for a fraction of a second. "Then go."

"Well, I can't go now," he said.

"Duke." She scrubbed at the eggs that hadn't made it to scrambled. "Can you just—can you go somewhere else, please?"

He stood there for another moment, maybe two, and then his footsteps echoed against the tile as he left the kitchen and went down the hall to the exit. The garage door slammed closed behind him, and Robin heard the rumble of the garage door as it lifted.

Robin wept as she cleaned up the kitchen, throwing all the leftovers straight into the trash. When she finished, she looked around at the gleaming, spotless surfaces, proud of the work she'd done.

She'd never believed husbands and wives should be apart for very long. Not for a job. Not for anything. And she and Duke hadn't been. She'd thought that was what had made their marriage so successful. Maybe it had only been part of it.

Maybe they could survive for just four months.

Robin had been clinging so tightly to what she believed—about marriage, about friendship, about Joel Shields—and as she stood in her kitchen, she felt her fist start to uncurl. Letting go was terribly hard, and Robin didn't know how to do it. She couldn't not go to Kristen's with a basket of her favorite treats, and she couldn't stop hoping that the Seafaring Girls would make it a habit to come back to Five Island Cove more often.

It was part of what made Robin who she was, but she realized as her pinky released its hold that she could change.

She *could* learn how to change.

"You can," she whispered to herself. And she let go of everything she'd been desperately holding so close, hoping she'd recognize herself when she came out the other side of all of this.

CHAPTER TWENTY-THREE

Alice crossed her legs as Eloise started the drive from Robin's to the lighthouse. "I hope she finds something highly breakable, and throws it," she said. "It'll really make her feel better." Alice knew. On a deep level, Alice *knew*.

"I've only seen her break down like that once before," Eloise said. "And I have no idea how to help her."

Alice suspected that was hard for Eloise, as she always knew the answer to a problem. "When was she like that before?" she asked.

"Remember when Robbie dumped her by asking Michelle Stevens out over the public address system at school?" Eloise cut Alice a glance, her fingers tightening on the wheel as she refocused her attention out the windshield.

"Oh, yeah." Alice looked out the window, her mind

wandering. "That was brutal. Poor Robin." She wanted to help Robin too, but she'd been trying to figure out how to show Kristen the letter now for two days. Maybe since the moment she'd found it.

Kristen had just brought up the folder and showed it to them. She'd cried instead of speaking, but for some reason Alice wanted to explain. Explain what, she wasn't sure. She'd told herself over and over that she wasn't her mother. She hadn't even known about the affair until last week; her father had never said a word about it.

Every time she thought of him, remembering back to those days and weeks and months following his wife's death, Alice grew a little more compassionate toward him. If she'd known what he was going through, she would've acted differently.

Alice was well-accustomed with regret, but this was unlike any other she'd felt before. She didn't know how to wrestle this kind of regret, the kind that she wished she could go back and make better. It felt like she'd never be able to pin it down and declare herself the winner, and no amount of shopping, or changing the furniture, or depriving herself of the best of Robin's cooking could make it go away.

Eloise turned with the road, and the lighthouse came into view. Alice honestly couldn't face it today, but she had to. She couldn't live another day with this secret on her chest. "You sure you want to do this?" Eloise asked, peering through the top of the windshield.

"I have to," Alice said. "Maybe I'll just hand her the paper." She looked at Eloise. Steady, strong Eloise, who had never led with her emotions, never worn her heart on her sleeve. She'd used her brain, and she was one of the kindest, smartest people Alice had the pleasure of knowing.

In fact, Alice didn't like anyone back in the Hamptons even half as much as she did the five women she'd been with for the past several days. She wasn't sure what that meant for her, but the thought of going back to her life for three more years until the twins finished high school felt like a death sentence.

"It's pretty self-explanatory, isn't it?" Alice asked.

"Yes," Eloise said, turning to go up the hill now. "Alice, this is not your fault."

"I know," she said, but something in her heart hurt anyway.

"I know I haven't seen you in a while," Eloise continued. "But I still know you, Alice Williams." She flashed her a smile, and Alice did like the use of her maiden name. "And I know you're blaming yourself for something you knew nothing about and couldn't have stopped anyway."

"I know," she said again, softer this time. She did know, intellectually. But making that lie flat in her mind and stay straight in her heart was much harder to actually do. She drew in a deep breath as the turn-off for the parking lot approached. "So, what are you and Aaron going to do today?"

"Oh, I don't know," Eloise said airily. "He said he'd plan something." She gave Alice a smile that radiated warmth and made the turn.

"Well, you deserve a man who treats you like a queen," she said as Eloise pulled into the parking spot closest to the lighthouse. "And don't you settle for anything less. I don't know if that's Aaron or not, but you'll know." She stared at Eloise, almost desperate for her to understand.

Eloise finally turned and looked at Alice, and so much passed between them.

"I love you, El," Alice said, her voice tight in her throat.

"I know." Eloise swallowed. "I love you too, Alice. Please, please don't let this hurt you too badly."

"I'm trying," Alice said, but having to go in there and present Kristen with the woman her husband had been cheating with *hurt*. It hurt a whole lot. She got out of the car and waved to Eloise, who backed out and left. Alice stayed on the sidewalk, watching the car leave, before she faced the lighthouse.

When her mother had dropped her off here, Alice couldn't wait to get out of the car. She'd barely wave good-bye or say thank you, and once her mother had lectured her for the entire trip back to Rocky Ridge about being grateful for the ride. "It's forty-five minutes one-way, Alice. The very least you can do is say thank you."

And she'd been right. Alice used the same lecture on

the twins, and her chest hitched a little tighter.

Alice wondered how many times she'd said thank you to her mother for dropping her off at the lighthouse, only to have her sneak around with Joel during the Seafaring Girls meetings. Her stomach roiled at the thought, because she hadn't noticed her mother being gone during any other evenings. She brought Alice to Seafaring Girls on Wednesdays, and hung around on Diamond Island until the meeting ended.

But Alice knew a lot more about the world now, and when Frank said he was "going to hang out in the city this weekend" instead of coming home, Alice knew there was definitely going to be some sex involved.

She put one hand over her stomach and couldn't get her feet to move. The folded letter in her pocket felt like a brick, and she held very still as Kristen came around the back of the lighthouse. Maybe if she didn't move, the woman Alice had adored as a teenager and still did wouldn't see her.

"I didn't think anyone was coming today," Kristen said, but she did not smile. Alice didn't blame her. She felt guilty for something her husband had done, and Alice seized onto that common ground between them.

"I have to show you something," Alice said, holding her head high as she dug in her pocket. "You're not going to like it." She pulled out the paper and extended it toward Kristen, though she was still several paces away. "I found this a few days ago, and I've been trying to figure out how to deal with it. How to show it to you without ruining everything between us."

Kristen stopped then, and tears pricked Alice's eyes. She shook the paper, nothing else to say.

"I don't want to see it," Kristen said, her voice haunted.

"You have to," Alice said. "I can't carry it any longer." She started up the sidewalk, but her legs shook. She hadn't eaten dinner or breakfast, because she simply couldn't stomach the thought of eating anything. Her time on Diamond Island was winding down now, and soon enough, Alice would have to be back at the gym to get rid of the five pounds she'd already gained by eating Robin's sugary French toast and all the rich seafood and creamed sauces on the island.

She reached Kristen and put the folded paper in her hand. "I'm so, so sorry."

Kristen didn't speak. She didn't look at the paper. She just stared straight ahead, and she looked beyond exhausted, with her eyes sunken in her head, the lines around her eyes deeper than Alice remembered.

"Do you want me to read it to you?" Alice asked.

"Absolutely not."

"Let's go make tea," she said, linking her arm through Kristen's. For some reason, now that she didn't have the letter in her possession, she felt lighter. She practically had to drag Kristen down the path to the cottage, and once inside, she looked around the kitchen, trying to get her bearings.

She could make tea; she'd done it before. Alice turned on the sink and filled the kettle with water before setting it on the burner. She kept Kristen in her peripheral vision at all times, because she needed to know when she opened the letter and read it.

She sat on the couch and let her hands rest in her lap, one of them still holding that folded paper. Alice left the water to boil and went to sit beside Kristen. The two women sat side-by-side in silence, and Alice literally had no thoughts in her head.

"Just tell me," Kristen said. "I can*not* stand to see something else in Joel's handwriting." She looked at Alice. "What did he do to you?"

"What makes you think it's about me?"

"You're the one who's here. He fixed Eloise's grades. He bought Kelli's father's business. He pushed AJ away, and lied to Robin, cheated on me. You're the only one left."

Alice nodded, her reasoning fairly sound. She drew in a breath, determined to just say it. "Joel cheated on you with my mother." She stared straight ahead, too weak to watch Kristen's reaction.

Kristen exhaled, her breath leaking from her in a hiss. She put the folded letter on Alice's leg, but Alice didn't touch it.

"I'm so sorry," Alice said, her voice cracking. She hadn't cried very often in her life, because she could make herself feel better with the right retail therapy and her children.

Kristen leaned into her, and Alice put her arm around her, and they cried together for a long, long time.

Hours later, someone knocked on the door, and Alice raised her head from the pillow and looked toward the entrance. Kristen looked that way too, but neither of them moved.

"Gotta be the food," Kristen said.

"Right." Alice groaned as she sat up. She'd dozed on and off on Kristen's couch, while she reclined in the armchair nearby. They'd put movie after movie on, and finally Kristen had said she needed to eat.

Alice had ordered pizza with a ton of cheese and meat, and she got up to get the door. She took the box from the teen boy standing there, passed him some money, and said, "Thanks."

She wondered if their melancholy had touched him, because he paused for a moment. Then he said, "This is a fifty-dollar bill."

"Yes," Alice said. "Keep the change as a tip for driving all the way up here." She tried to smile but didn't quite pull it off.

She closed the door and took the pizza into the kitchen, all the lights in the cottage glaring too brightly in her face. She felt removed from everything, despite the world spinning around her.

"You want some?"

"Yes, please," Kristen said, and Alice managed to find a plate and put two pieces of pizza on it and took it to Kristen.

"What else, my friend? Water? Wine?"

"I wish I had wine," Kristen said. "Remember how Robin dumped the vodka down the drain?"

Oh, Alice remembered, and she turned back to get another plate and some pizza for her. She hadn't eaten much for twenty-four hours, and her clothes still fit fairly well. She could have a piece of pizza, and she sank back onto the couch. She'd taken two bites before her stomach revolted against eating any more.

She wasn't sure why; she should be hungry. But she felt so overwhelmed mentally that she couldn't handle eating too.

Her phone buzzed on the only end table Kristen had kept, and Alice swapped her plate for her phone. Charlie had texted, *Mom, Grandpa wants me to come live here in the summer and work on the shrimp boat. Can I?*

"Not a texting conversation, Charlie," she murmured as she typed the words. Not only that, but Alice would need to have a word with her father about acceptable summer jobs for her fifteen-year-old. Working on a shrimp boat was not on that list, at least not for Alice. She knew what happened on those boats, and Charlie did not know how to work the way he'd be expected to.

So it might be good for him, she thought.

"Is it Robin?" Kristen asked, and Alice looked up from her phone.

"Surprisingly, no," she said. She didn't want to give away Robin's episode from that morning, because that would only hurt Kristen further. "She's dealing with a lot right now."

"I'm sure she is. She internalizes everything so much."

"That she does," Alice said. "It's Charlie, and he wants to have a serious conversation via text." She turned off her phone and set it down. "Feeling better?" She got up and took Kristen's empty plate. "More pizza?"

"No, I'm good, dear," Kristen said. "Thank you so much for being here with me."

"Of course," Alice said.

"Tell me how you really are," Kristen said.

Alice put the plate in the sink and sighed, leaning into the counter in front of her, looking out the window and realizing it was almost completely dark. Where had the whole day gone?

She and Kristen hadn't talked hardly at all about the contents of the letter. Alice had taken it and ripped it into tiny pieces; Kristen hadn't read a word of it. Alice had thought she'd need to explain the situation, tell Kristen everything she'd learned from her father.

But once she'd said Joel's mistress was her mother, that was all the explanation she'd needed to give.

They'd cried for a while, and Alice had felt stronger afterward.

"Alice, you don't have to," Kristen said, and Alice pulled herself back to the present. She went back into the living room and laid back down on the couch, pulling the blanket over her body again.

"I'm okay," she finally said, her mind flowing forward to next week, when she'd be back in a house ten times this size, utterly alone.

"I worry about you."

"Thank you," Alice said. "I'm going to worry about you here, too. What are you going to do when we all leave?"

"You know what? I don't know. So much of my life has been wrapped up in this place, and I feel like we threw it all away." Kristen sounded like she was going to start crying again. "Maybe I'll start learning a new skill. I think women my age sew, don't they?"

Alice let a moment of silence go by, and then she burst out laughing. "Sewing," she said between laughs, and Kristen started laughing too. Alice laughed and laughed and laughed until she couldn't breathe and she had tears rolling down her face.

She sighed and sat back against the couch. "I'm going to stay the night, if that's okay."

"Oh, I was hoping you would," Kristen said. "I've been sleeping at the lighthouse, because I'm not sure how to be by myself yet."

"You'll figure it out," Alice said. "Trust me, you'll figure it out."

CHAPTER TWENTY-FOUR

E loise breathed in deeply, trying to commit this ferry ride to her permanent memory. The crisp air rushing by her face. The way she smiled as she reached up and gathered her long, dark hair into a ponytail at the nape of her neck and held it because she didn't have a rubber band. The sun shining nearly directly overhead; the puffy white clouds hovering on the horizon over the mainland in the distance.

The sound of the water slapping against the ferry. The way Aaron shifted closer to her, easily sliding his hand along her back and around her waist. Eloise leaned into him, and the musky, oaky scent of his skin started a new memory.

"Do you have a favorite place to eat on Sanctuary?" he asked, his voice right at her ear.

Eloise turned toward him, finding his face only inches

from hers. He'd shown her around the police station with a goofy grin on his face, but that excitement had been replaced by a straight-faced Aaron with a heavy glint of desire in his gaze. He peered right into her soul, and Eloise wanted him to know all of her secrets.

"Yeah, sure," she said, turning to face the water again and moving her foot so it rested on the other side of his. He put his other hand on her arm, and she stood within the safety and comfort of his arms, more content with a man than she'd ever been.

If only she could take some of this just-right-ness into other aspects of her life. Her thoughts stormed over Robin and Alice, Kristen and Kelli, and AJ before she chased them away. Kelli and AJ had gone dark, and they probably needed it. Robin had broken down. Alice had an impossible task in front of her. They all needed time away from the situation, and Eloise was determined to enjoy her day with Aaron.

"Are you going to make me guess what it is?" he asked, chuckling in a low, throaty voice that sent pleasant shivers across her shoulders and down her back.

She giggled too and said, "Have you heard of The Chubby Pancake?"

"Yeah, of course," he said. "Lifer, you know? But don't they just do breakfast?"

"All day breakfast," she clarified. "And they have this smoked salmon bagel that is one of my favorite things on the planet."

"Ah, I see," he said. "Fancy breakfasts."

"Does that sound okay to you?" she asked.

"Anywhere is fine with me." Aaron's arms tightened around her, and while Eloise would've never put her affection for a man on such public display, she found she didn't care if people saw her with him. She'd only had six days with him, and she only had a few more. Then, they'd have to work something out, and Eloise tried to quell the nervous pit in her stomach that seemed to open every time she thought about returning to Boston.

"Serious truth," she said.

"All right," Aaron agreed. He'd been the one to introduce the game they'd been playing for the past couple of days since their talk on the beach. He'd said they'd have to find a way to stay close once she went back to Boston, and they had phones to call, text, or video chat. So he'd told her about Serious Truth, where they got to ask each other questions that were answered truthfully and seriously.

She'd learned that his ex-wife had crazy high expectations for him and the kids, and about the time their first daughter went to kindergarten and didn't know everything immediately, she'd packed a bag, said motherhood was not for her, and left the cove. Completely gone, in just a day.

He'd been raising the girls alone ever since, and when they asked about their mother, he told them the truth: he didn't know where she was or if she'd ever come back.

Eloise could not imagine doing that to her own offspring. To any child, really.

"Did you always want to be a cop?" she asked.

Aaron drew in a deep breath, his chest pressing against her back. "Uh, yes and no? I grew up fascinated with policemen, firefighters, paramedics. You know, all the heroes. I wanted to be like them. But I went to college for a year or two before I realized that I hate sitting behind a desk. I hate reading. Don't laugh."

Eloise had started to giggle, because she was the exact opposite. If she had to go outside, it was only to get from point A to point B. No sense in getting sunburned or wind chapped lips. Not to her. "Sorry," she said. "It's not what you said."

"Another opposite for you?"

Eloise sobered, because yes, it was another opposite for her. Were her and Aaron simply cut from two different stripes? Could they make a relationship work when they liked hardly any of the same things? And not just a relationship, but a long-distance relationship.

"Yeah, I love sitting behind the desk, and I literally read for enjoyment in my spare time." She wanted to turn and see his reaction, but his lips landed on the back of her neck.

"So you'll do that while I take the girls hiking, and then I'll make dinner." He had an answer for everything, and Eloise really liked that. She felt like he could integrate easily into her life, but Eloise knew that if they had any chance of a real relationship, she'd have to move back to Five Island Cove.

And right now, that wasn't even something she could fathom. There was no university here. One high school, where the same teachers held the jobs for decades. What would she do all day without a job? Read? She didn't like it that much.

"Anyway," she said. "You found you didn't like the desk or reading."

"Right. So I decided to give the Police Academy a try. It was a much better fit. I was done in a year, and I moved back here when an opening came up on the force. I worked in Maryland for about three years before that happened. That's where I met Carol."

So he had lived somewhere else. Perhaps he would consider relocating. Even as Eloise thought it, she banished the idea. She was thinking too far ahead. Way too far ahead. She just needed to ground herself in this moment, this right now, this conversation.

"I've got one for you," he said.

"Go." A slip of unease moved through her, because he could literally ask anything, and Eloise did want to be truthful and serious with him. But she still had things she hadn't told him, and she wasn't ready to make a serious commitment on the ferry from Diamond Island to Sanctuary.

"Do you like kids? I mean, did you ever want children of your own?"

"Sure," she said, relieved the question was an easy one. "I was only married for a couple of years, and we didn't have kids. We wanted them, but it wasn't meant to be, and then I was so busy with my doctorate that the time wasn't right." Eloise's memory flowed back to her younger days, and the amount of stress she carried on her back. Classes, thesis work, dealing with a dysfunctional marriage...she was amazed she'd survived those years.

"And then I got divorced, and well, I never married again." She shrugged, though she'd had a few years in her thirties where her lack of children had definitely been a plague for her.

"And you like girls, right?" Aaron asked.

Eloise faced him then, turning easily in his arms to look at him. "Sounds like you're thinking way down the road. I thought we agreed we weren't going to do that."

"I'm just asking," he said.

"I've met your girls, Aaron," she said. "They were great." Eloise had no idea how to be a mother, but she had Robin's number, and she could ask for help if she needed it. Alice seemed to adore her children too, and they'd displayed such good manners that Alice must've done something right with them.

He nodded, suddenly leaning down to kiss her. Eloise didn't fight for control, and she let Aaron's passion flow through her as he kissed her more roughly than he had previously. He pulled away just as quickly as he'd leaned down, and he raised his head so he was looking out at the water.

"I sure do like you, Eloise," he said, and he sounded absolutely miserable about it.

Eloise wrapped her arms around him and pressed her cheek to his heartbeat. His pulse raced slightly, and Eloise enjoyed the rhythm of it. She liked the solidness of him in her arms, and the way he was carving a place for himself in her heart.

"Serious truth," she said again. "What are you worried about?"

"Worried about?"

"Yeah." She looked up at him again, but he wouldn't meet her eye. "You just said you liked me, but you sounded like it was a terrible thing. What are you worried about?"

He looked at her then. "Honestly?"

"Serious truth."

"I'm worried that I'm not a big enough prize for you," he said. "That you'll go back to Boston and realize how amazing your life there is, and I'll...fade away. Out of sight, out of mind."

Eloise blinked, because she had not realized Aaron didn't see himself as a purely brilliant catch, especially for a woman like Eloise. "I'm not sure what you think my life in Boston is like," she said. "But it's not that great."

"I know you left the cove for a reason."

"It was time," she said.

"And you don't visit very often."

Eloise turned around again, because she didn't want to talk about all of this right now.

"Serious truth, El."

"I want to pause the game," she said. "Can it wait until I show you the...what I want to show you on the island?"

"Okay," Aaron said, and Eloise appreciated that he could be patient though she was sure he didn't want to be. As the ferry continued chugging along toward Sanctuary, Eloise couldn't help wondering if she'd made a huge mistake in asking Aaron to come with her to the Cliffside Inn.

She searched for something else to show him, but she didn't have anything else. And she didn't want to lie to him. They spoke little for the rest of the trip, and once Eloise had her smoked salmon bagel in front of her, the tension finally broke as she lifted it, smiled, and said, "Isn't that the most beautiful thing you've ever seen?"

Aaron laughed, shook his head, and dug into his chicken fried steak and eggs. The conversation picked up again, and breakfast-for-lunch ended far too quickly. Aaron tossed a couple of twenty-dollar bills on the table and looked at her.

"Are you ready? Do we need a car?"

"We definitely need a car." She took one more sip of water and put her napkin on her empty plate. She met his eye, her chest buzzing with nerves. "And I guess I'm ready."

"I'll get a car." He started tapping, as the island network used a car service app for people who didn't bring their cars on the ferry. "Five minutes."

Eloise nodded, and they got up and went outside. The sleek, black car pulled up and the driver said, "Aaron?"

"Right here."

"Where to?"

He looked at Eloise, who swallowed hard. "Uh, the Cliffside Inn? Do you know where that is?"

"No idea," the man said, and Eloise didn't blame him. The Cliffside Inn wasn't open, and hadn't been for over twenty years. This guy probably wasn't even thirty years old yet.

"It's up on Cliffside Drive," she said. "Last building at the top of the road."

"I thought Cliffside Drive was closed," the driver said.

Eloise's heart pumped out extra beats. "Is it? I hadn't heard that." She slid into the car, and the driver got behind the wheel again.

He tapped on his phone for a few seconds. "Oh, that must have been temporary. Landslide last winter." He set his phone in a holder attached to the air vent. "All right, here we go. Says twenty-one minutes."

Eloise smiled and looked from the side of his face to Aaron's, who wore a curious look on his face. Thankfully, he didn't ask her any questions during the drive, and Eloise was left to stew in her own thoughts.

A landslide didn't sound good, and she wondered if

the inn had suffered any damage. Her stomach churned around the bagel, cream cheese, and salmon, and she almost wished she hadn't eaten right before this overdue visit.

Before she knew it, the driver turned onto Cliffside Drive and started going up. Up, up, and then the road leveled to the highest point on Sanctuary Island. "Wow," he said, looking out his window. "I've never been up here." He passed a house and added, "Huge houses up here."

"It is beautiful," Aaron murmured, his gaze out the window too.

Eloise had the picture-perfect image of this place in her mind, and she closed her eyes and saw it expand in every direction. The blue sky. The white-tipped water below. The pine trees that protected the homes up here. The gray and black and white rocks. The pristine swimming pool. Perfectly decorated guest rooms. Delicious meals twice each day.

"Here we are," the driver said, and Eloise opened her eyes, the gleaming, white building that was the Cliffside Inn disappearing the moment she did.

She got out of the car. While Aaron paid the driver, she stood in the cracked and crumbling drive of the Cliffside Inn, which wasn't anything like the shiny, black asphalt with clearly marked white arrows directing guests which way to go to get in and out of the inn that existed in her mind.

The building didn't gleam in any color, and it wasn't

white anymore either. She stared at the siding that bore dirt, water stains, and other organic matter that Eloise could only classify as algae. Slime. Something.

The car drove away, and Aaron came to stand beside her. "Wow," he said, staring at the building too.

In Eloise's mind, the front yard of the inn glowed an emerald green, with rose bushes lining the front of it. Several carefully placed trees had flowers growing around their trunks, and when someone arrived at the inn, they were immediately charmed by its appearance.

Weeds overran the grass, with scrub trees shooting up wherever they wanted. The sight of it didn't charm Eloise, but rather, made her want to hurry past to find somewhere else to stay.

The building in front of her looked exactly like it should—like someone had abandoned it. And then someone else had bought it and forgotten about it for two decades.

"So," she said, glad Aaron hadn't prompted her. "I own this place. My dad owned it when I was a girl, and when he and my mom finally got divorced, he closed it. When he died, it went into foreclosure, because he refused to let anyone have the inn but him." She spoke in a dead voice, one that didn't inflect up and down. "I bought it in the auction." She looked at Aaron and away quickly. "I did not like my father much."

She folded her arms and hugged herself, because she

didn't talk about this. But that door in her mind was open now, and dozens of things were emerging.

"He hit my mother for years, and when he turned his wrath on me one night, that was when she finally got the courage to kick him out."

"Eloise." Aaron stepped in front of the inn, blocking her view of it. He gathered her into his arms, and she hugged him instead of herself. "I'm so sorry."

"The inn sat empty for a few years before I bought it," she said. "I was twenty-six and newly divorced. I've made the payments all these years, and I've only been back every now and then to make sure it's still standing."

Why, she didn't know. Perhaps everything would be better if she burned it down, said good-bye to it for good.

"Why?" he asked.

"I don't know," she said, stepping back. She took his hand and tried to put a smile on her face. It wobbled though, and she let it fall off. They faced the inn again. "I think...I had great memories here as a little girl. The inn was only open in the summer, and I'd get to come up here with my dad, and he was...different somehow."

"How?" Aaron asked.

"He didn't drink or gamble while at the inn," Eloise whispered, only realizing it in that moment. "My mom never came to the inn, and it was like...my dad came alive without her." She shook her head. She didn't know what she was saying. She cleared her throat. "Do you want to go inside?"

"Yes," Aaron said, squeezing her hand. "Show me your happy times, Eloise."

She looked up at him, and she knew it was ridiculous to start to fall in love with someone after only six days. But she definitely felt herself falling for a moment. "I haven't told anyone about this, Aaron. Not Robin, or Alice, or Kristen. Not even my mother knows I own the inn."

"Then thank you for trusting me with it." He leaned down and touched his lips to hers in a sweet, chaste kiss so unlike the one they'd shared on the ferry.

They faced the inn again, and Eloise took the first step toward the double-wide front doors, hoping with everything she had that she wouldn't fall through one of the floorboards during the tour.

CHAPTER TWENTY-FIVE

Kristen tiptoed past Alice sleeping on the couch, the memory of the one and only time the girl had done so before. Both Alice and her mother, Denise, had stayed the night at the lighthouse once, when a storm had blown through Five Island Cove, and they'd been stuck on Diamond Island.

Alice had been thirteen then, and Kristen hadn't even suspected Joel of stepping out on her. Could it have been that night when he'd first started feeling things for Denise Williams?

She shook herself as she unlocked the front door and went outside. She didn't want to think about Denise Williams. She didn't want to remember how she'd mourned the woman's death, how she'd gone to talk to Connor about taking better care of his children, how often she'd discussed Alice with Joel after the funeral.

Pure foolishness filled her, and she'd really rather not wallow in that. She had never seen him act strangely about Denise's death, though surely he'd mourned her too. Didn't he?

Kristen did not want to believe that her husband was so past feeling and so cruel that he didn't. At the same time, he'd left behind enough secrets to destroy her without the luxury of being around to provide answers and reasons and explanations as to why.

That was all Kristen wanted to know. Why?

Why doctor Eloise's scores? Why was he so unhappy with her that he had to find another woman? Why had he focused so much on other kids instead of his own? Why had he deceived Guy Watkins and watched the man crash and burn?

Why? Why? *Why?*

The word screamed through her head as she walked, and she didn't specifically pick a direction to go. So when she realized the path ended in one more step, she looked up from the bumpy concrete she'd been walking on. The lighthouse stood to her right, about half of it visible above the tops of the trees separating her from it.

She felt separated from everything and everyone in her life right now, and she reached out to hold onto the railing marking the overlook of Sea Lion Point. Hardly anyone knew this gem existed, but Kristen had been here many times before. When she'd lost her third pregnancy, she'd fled to this point. When Joel had been diagnosed with cancer, she'd come here. It seemed like every time Kristen needed to find herself, discover a new path for her life, she ended up at Sea Lion Point.

The best time to actually see sea lions on the long strip of beach below was in September and October, but Kristen took a few minutes to search the sand anyway. The only way to get to the sand below was by boat, and only tour groups did it in the peak of summer tourism. Kristen herself had never actually been on the beach, though she'd imagined herself down there many times.

Alone, where no one would bother her.

When her kids had been small children, and they were driving her nuts, she'd lock herself in the bathroom, close her eyes, and transport herself to the beach with the sea lions. Then, there were no crying children. No one who just needed to "ask her something real quick." No paperwork, and no seafaring lessons, and no worry about bills she and Joel didn't have the money to pay.

Just miles of sun, sea, and sand.

She sighed, but she didn't cry. She felt like she'd shed more tears in the past week and a half than any human should have to. Her tear ducts felt dry, and she was glad she didn't have anything left to give.

"A few more days," she told herself. The funeral was on Saturday, and once it was over, Kristen's life was nothing but a blank slate. Because of Robin's excellent organizational skills and absolute determination to get the five of them back to the cove to help, the cottage was cleaned out. The lighthouse was nearly there. Kristen wouldn't have to lift a finger once Joel went into the ground.

She also had nothing else to occupy her time. So much of the last five years had been spent taking him to the doctor or the hospital, getting his medications, making sure he took them, monitoring his health, making and bringing him food. And Kristen had been happy to do it, because she loved him.

She'd thought he loved her.

Now, as she thought about how stressful his care had been and how much of herself she'd given him, a new kind of anger simmered in her veins. This dangerous, dark feeling had been creeping up on her for days now, and Kristen pushed it away. She did not want to think the last fifty years of her life had been a lie.

She'd had plenty of happy times. Plenty of learning and growth. She'd felt plenty of love from Joel, and she didn't want those memories and times to be tainted by the secrets she'd discovered over the past week.

Maybe the fact that Joel hadn't told her was actually a blessing. Maybe he'd wanted to preserve her happy life. Her thoughts went round and round, because she eventually landed on, *Then why didn't he destroy all the evidence of his indiscretions?*

Perhaps he'd meant to, and then been too sick.

Kristen straightened away from the railing, because she did not want to make excuses for him.

She faced the path she'd already trod, feeling like she had a very long road ahead of her. Her phone rang in her pocket as she left the overlook behind, and she pulled it out to see the funeral home's number on the screen.

"Hello?" she asked, slowing to a stop. She normally liked to watch the ground while she walked, as this path wasn't well-maintained, and she was seventy-six-years-old.

"Kristen," a man said. "It's Sydney Martin at Martin Mortuary. How are you?" He spoke in a smooth, professional voice, and Kristen appreciated that.

"I'm doing fine," Kristen said. "What can I help you with?"

"I'm just looking over this final plan you submitted via the portal." He paused, and Kristen wondered what she'd done wrong. "And I'm afraid I had you pick out the wrong casket. You get a gold level casket, and you chose a silver."

The thought of going back to the funeral home and picking a different casket made her ill. "Joel picked the casket," she said. "It's fine. I don't care."

"I'm afraid I can't refund any money."

"That's fine," Kristen said. "I'm not asking for a refund."

"Are you sure?"

"Positively."

Sydney let a couple moments go by, as if he expected her to change her mind. She wouldn't. "All right," he said. "Other than that, I think we're ready for Saturday morning."

"Sounds great," Kristen said. The call ended, and she wished Saturday morning had already come and gone. She started walking again, her thoughts revolving around the funeral arrangements now. She'd meant to call Patricia back about the food for the family luncheon too, and she hadn't.

The woman ran the community outreach arm of the church Joel and Kristen had attended for many years, and she wanted to host a luncheon for everyone after the funeral and the burial, and Kristen had agreed to it.

Why she'd agreed to it, she wasn't sure. Patricia had probably caught her in a weak moment. She'd heard nothing from the woman for a while, so maybe the luncheon wasn't happening. But Kristen knew Patricia better than that, and she'd probably planned a three-course meal.

Kristen thought perhaps she could get more involved in her church once the funeral was over, once her girls left the cove again. She detoured down the path toward the picnic table, and sat down, intending to make a few phone calls and tie things up with the loose ends still hanging down as they related to the funeral.

She first called Patricia, and the woman answered on the first ring. "Kristen, hello."

"Hello."

"You must be calling about the luncheon," she said. "I didn't want to bother you, because I know you've had so much going on, but I want you to know that it's going to be great. We'll have a full lunch ready for when you're finished at the cemetery, and I even got LisaAnne to make her steamed mussels."

"Wow," Kristen said, feeling her spirits start to lift. "That's amazing, Patricia. Thank you."

"I only need one thing from you, and that's an estimate of how many people you think you'll have at the luncheon."

Kristen wasn't sure how to count. "Well, Joel was the only member of his family left. We've got our kids, their spouses, a few of my really close friends." Even as Kristen spoke, she didn't even know if Clara would be there, or Jean, Rueben's wife. But she wanted Alice and her twins there. Robin's family. The other girls.

She had a couple of friends at the community center, from her years working in the Seafaring Girls program.

"I would say there won't be more than twenty-five," she said. "Is that okay?"

"Totally okay," Patricia chirped. "Thank you for letting us serve you this way."

"Of course," Kristen said, trying to be as proper as Patricia. As soon as the call ended, she deflated. Talking to people was too hard, and her idea to do more volunteer work with the church fled.

But she had one more call to make, and she stayed seated, because she needed all the strength she had to talk to Clara.

"Hey, Mom." At least her daughter had answered this time.

"Hello, dear." Kristen wasn't sure what else to say. She didn't want to ask Clara if she was coming to the funeral or not. Her daughter knew Kristen wanted her there. "Tell me what I can do for you."

Clara sighed, and Kristen just waited. Clara needed some time to put her words in the right order, and Kristen had learned that if she just waited long enough, she'd start talking.

"Did you know Joel asked me to read his eulogy at the funeral?" Clara asked.

"Yes." Kristen bristled when Clara called her father Joel, but she'd given up on correcting her. "He told me."

"Did he tell you he wrote the eulogy?"

"He planned everything," Kristen said.

"I hate it," Clara said, the words bursting from her in a rush. "It's not the man I knew at all, Mom, and I just thought if I didn't come, then I wouldn't have to read it."

"Is that what's keeping you from coming?"

"Mom, I'm on Pearl. I've been staying with Ebony."

Kristen's chest simultaneously stung and collapsed. She struggled to breathe against the fact that her own daughter didn't want to stay with her. Kristen thought they could've had some real opportunities to bond over the past week and a half, the way she'd seen her Seafaring Girls do.

"Don't read it, then," Kristen said, glad her voice stayed somewhat steady.

"I don't want to disrespect his wishes."

"What?" Kristen asked, because Clara wasn't making sense. "You call him Joel, Clara. I think that's more disrespectful than not reading the eulogy." As soon as she said it, she wished she could suck the words right back down her throat.

But Clara said, "I know, Mom."

Kristen had no energy left for this conversation. It was amazing how quickly she drained these days, and she leaned her head in her hand not holding the phone. "Clara," she said. "I'm sorry. That wasn't very nice. Listen, honey, I love you. I want you here. Change the eulogy if you want to. He's not here, and he's not going to know."

"You think I can?"

"Yes," Kristen said. "Do what you need to do so that you can come. Please...just come if you can."

Clara sniffled, and she said, "Okay, Mom. I love you."

"Love you too." She put her phone down on the table, relying on Clara to end the call. She didn't like it when her daughter cried, because it squeezed her heart so tightly. She didn't think she had any tears left—and for herself and her situation, she didn't.

But for her daughter, she had plenty of tears to cry.

By the time she composed herself and made it back to her cottage, she found a hash brown casserole sitting on the stovetop, with a note on the counter beside it.

I had to run, Alice had said. *Thank you for showing me how to be strong and how to forgive. I love you, and I'll check on you later.*

Alice

Kristen wanted more notes like this. Why couldn't Joel have left notes like this for her to find after he'd gone?

She pressed the paper to her heart, almost able to smell Alice's expensive perfume embedded in the fibers. Oh, how she loved Alice, no matter how much money she had or what kind of house or what her last name was. She hoped Alice knew that, and Kristen determined that, once this was all over, she'd make sure she told all of her girls what amazing women they were and how much she loved them more often.

CHAPTER TWENTY-SIX

Robin poured the drained spaghetti into the cream and herb sauce she'd put together. With a pair of tongs, she mixed the pasta with the sauce and used two hands to move the pan to the island counter behind her.

"Okay," she said. "We're ready." She suddenly remembered the garlic bread in the oven, and she cursed under her breath as she yanked open the oven. Thankfully, the toast was just starting to sizzle and brown, and maybe for the first time in her life, she thanked the stars above that her oven was so old.

She pulled the cookie sheet of garlic bread out and put it on the stovetop, because she didn't have a fancy trivet to put it on. She usually threw down a couple of pot holders to protect the countertop, but tonight, her family could come over to the stove if they wanted carb on top of carb for dinner.

The atmosphere around the house had been cinched tight since yesterday morning, when she'd asked Duke to go somewhere else. He'd returned with the girls after school, and Robin had treated them all civilly. She'd slept in the same bed with Duke, and she'd simply said she didn't want to talk about Alaska until she was ready.

He'd said, "Okay, Robin. You tell me when you're ready," rolled over, and gone to sleep. She wished she could shelve all of her cares and worries like that, but she'd lain awake for at least an hour before she'd fallen asleep out of sheer exhaustion. At least she didn't take pills to cover her problems, and she'd spent about a minute thinking she needed to find something strong to drink before dismissing the idea.

Duke had gotten up as normal, showered as normal, driven the girls to school as normal. Robin had made breakfast as normal, cleaned up as normal, and gone into her office as normal.

But nothing in her life was normal anymore, because she needed to establish a new normal. She'd taken one look at the scattered sheets and cards, turned around, and gone to the freezer for an ice cream bar.

She'd spent the day alone, and her skin was starting to itch with the need to make an adult connection with someone. Being involved in other people's lives had given Robin a sense of purpose in her own. She liked having friends, and she didn't think that was a flaw.

But she wanted to give Kelli the space she obviously

needed. She was grateful Alice had taken on the care of Kristen. But AJ hadn't checked in, though she'd said she would. And even Eloise hadn't come home—back to Robin's—last night. She'd at least texted to say she was staying on Sanctuary, so Robin hadn't needed to worry. Likewise, Alice had said she needed some time with her family, and Robin wasn't surprised she hadn't shown up for dinner.

"Mom?"

Robin shook her head, pushing her friends onto the back burner so she could focus on her family, who all stood on the other side of the island, waiting for her to say what was for dinner.

"It's creamy pesto pasta," she said. "And garlic toast. Let's eat."

Mandie picked up a plate, and she got things started as she mentioned the theater company tryouts happening next week.

"Oh, are you going to try out for that?" Robin asked, standing out of the way like she always did.

"Yeah, I think so," Mandie said.

"What prompted that?" She glanced at Duke, expecting him to go in front of her. He didn't particularly like pasta meals, because there was no meat, but she couldn't feed his red meat habit every night.

He gestured for her to go in front of him as Mandie said, "Well, there's this boy, Sam..."

"Sam Corring?" Robin asked, still looking at Duke. He

flashed her that sexy smile that Robin loved so much, and she stepped in front of him. She reached for his hand, glad when he pressed in close to her while she reached for a plate.

"Yes," Mandie said, unaware of the delicate dance Robin and Duke were doing. They'd talk later, and Robin really wanted to build a new bridge between them—even if that meant he went to Alaska for four months.

"He's cute, Mom."

"Oh, I know he is," Robin said, picking up a small piece of garlic bread. "So what do you have to do for auditions?" They sat at the table, and they had a normal conversation for their family. Mandie even told everyone how she'd decided not to kiss Brady, and their relationship had been defined as *just friends*.

Soon enough, Jamie went down the hall to get her math homework, and Mandie went down the hall to the small office off the front of the house, where they had a piano they hardly used. She hummed along as she plunked out a tune, and Robin finally looked at Duke.

He hadn't left the table like he usually did, going off to check on something in the backyard or garage until she called him in to sit with her while they watched a movie.

Her heart softened as it thumped harder, and she reached over and covered his hand with hers. "I'm sorry about yesterday. It's been a very stressful time since Joel died."

"I know."

"And you..." No, she didn't want to blame him. But he hadn't seen her when he'd gotten home yesterday morning. "I want you to see me," she said instead.

"I see you."

"Do you, Duke? When you walked in yesterday, I'd just destroyed my office, screaming at the top of my lungs. And what was the first thing you asked me?"

Duke blinked at her. "I don't remember."

Robin wondered what that would be like. She carried around so many little things, and she needed to start learning how to set them down. "You asked if we had any leftovers. Then you yelled at me from the kitchen to come find something for you, and then you hit me with Alaska." Robin tried to tame her voice so it didn't sound accusatory.

"I'm sorry," Duke said. "I guess I didn't know."

"I know you didn't know, and I just...I just wonder *why* you didn't know." She shook her head. "It doesn't matter. I get men and women are different, but I want you to know that yesterday was not all about Alaska."

"I know you don't want to go to Alaska."

"No, I don't," Robin said. "But—I'm trying to have an open mind, and I do want what's best for our whole family." She drew a deep breath and pushed it out. "So, with all of that said, I've been thinking about it pretty much nonstop, and I think you should go to Alaska in May."

"Robin," he started.

"I know you want to, and I think it would be great for

our family. I know you just want to do the best for me, and Mandie, and Jamie, and I love you so much for that." She met his eye, and the hint of agony in his gaze made her fall in love with him all over again.

"I'll try to notice what you're doing more," he said.

Robin smiled, because they'd had this part of the conversation before. "Do you really think you can make as much in Alaska in four months as you make here all year?"

"Yes, babe," he said. "I really think so."

"Even if you're *not* here for the summer?" It was his busiest season, and Alaska would have to be something special for him to leave the cove during the summer.

"Even if." He looked at her with pure honesty in his eyes, and Robin had to trust him. She always had before, and she saw no reason to stop now.

"All right," she said, standing up. She stepped around the corner and leaned down to kiss him.

He took her face in both of his hands, stopping her before her lips could touch his. "You know you're my queen, right?" he asked, and Robin's chest expanded as her heart grew two sizes. "I know I'm not great at saying it or showing it, but I love you more than anything, and anyone, and more than Alaska."

"More than fishing?" she teased.

"Oh, now, come on," he said with a smile, finally bringing her face to his so he could kiss her.

Part of Robin's life that had exploded yesterday

morning got put back where it was supposed to be, and as soon as Duke finished kissing her, Robin's thoughts immediately turned to her friends. She needed them back in this house too, because this house was a home to everyone who stepped through the front door.

"I lost you," Duke said, and Robin turned from where she stood at the sink.

"Sorry," she said. "Just thinking about the girls."

He put his plate in the sink with one hand and slid the other one along her hip. "Could you put the girls on hold for a minute while you take me to bed?"

Robin nudged him with her hip, though she did want to go down the hall and make love to her husband. "It's seven o'clock," she said.

"So?"

"So Mandie and Jamie are awake." Robin kept rinsing the dishes, and Duke opened the dishwasher and started loading them into the racks.

"So we'll say we're watching a movie in the bedroom," he said. "We've done it before."

"Keep loading," Robin said. "And you'll probably get your way."

He chuckled, and Robin laughed with him. Once the kitchen was clean and all the leftover pasta put away, Robin went down the hall to tell Mandie she was tired and was going to go lie in bed and watch a movie with her dad.

"Okay, I'll make sure all the lights are off," Mandie

said, none the wiser. Robin gave the same speech to Jamie, who said she'd just finished her homework and she was going to turn on her TV show and go to bed.

Robin went into her bedroom and locked the door before facing her husband. She could shelve her friends for right now, because she could learn, she could change, and she could adapt, but she needed Duke by her side to do it.

THE NEXT MORNING, AFTER HER RUN ALONG THE BEACH, Robin set boxed cereal on the counter and put out bowls and spoons. "I'm going out to the front porch," she said. "Have a great day at school." She dropped a kiss on Mandie's cheek, and Jamie's forehead, but Duke took her in his arms and growled as he kissed her flush on the mouth.

She giggled and swatted him away from her, taking her phone down the hall and out the front door. The morning air went down cold, as the front of the house faced west and took all the afternoon warmth from the sun.

She had four choices of who to call first, and she dismissed Alice and Eloise immediately. She knew where they were and that they were probably okay. So she dialed AJ, thinking Kelli would only be pushed farther away when she saw Robin's name on her screen.

AJ didn't answer either, and Robin felt her spine bend in the wrong direction. She took a deep breath. This was not going to break her. She dialed AJ again, because it was early in the morning, and maybe she was still asleep.

"Robin," she said after three rings. "I'm so sorry we've gone off the rails."

"Where are you guys? Are you okay?"

"We're on our way back to Diamond," AJ said. "Or we will be in a little bit. Kelli's still asleep."

"I'm sorry I called too early," Robin said. "I was just worried, and I...want everyone here for dinner tonight." They only had one more full day before the funeral, and Robin needed to know where everyone stood.

"I need to get up and get going anyway," AJ said. "I'm sorry to worry you, Robin. We've been dealing with a lot here, and Nathan called yesterday, and I spent a lot of time talking with him."

"I'm sorry," Robin said. "Good talking?"

"Uh, I'm not sure yet," AJ said. "Anyway, Kelli and I talked last night, and we're definitely coming back to Diamond today. We'll definitely be there by dinner."

"Okay," Robin said. "Requests?"

"Can that hot husband of yours get us some lobster?"

Robin laughed with AJ, and she promised she'd send Duke to get some lobster for dinner. She could hear the money draining from her bank account, but she wasn't going to say anything. She'd figure out the checkbook after everyone left town again.

Her breath hitched at the thought of being the only one left in the cove, but she pulled back on those emotions.

"All right," she said. "Well, I'm not going to Kristen's today, so come by whenever you get here."

"Will do," AJ said. "Oh, my boss is calling. I have to go."

Robin hung up and watched the street in front of her house. She lived in a peaceful neighborhood, but it was a little too early to see parents walking their children to the bus stop or going on walks with one another.

She decided she didn't need to call Alice or Eloise, and she sent a text to the group string. Lobster dinner at six tonight. My house. Everyone is invited. If it's not just you, let me know how many.

She worked through the morning, putting her office back together, showering, and planning the sides to go with the lobster she'd sent Duke to get. He'd boil them up, as he was a pro with shellfish, and she started shredding cabbage about three o'clock. Not five minutes later, the front door opened, and Alice called, "Hello? We're here."

"In the kitchen," Robin called back, elbow-deep in feeding chunks of cabbage into the food processor.

Alice spoke all the way down the hall, and she came into the kitchen with her twins, as well as Eloise and Aaron. Robin teared up at the sight of them, and she abandoned the cabbage.

"Oh, you're here," she said, pushing the button on the

food processor to get it to stop. She flew into Alice's arms, reaching for Eloise at the same time. They embraced, and Robin squeezed her eyes shut, smelling the lavish rosy perfume that was the epitome of Alice, and the soft powdery scent that would forever be Eloise.

"How are you?" Alice asked, stepping back and holding onto Robin's shoulders.

"Really good," she said. "Really." She switched her gaze to Eloise. "Did you guys have a good couple of days?"

"I did," Eloise said, linking her arm through Aaron's.

"Tuesday was rough," Alice said. "But we spent Wednesday and most of today eating and shopping our way across two islands to celebrate the twins' fifteenth birthday." She smiled at her kids and put her arm around her daughter's shoulders. "And that was fun."

"Is Mandie here?" Charlie asked, and Alice narrowed her eyes at her son.

"She'll be home from school in about a half an hour," Robin said, not terribly upset by the boy's crush on her daughter. In fact, Robin knew Mandie thought Charlie was cute too, and she should probably pause in her prep of the slaw to text her daughter that the boy was here. She could fluff her hair or add more lip gloss before she came into the house.

Robin reminded herself that it wasn't the eighties anymore, and Mandie would never fluff her hair for a guy. Robin would've ratted her bangs to the height of the sky before meeting a cute boy, and she smiled at the memory.

"Tell us what to do to help," Eloise said.

"You can shuck the corn," Robin said. "And someone can peel the carrots and potatoes for the veggie fries." She indicated the vegetables on the counter beside her. "And I have a box of biscuit mix someone can be in charge of."

"Corn," Alice said. "Come on guys, grab the garbage can and let's get this done."

"We'll do the veggie fries," Eloise said, and Robin smiled at Aaron as he happily went along with her.

"I'll put my girls on the biscuits," Robin said, feeling herself tense up by having other people in her kitchen with her. She was used to being the top chef, and she kept bumping into people and trying to tame her irritation.

She forced herself to calm down, and she thought about uncurling that fist and letting go of the control she'd always wielded in her kitchen.

"We're home," Duke said, and Robin realized she'd forgotten to text Mandie. Her daughter came around the corner and froze, prompting Duke to add, "Don't stop, baby. I'm right behind you."

She stepped out of the way, and Duke came into the kitchen with a huge crate of live lobsters.

"Oh, bless this man," Alice said, eyeing the lobsters. "No wonder Robin married you." She grinned as Duke smiled back at her and kissed Robin while she stirred the cole slaw.

"Taste," she said, scooping up a forkful of slaw for him. He opened his mouth and she slid the fork in.

"It's good," he said, and Robin took a taste too, catching Mandie hurrying out of the living room as fast as her feet could carry her.

"I think more celery seed," she said, tapping in another pinch or two. "And salt."

"You're the genius," Duke said. "I'm going to get the fire going." He wisely got out of the fray of women, nodding to Aaron as he passed. "Do you want to join me in the backyard?"

"Sure," he said, and he didn't ask Eloise if it was okay with her. Robin liked that, because it spoke of a healthy relationship that had started between the two of them. He did step over to her and lean into her as she continued to peel the potato in her hand. He grinned, and he was just so cute with that dimple in his right cheek. He said something, and she nodded, and Aaron went out into the backyard with Duke.

Robin waited until the door clicked closed before she said, "Eloise, five minutes. Tell us everything."

Eloise shook her head, and Robin couldn't see her face as she had her back to her. "There are minors here," she said.

"You did something you can't say in front of fifteen-year-olds?" Alice asked, "Eloise." A peal of laughter filled the kitchen, and Robin peeled off a piece of aluminum foil and covered the bowl of cole slaw before putting it in the fridge. The flavors would marry as they chilled, and she faced the kitchen.

"Of course not," Eloise said. "I leave in three days."

"So you went to Sanctuary?" Alice asked. "Did you take Aaron?"

"He came on Tuesday," Eloise said. "He has two girls at home, and he's the only one to take care of them."

"His parents are still alive," Robin said. "They could've kept the girls. That's why I asked."

Eloise rinsed a potato and put it on the towel next to the sink. She turned off the water and faced the kitchen. She wore a look on her face that broadcasted a clear message.

"Jamie," Robin said. "Go out to the garage and get me the big bag of paper plates." That would give them five minutes.

"Charlie, you and Ginny go see what those men are doing in the backyard," Alice said just as Mandie came back into the kitchen. She definitely had more lip gloss on now, and she'd changed her shirt.

"You go with them," Robin said, and all the teenagers left the kitchen. "You've got two minutes left."

"Nothing happened with Aaron," she said. "We're still committed to the long-distance relationship. This is about something else."

"Okay," Alice said, the corn silk and husk-free now.

"I bought the Cliffside Inn," Eloise said, pressing her palms together. "I've owned it for eighteen years, and I took Aaron to see it."

Robin's breath left her body, and she didn't know how

to respond. Eloise's father had left the cove while she and her mother stayed to pick up the broken pieces of their lives. He'd closed the inn, and it was only after his death that the bank had repossessed it and sold it at auction.

"Good for you," Alice said, nodding.

"Yeah," Robin chimed in. "That's amazing, Eloise."

"I'm going back to Boston on Sunday," she said. "But I'm not teaching again until fall, and I might be back to start fixing it up."

Robin's eyebrows shot toward her hairline. "Really?"

"I hardly ever teach the summer semester," Eloise said. "And it's a summer inn. I could open it when I'm not teaching."

"Wow, Eloise," Alice said, and that echoed Robin's thoughts.

"Hey," AJ said, and Robin swung her attention to her and Kelli, who'd appeared in the kitchen without making a sound.

Exclamations of "Kelli," and "AJ," and "Thank the Lord," filled the kitchen, and Alice, Robin, and Eloise swarmed Kelli and AJ, the five-way hug that followed made Robin's heart calm even more.

Oh, how she loved these women.

"Guys," Alice said. "Can we go to Rocky Ridge tomorrow?"

"We have to go to the lighthouse too," Robin said. "We need Kristen to know we still love her, even though Joel has turned out to be someone we barely knew."

"Lighthouse in the morning," AJ said, looking around at the others. "Rocky Ridge in the afternoon?"

"It's a plan," Eloise said, and the others agreed.

"Babe," Duke said, and Robin lifted her head out of the huddle. "I need the salt." He caught her eye and came into the house. "I'll get it myself."

Robin rejoined her ladies, her friends, her sisters. "That's right," she muttered. "He'll get it himself."

Two beats of silence passed, and then all five of them burst out laughing together.

CHAPTER TWENTY-SEVEN

AJ folded her long legs underneath her, her stomach full of buttery lobster and the fattening cole slaw Robin had made. She'd always been good in the kitchen, and AJ couldn't remember a time the girl had ever burned her cookies in all the times they'd made them to bring to the lighthouse.

AJ had been helpless in the kitchen, and when they'd finally entered their senior year, she'd started stopping at the grocer to buy cookies before going to the lighthouse. So much had changed that year, but not her friendship with these four women.

"Thanks for dinner, Duke," she said as the man bent over and kissed his wife. AJ had never really wanted to be Robin until that moment. She didn't want to live on this island. She didn't want to run along the beach—she'd done that plenty of times. She didn't want to be responsible for knowing where every little item her family owned was.

But she did want a man who adored her as obviously as Duke adored Robin.

"Yeah," he said, smiling at AJ. "Thanks for coming, all of you." He straightened and smiled around at everyone before looking back at Robin. "I'm taking the kids to the movies."

"Dad, I want to do laser tag," Mandie said, a hopeful look on her face, and AJ couldn't help wondering what a daughter of hers would look like. She'd never know, because she was too old to have a baby now. Nathan didn't want children—at least not more than the three he had with three other women.

"It's all in the same place," Duke said without looking at her. "Alice, is it okay if your kids come with us?"

"Of course." Alice probably never said things like, "Yeah," or "yes." She wore clothes that cost as much as AJ's rent every month, and AJ hadn't seen a hair out of place since she'd arrived, though they'd worked some long hours in the lighthouse, going through dusty, old files. But Alice had always been the picture of poise and beauty, and AJ thought she could learn something from her that would help her while she spoke to the camera.

Aaron leaned down and kissed Eloise's forehead. "I'm going to take my girls with them. Okay?"

"Sure," she said, setting her can of diet cola on the coffee table in front of her. "I'll walk you out." She possessed a glow, and AJ wondered if she'd ever shone like that around Nathan. If she had, it had been a long, long time.

Duke grabbed his keys and followed Aaron and the kids down the hall to the garage exit. AJ settled into the couch, warm and full and comfortable. How long had she felt like this? She couldn't remember the last time, because her apartment didn't have plush, comfortable furniture like this couch. Nathan liked modern, and all AJ knew about modern was that it wasn't worth sitting on.

"Oh," Alice said, jumping up from the couch and almost knocking into the table. She held a cup of coffee, and not a single drop of it spilled while she hurried down the hall too.

"Where's she going?" Robin asked.

Neither Kelli nor AJ answered, because Alice was as unpredictable as she was beautiful. She pulled something from her purse and brought it back into the living room while AJ let her eyes close.

She was very good at pretending, as she'd been doing it for years. Decades. When she didn't feel confident behind the news desk, she faked it. When she broke out because of stress or the hormonal issues she'd had, she pretended like she didn't think about the acne during the interview.

There was always time to scrutinize everything she said and did later. In the moment, she pretended like everything was perfect and wonderful. That *she* was perfect and wonderful.

But when she got back to the dressing room or to the safety of her apartment, she could take off all the makeup, and unfurl the scarves that hid the unsightly scar on her neck, and go a couple of days without showering to make her hair straight, silky, and shiny.

Something bubbled in her stomach, and she wasn't sure how long Robin would let her go without asking for a report about where she and Kelli had been and what they'd been doing.

"Alice," Robin said, a measure of chastisement in her voice. "You don't owe me any money."

AJ opened her eyes to find Robin holding an envelope and peering down into it and then up at Alice.

"Yes, we do," Eloise said, returning to the living room.

She and Alice sat in unison, and Alice added, "We don't expect you to pay for everything, Robin. You make a hot breakfast in the morning, for crying out loud."

Robin still wore a look of doubt, but she closed the envelope and nodded. "Well, thank you. It will help with the lobster feast we had tonight."

"Which was amazing," Kelli said, lifting her own can of soda to her lips.

"It really was," AJ added. She cursed herself for speaking when her comment drew Alice's and Robin's attention. "What?" she asked.

"I think—if you're comfortable," Alice said,

exchanging a glance with Robin. "You should tell us why you didn't want to come to the funeral."

AJ's stomach flipped and shrunk, making all that she'd eaten way too much. She shot a look at Kelli, who just nodded quietly.

So not fair, AJ thought. Kelli hadn't told anyone about the house on Seabreeze Shore, though if they searched their memories hard enough, they'd probably all remember where Kelli grew up.

"It's the last secret," Robin said. "And I think we need to know them all, so we can find some closure." She sounded so reasonable, but AJ was certain that if she was the one harboring the secret, she wouldn't think that.

"We all love you, AJ," Alice said. "No matter what."

AJ shifted on the couch, drawing her knees to her chest, almost like a shield between her and the others. The problem was, she had no shield against her thoughts. When she focused on work, she didn't have to think about Five Island Cove.

All of her siblings had moved from the cove fifteen years ago, and AJ didn't speak much to her father, though he still lived here. She really had no reason to come back to this little group of islands—except for the women in the room with her. She thought she'd like to spend more time with them, as she didn't have very many friends in Atlanta, at least not female friends.

She wanted to keep this renewed friendship going, and she could trust them with this. After drawing in a deep breath, she said, "Joel...was a cruel taskmaster. Everyone loved him as a coach, but he pushed me harder than everyone." Her voice grew in strength, and she stared at a spot on the floor just past the coffee table. Perhaps if she didn't look at anyone, the story would just flow from her.

"Which is fine. I was beat up in college too."

"Beat up?" Robin asked. "Like, he physically beat you up?"

"No," AJ said, remembering how there were never any physical marks. Only complete mental exhaustion, crippling self-doubt, and anxiety that she'd never be good enough for Joel. "Just mental, verbal, that kind of thing. One of the last things he said to me was how surprised he was that I'd gotten my scholarship to the University of Miami." She shook her head. "But that's way at the end of the story."

No one said anything, and AJ hated the silence. She'd rather they fire questions at her than just wait for her patiently to explain.

She just needed to blurt it out. Rip it off like a bandage. AJ didn't want to cry, but she knew she would, and she hated the hot-eyed feeling of tears. Her chest *hurt*, and she struggled to breathe against it.

"He made a pass at Amelia," she finally said, her voice loud and echoing in the silence. AJ looked nervously at Robin, then Kelli, and then Alice. She could see her fair-haired sister when she looked at Kelli, and AJ could not even imagine what might have happened had she not shown up early to pick up her younger sister from soccer practice.

"You're kidding," Alice said, her voice made of air. Her eyes had widened, and she held her coffee cup very, very still.

"I'm not," AJ said. "He had her pressed up against that crappy truck he used to drive, and he had his hands all over her." AJ shoved against the images in her mind. "I lost it. I honked my horn—I was driving into the parking lot when I saw them. I nearly crashed my dad's car, trying to get out." She could see it all again, and she let her voice trail into the stunned tension now filling the room.

She couldn't tell any more of the story, mostly because she'd gone blank after springing from the car and running toward Amelia and Joel. She'd been so angry. She'd never been that angry before or since, and she'd simply lost those memories, as if someone had gone into her mind while she slept and scrubbed them out with a black marker.

"When did this happen?" Eloise asked.

AJ swung her head toward Eloise, who sat right beside her on the couch, feeling like she was underwater and couldn't move as fast as she'd like. "Almost the end of senior year," she said. "I got Amy out of there, and I told my dad. He moved her to a different soccer club after that, one that cost a lot more and involved a lot more travel. But at least Amelia wouldn't be dealing with Joel again."

Robin started to cry, and AJ teared up too. That annoying, hot sting in her eyes she hated so much. She pulled every lace inside her as tight as she could, and she started reciting the University of Miami fight song to give herself something to focus on. The tears dried right up as Alice got up from the other end of the couch and went to comfort Robin in the armchair.

AJ watched them as if from behind a sheet of waxed paper. She wanted to cry and mourn over the fact that Joel Shields had turned out to be someone quite different than she'd known. But AJ had already done her crying. She already knew what kind of man Joel Shields was.

And she still didn't know if she could go to the funeral and hear glowing, kind things said about him. She also couldn't tell Robin that right now, as the woman was desperate to have them all there to support Kristen.

Right then, in that moment, from behind the filmy drape that separated her from everyone else, AJ knew she'd put aside her feelings for Joel and go to support the woman who had always been there for her. She'd seen Nathan choose himself and his interests over everyone and everything else for years now, and she didn't want to be that kind of person.

She got up too, broke through the waxed paper, and went to kneel in front of Robin. She put her hands on Robin's knees, and she looked up into her friend's teary face. "I'm so sorry," she whispered.

"You have nothing to be sorry for," Alice said, patting AJ's shoulder.

"I just can't believe it," Eloise said. "How did he hide all of this so well?"

"They're really isolated up there at that lighthouse," Kelli said. "He always had a smile for everyone. Why would anyone suspect anything?"

"Secrets are easy to keep when your nearest neighbor is a mile away," Alice said. "Sometimes even when they're right next door."

AJ looked up at Alice, because she sounded like she spoke from experience. "True," AJ said. "Do you think we need to tell Kristen?"

"No," Robin said quickly. "She doesn't need to know this. Maybe I'll tell her in a few months or something, if it feels right."

AJ stood up, her hips starting to ache. She hadn't been on a competitive field for years, and while she still worked out most days, she had to stretch for as long before and after now that she'd reached her mid-forties.

Robin got up too, and she latched onto AJ, hugging her tight. "You're an amazing person," she whispered, and AJ closed her eyes and let the words wash over her, believing them for maybe the first time. She pulled back and leaned her forehead against Robin's. "If that were true, you'd think I could get Nathan to marry me."

"He's not the right guy for you," Robin said.

"I agree," Kelli said, though AJ wasn't even sure how

she'd heard from all the way across the room. "AJ, I've told you that a dozen times. If he was the right one, he'd want you to be his instantly."

AJ nodded as she backed away from Robin, sliding her hands down the front of her joggers. "I know. I'm going to do something about it." She returned to her corner of the couch, where Eloise reached over and took her hand, her smile soft and timid. AJ felt her phone against her stomach, and she wished it had vibrated or rang and had Nathan's name on the screen even once while she'd been in the cove. But it hadn't.

"All right." Robin took the paper towel from Alice and wiped her face. "Kelli, how are you? What can we do for you?"

AJ hugged her knees to herself and looked at Kelli. She deserved the very best in life, and it seemed so unfair to AJ that she didn't have it all. She put on a brave face, though, and AJ would've never known about her anxiety and marital problems if she hadn't spent a couple of days with her, sitting on the back porch, watching the newly budded leaves on the trees sway in the breeze.

The backyard at the house had a long trail with dozens of stairs that led down to a beach where AJ would spend almost all of her time if she lived in the house above it.

"I'm okay," she said. "I talked to Julian, and we're going to take a short vacation when I get home. His mother is going to keep Parker." Kelli took a deep breath, and AJ saw what it cost her to leave her son behind. They'd talked a lot about it at the house, and AJ had told her she deserved to be Kelli Thompson too, not just "Parker's mom."

Kelli had agreed. She wanted to be both, and she knew she needed to take care of herself in order to be the best mom to Parker she could be.

"That's great," Alice said, smiling at Kelli. She switched her gaze to Robin. "Now, do you have any rosé? I think we could all use some alcohol."

Robin blinked at her, and then trilled out a laugh. "I don't keep wine in the house, but let's go out and get a drink at the Island Seasons."

"Ooh, do they still have that long bar made out of abalone shells?" Eloise asked, and AJ watched her face light up.

She could admit the night would get much better with something fruity and full of vodka in front of her, and she said, "If we go, I'm not changing out of my joggers."

"I have the perfect pair of pumps to wear with those," Alice said, heading for the stairs. "I'll be right back."

"Alice," AJ said, but the woman was fast for her age. "I'm not going to wear heels." She looked around at the others. "I already tower over all of you."

"Oh, wear them," Kelli said, standing and extending her hand to help AJ off the couch. "Isn't that what you told me? Own what you have and who you are?"

AJ had said that, but she didn't appreciate it being thrown back in her face. Though Kelli never really did throw any of her words, so AJ could only smile at her as she stood. "Fine," she said. "But don't complain when I'm literally a foot taller than you."

Alice came back downstairs carrying a beautiful pair of matte black heels. "Here you go."

AJ took the heels, noting the pristine condition of them. "When were you going to wear these?" She glanced up at Alice, a giggle gathering in the back of her throat.

"You never know," Alice said, shaking her shoulder-length hair to fluff it up. "You can never go wrong with a pair of black pumps."

"These are heels," AJ said, shaking them at her.

"No," Alice said, squaring her shoulders. "A pair of black *pumps* can make any outfit extra-special. Put them on. You'll see."

AJ put the shoes on the ground and stepped into them, gaining two inches and expecting the familiar pinch that came with every pair of heels she'd ever worn. But this time, it didn't come. "Wow," she said, gazing down at her feet. "These are amazing."

Alice beamed at her, a hint of self-righteousness in her eyes. "See? There's a difference between pumps and heels."

"Yeah," Eloise said, shrugging into her jacket. "Two thousand dollars."

That elicited a moment of silence and then a roar of laughter from everyone in the room, including Alice.

When they quieted, AJ said, "Who's driving? I'd like to drink tonight."

"Me too," Alice said.

"I don't drink much," Robin said. "I'll drive and be the designated mother." She pointed at Alice. "But I need a verbal commitment that you'll stop when I say stop. We have a full day tomorrow."

"Yes, Mother," Alice said in a hoity-toity voice before she strode toward the garage, a pair of beautiful wedges strapped to her feet.

AJ grinned at Robin. "Deal, Robin." She grabbed onto her and hugged her, whispering, "Thank you for everything." She wanted to say more, like how wonderful she was, how kind, how accommodating, what a great example. But Robin got the message, AJ was sure.

She hoped Robin would let her have at least three drinks tonight, because she had to face Kristen again tomorrow, and then the funeral the morning after that. She could survive.

She *hoped* she could survive.

CHAPTER TWENTY-EIGHT

A lice groaned as her alarm went off, because Robin had not cut her off as soon as she should have. She rolled over in bed, teetered on the edge of the mattress, and barely kept herself from falling to the floor.

"Mom," Charlie moaned, and Alice finally got the alarm to stop chirping. "Do we have to get up?"

Alice didn't know. The twins had been asleep on a couple of air mattresses in her bedroom when Eloise had finally delivered her to her room. She knew they had plans to go to the lighthouse this morning, and she'd somehow set an alarm, so she must've known what time she had to be ready at some point last night.

"I'll find out," she said, her tongue feeling like she'd put a handful of sand in her mouth and tried to swallow it all. She slipped out of the room without taking anything with her, relieved the bathroom was free.

Robin had a lovely home, with five bedrooms and three bathrooms, but Alice usually didn't share a bedroom or a bathroom. She didn't mind doing so here either, and she grabbed a washcloth and put it in the sink to run hot water over it. She refused to look at herself until she'd melted the sleep out of the corners of her eyes and had taken a deep breath of steamy air.

Then she looked right into her light brown eyes, and she recognized the shape, the color, the way her eyelashes looked a little thrashed. On the outside, she looked the same, and it wasn't as miserable as she felt.

But inside, Alice felt like a completely different woman. For the first time in years, she'd enjoyed the twins' birthday, and she knew it was because she knew she didn't have to deal with Frank. She hadn't had to call him six times during the day to find out if he'd left the office yet. She hadn't had to make sure Ginny and Charlie received a separate gift—that she'd bought— from him. If he had to buy something for either of them, he wouldn't get them something they liked. So she'd buy the sweater Ginny had eyed at the boutique and put it in a plain bag and put Frank's name on it. Last year, for Charlie, she'd put a dirt bike in the garage with a blue bow on it with Frank's name dangling from the handle-bars. He'd almost hit it as he pulled into the garage an hour later.

"I don't want to go home," she whispered to herself. In fact, the Hamptons didn't even feel like home now that she'd been here, though her days here had not been easy in any way, shape, or form.

She couldn't stay in the cove. Her kids needed to get back to school, and Alice did have a library board meeting next week. As she got in the shower, she told herself she'd simply distract herself from her life by planning the vacation to the cove in June.

Her mind ran through details, and she told herself to slow down, because none of the other women even knew about the summer sand pact Alice wanted to get them to agree to. They'd all agreed to go to Rocky Ridge with her easily, but she knew convincing AJ and Kelli to come back in only six weeks would take some serious work.

She got out of the shower and wrapped a towel around herself to get back to the room. As she reached for the doorknob, the door further down the hall opened, and Kelli came out. She had her hand over her eyes, and she almost ran into Alice before she saw her.

"Hey." Alice hugged her, glad when Kelli gripped her shoulders too. "What did we decide to do today?"

"Leaving for the lighthouse at nine," Kelli said. "Duke is taking the kids to Pearl for a surfing lesson, though it's a school day. Robin still isn't happy about it."

"My kids don't need to be entertained," Alice said. They could come to the lighthouse, and she could take them to her father's that afternoon.

"She knows that." Kelli smiled at her and continued down the hall. Alice slipped into the bedroom and started rummaging through the closet, where she'd hung all of her garments the first night she'd been here. She'd learned quickly that she couldn't leave silks and wools folded in a suitcase and expect to look polished and poised when she got dressed.

She dressed quickly, keeping her eyes on her twins as they slept. The clock on her phone read eight-fifteen, and she bent down to pick up Ginny's phone. She had no alarm set, and Alice put one in for eight-forty. That should give the twins enough time to get up, brush their teeth and hair, and put on clean clothes.

Alice left the room again and went downstairs, hoping Robin had gotten up and made coffee. Very strong coffee. But the kitchen sat quiet and empty, so Alice opened the cupboard above the coffeemaker, having seen Robin brew the liquid caffeine the night before.

She set about making the coffee, though she had no idea what else to get out to make for breakfast. She wasn't hungover, and she didn't need a greasy breakfast sandwich to function this morning.

Robin needed a new coffeemaker, because hers took forever to drip the drink Alice desperately needed. At least now Alice knew what to get her friend for her next birthday. She'd just put a dash of cream—no sugar—in her coffee when she heard someone else coming down the steps.

AJ came into the kitchen, and Alice nodded at her as she took her first sip. Relief moved down her throat as the hot liquid did, and she reached up to get a mug down for AJ. "Coffee?"

"Yes." She sighed as she sat at the bar. Her long hair wasn't wet, which meant she hadn't showered, and yet, she still looked fresh and ready for the day. Alice wasn't sure how she pulled that off, but AJ had always had the most spectacular beach waves, while Alice's hair couldn't hold a curl for more than ten minutes.

She poured AJ's coffee and pushed the cream and sugar toward her, envious of the two healthy spoonfuls of sugar her friend stirred into her cup. Eloise arrived in the kitchen and opened the fridge.

"Who wants eggs?" she asked.

"Pass," Alice said, moving into the living room to nurse her coffee, all the breakfast she needed. Eloise chatted easily with AJ as she cracked and scrambled, and by the time the eggs hit the table, Kelli had come downstairs. Not long after that, all the teens arrived, but there was still no sign of Duke or Robin.

"Could she have overslept?" AJ finally asked when there were only ten minutes before they were supposed to leave.

Alice glanced at Charlie, Ginny, and Mandie as they sat at the table on the back patio, wishing she could hear what they were talking about. She needed to ask her son what, if anything, was going on with him and Mandie, but Alice didn't want to embarrass him.

"I'll go check on her," Eloise said, and Alice finished

the last of her coffee as Eloise went down the hall. She felt conflicted this morning, and she made no attempt to speak to anyone.

"She's coming," Eloise said as she reappeared in the living room and kitchen. She grinned around at everyone. "I think she did oversleep."

"And she didn't even drink," Kelli said with a small smile.

"At least we know she's human," Alice quipped, and that got AJ to chuckle. Eloise set about making more eggs, and Robin and Duke came down the hall together a few minutes later.

"I'm so sorry," Robin said, glancing around at everyone.

"It's fine," Eloise said, scooping eggs onto a couple of plates. "It's not like we have a deadline."

But Alice would like to get going. She hated sitting around, waiting to do whatever needed to be done that day.

"We do need to leave on time," Duke said, picking up the plate and taking it with him. "Our lesson is at ten, and if we miss the ferry, we'll be late." He opened the back door and said, "Hey, let's get in the car." He shoveled a few bites of eggs in his mouth and put the plate down. After chewing and swallowing, he grabbed a protein shake out of the fridge, thanked Eloise for breakfast, and kissed Robin good-bye.

Robin ate her eggs slower, but she did pour her coffee

into a to-go thermos so they could go. The five of them piled into Eloise's car, and the drive to the lighthouse began. In the front seat, Eloise and Robin chatted about the final funeral arrangement. Beside her, AJ and Kelli talked in hushed voices too, and the feeling of being a fifth wheel overcame Alice.

She could do something about it; she knew how to interject herself into a conversation and take command of it. She simply didn't want to talk right now.

Before she knew it, they'd arrived at the lighthouse, and Robin got out easily. Alice hesitated for a moment, and neither AJ nor Kelli moved at all. "It's okay," Alice said as she opened the door. "She's not mad."

"I just feel stupid," Kelli said. "She called me a couple times, and I didn't answer."

"She loves us," Alice said, surprised the words came from her. It was more Robin's role to give mini-lectures about how someone else felt, as if that changed how awkward a situation was.

She got out and held the door as Kelli scooted across the seat and emerged from the car too. "Are you going to have her sign the glassworks shop over to you?" Alice asked.

"I'm not going to bring it up," Kelli said. "If she says something, I guess I'll have to figure out what to do then."

"It's at least property," Alice said. "On a beautiful island. You could build a vacation home here like all my friends in the Hamptons."

Robin hadn't gone very far, and she said, "You should do that, Kel."

Kelli cleared her throat and adjusted the strap of her bag over her shoulder. "I, um, have a house on Bell."

Alice froze, blinking rapidly for a few seconds. Thankfully, it was Robin who said, "You do?"

"The house I grew up in," Kelli said as AJ came up beside her. "That's where AJ and I went the past few days. It's a mess, and I'd probably need to do a ton of work to actually live in it, but I do have it."

"Then you should get the Glassworks too," Alice said, catching up to her senses. "It's on the same island, and even if you don't use it like your father did, it's worth something."

"And I don't want it," Kristen said. Everyone turned toward the lighthouse to see Kristen standing there. She wore her black cotton pants and a long-sleeved blue blouse, and she looked positively maternal.

Alice moved first, stepping around Robin and Eloise, who had created a wall between Kristen and everyone else. "Good morning," she said, stepping into her and hugging her.

"Morning, dear."

Alice pressed her eyes closed and pulled in a breath of Kristen's powdery scent.

"Kristen," Kelli said, her voice breaking, and Alice got out of the way so she could hug Kristen too.

"I'm so sorry, child," Kristen said. "I didn't know, and

I've already signed the deed over to you. It's in my cottage."

Kelli said nothing—at least, nothing Alice could hear, and she stayed out of the way while everyone had their turn giving Kristen a good morning hug. This was why she'd called the pilot the moment she'd gotten off the phone with Robin last week. To be here to see the six of them together again, to see all the distance between them narrow to nothing, to realize that forgiveness was possible, and reconciliation could happen, even with six of the strongest, most stubborn women on the planet.

"ALL RIGHT, ALICE," ROBIN SAID HOURS LATER. SHE PUSHED away her plate with half a lobster roll still on it and folded her arms. "Tell us why we had to take two ferries to get to Rocky Ridge this afternoon."

Alice had finished her lobster bisque and oysters a while ago, but she'd enjoyed the ferry rides and the lunch at the premier seafood restaurant on the island. She looked from Robin to AJ, who also wore a look of curiosity.

"Okay," Alice said, putting a smile on her face. "But everyone has to listen all the way to the end."

"Oh, boy," Eloise said, leaning back in her chair and folding her arms.

"I'm just saying," Alice said. "Robin tends to interrupt, and AJ tends to scoff."

AJ scoffed, and Alice couldn't have planned it any better. "I do not scoff."

Kelli giggled and said, "AJ, you literally just scoffed."

"Fine," AJ said. "I won't make any noise until the end."

"I won't interrupt," Robin said, gesturing for Alice to go on.

"I want us all to come to my vacation house in June," Alice said bluntly. "Two weeks, on the black sand beach. Our summer sand pact." She looked around at everyone, and the only one who looked like she might actually come was Eloise.

And Alice knew Aaron Sherman had a lot to do with that.

"Robin, you live here," Alice said. "It's easy for you to come. You'll bring the girls while Duke's out on the boat, and he won't even know you're gone. Eloise, I'll make sure there's plenty of free time for you to see Aaron. Kelli, you can bring Parker—and Julian if he'll come. There's plenty of room, and we could use more boys in our kid group."

She looked at all of them, and Robin now had her arms folded too. Her bright blue eyes blazed, but with an emotion Alice couldn't name.

"And AJ, if you put in your vacation now, I know you can get it off. You've been away from the cove for so long, and I think it—well, I don't know. I just know we made a summer sand pact, and we've only kept it once. Once." She held up one finger. "One summer. Maybe two."

She drew in a deep breath and looked around at everyone.

"I don't work in the summer," Eloise said. "I'll come." She swatted Alice's arm. "I didn't know you had a vacation house on Rocky Ridge."

"You didn't? I thought everyone knew that. It's on the north side of the island, and the sand isn't quite the same as the black sand beach down by my father's, but we can go to the black sand beach easily."

"How big is your house?" Kelli asked.

"Sixty-five hundred square feet," Alice said. "I have a management company that rents it when I'm not using it, and it sleeps eighteen." She hadn't done the math yet, but there was no way there'd be more than eighteen of them. If everyone brought their whole family—husband and children—there would be sixteen of them. And that was with Aaron and his girls, and AJ's boyfriend.

Seventeen if Frank came, which he wouldn't. Alice wasn't even planning on telling him about the vacation until she'd left the Hamptons.

"And I can bring in more beds if we need them." She reached for her water glass, her heart pounding. They had to come. They just had to.

"I'll talk to Duke," Robin said, and that was as good as a commitment. Robin did have a partnership in her marriage, but Alice knew she'd get her way if she really wanted it.

"Kelli?" Alice asked. If she could get Kelli, she might be able to get AJ too.

"I don't know, Alice." Her eyes opened wider, and she seemed so anxious. Alice wished she could do something to help the woman, because she didn't want to cause this feeling in her friend. "I'll have to see how things go at home before I can say for sure if I can come or not."

"That's fine," Alice said. She refused to look at AJ. "I just think this has been so amazing, and we've needed this time together. Think how much fun we could have if we weren't dealing with secrets and grief and a funeral." She smiled at her friends. "And I don't know about you, but I need some fun in my life. I *need* you guys."

She'd needed these girls when she was a teenager, and she still needed them. How she hadn't know that and had let herself drift so far from them, she didn't know. She supposed life had just gotten busy, for everyone.

"Why not?" AJ said, scoffing loudly. "I'm in. I'm probably going to break up with Nathan when I get back to Atlanta anyway, and having this to look forward to might be the only thing that keeps me going."

"Oh, no, really?" Kelli asked.

"He hasn't called or texted once," AJ said miserably, and Alice knew exactly how AJ felt. She knew *keenly* how she felt. But she let the other girls console AJ, because

Alice had some serious thinking to do about her own marriage.

In some ways, AJ's situation was easier, as she and Nathan weren't married. But Alice had her whole life tied in with Frank's, and she couldn't see through the web of their lives to see the light at the end of the tunnel.

She drew in a deep breath and pushed Frank and her miserable marriage out of her mind. If AJ was in, Kelli would find a way to be there, and Alice needed to start planning for the best two weeks any of them had ever experienced.

"Okay, enough." AJ shook herself and ran her hand down her face, effectively erasing her emotion. She put that hand into the middle of the table, the way a team did to yell their cheer. "To the summer sand pact."

Alice threw her hand in and put it on top of AJ's. Robin did, and Eloise, and finally Kelli.

"The summer sand pact," they said together, throwing their hands up. Alice laughed along with everyone else, hoping this vacation actually came to pass.

She'd simply make sure it did.

CHAPTER TWENTY-NINE

Robin left the other ladies on Rocky Ridge, where they were going to stay at Alice's house, though none of them had any clothes. The funeral began at ten a.m. the following morning, and they'd have to be on the ferry by seven-thirty, but they'd wanted to stay.

Robin needed to stop by Kristen's to make sure she had everything she needed for tomorrow. She'd asked her how things were going, and Kristen had avoided the question, which indicated to Robin that she wasn't ready. Robin didn't know what else needed to be done, but she wanted to make sure that all Kristen had to do in the morning was shower, get dressed, and drive to the funeral home.

The ferry ride back to Sanctuary and then Diamond wasn't nearly as fun by herself, but she'd ridden on so many ferries, Robin thought she could do it in her sleep.

By the time she'd returned to the lighthouse, the sun painted the sky pink and gold, with streaks of navy and white in there too.

A sigh moved through Robin's whole body, because a sunset sky above an ocean was like manna from heaven to her soul. She got out of the car, noting another one in the parking lot she hadn't seen before.

She glanced to the lighthouse, which had two of the tiny windows along the bottom third of it lit up, and then she faced the path that wound down to Kristen's cottage. She went that way, her muscles tight and tired. She wouldn't run tomorrow, and that would be a relief.

She knocked on Kristen's door and heard multiple voices inside. Her heart skipped over its beat, and someone yanked open the door.

"Clara," Robin said, plenty of surprise in her voice. She moved instantly to hug the woman who was five or six years older than her. "Oh, it's so good to see you." She embraced her tightly, getting the same response from Clara. "Did your family come?"

"Yes," she said, stepping back and wiping her eyes quickly. "Scott and Lena are up at the lighthouse with Rueben."

"They're finishing dinner," Kristen said, opening the door further. She leaned forward and touched her cheek to Robin's. "Come in. I'm just pouring the coffee, and the others should be down soon."

"I don't think they're coming, Mom," Clara said. "I

know Lena needs to get to bed." She looked at Robin. "She has a sinus infection, and the pressure on the airplane really hurt her ears."

"Oh, that's too bad," Robin said, entering the cottage.

"Well, they should," Kristen said. "I made my peanut butter chocolate chunk cookies this afternoon."

Robin's mouth watered, though she certainly didn't need the extra calories. But funeral-calories didn't count, and Robin was going to stick to that.

"You'll come to the family luncheon tomorrow, won't you?" Kristen asked, offering Robin the plate of cookies.

"I didn't know we were invited," Robin said.

"You are," Kristen said. "The whole family. Patricia says the ladies at the church have a ton of food."

"Sure," Robin said, though she wasn't sure she'd be able to drag Duke and the girls to a luncheon after the service and the burial at the cemetery. She'd play it by ear, because Duke needed to get back out on the water. At least that was what he'd said. She picked up a cookie and took a bite, her taste buds rejoicing.

She knew she'd interrupted something, as Kristen wouldn't even look at her. Robin glanced at Clara, who'd picked up a magazine and started leafing through it while she sat at the kitchen table. There was no way she was reading anything on the pages, though, and an extreme sense of discomfort moved through her.

"So what are you guys doing tonight?" Robin asked. "Is there anything last-minute that I can help with?"

"I think we're ready," Kristen said.

"You know what?" Clara asked. "Maybe she can be the deciding vote on the eulogy." She abandoned the magazine and got up from the table, her eyebrows up in a challenge.

"The eulogy?" Robin asked as Clara strode toward the front door. She rummaged through a purse there, pulling out a wrinkled piece of paper.

"Yes," Clara said. "Joel wrote it, and he asked me to deliver it." She came back through the living room and extended the paper toward Robin.

Robin looked at Kristen, who wore a disgruntled look on her face. "I told you to change it, if you needed to," she said.

"But you didn't like the changes."

"I just don't think we need to air the family laundry at his funeral."

Clara shook the paper, which had clearly been crumpled, smoothed out, and balled up again. Robin reached for it slowly, taking the rough paper in a couple of fingers. She looked around at everyone, the tension in the small cottage higher than anything Robin had experienced before, even when Kristen had first blurted that Joel had cheated on her.

That declaration felt like it had happened ages and ages ago, but it was less than two weeks old.

Robin went over to the kitchen table and sat with her back to the rest of the kitchen and most of the living room.

She started to read the eulogy, and it started out inno-cently enough. Joel had listed when he was born, where he'd grown up—and Robin learned he'd been born and raised in Cape Cod—and how he'd come to Five Island Cove.

From there, he'd mentioned the lighthouse, the coaching he'd done, his wife, and kids. Clara had made plenty of notes, crossing some things out and writing in new things she wanted to say.

She'd written *no* in capital letters in a couple of spots and left nothing to replace what she didn't want to say. Robin finished the eulogy and started over at the begin-ning. Her heart thumped in her chest as she read the new parts in where they were supposed to go.

No wonder Kristen didn't want her daughter to read this at the funeral. Clara had put in some things about how Joel wasn't perfect, and that he'd single-handedly driven both her and Rueben from the cove with his belit-tling comments and threats to make sure they didn't have anything to inherit since the cottage, the lighthouse, and all the land they sat on was one inheritance.

She pushed out her breath and looked up. The wall several feet in front of her didn't provide the answer, and she stood to face the mother and daughter pair that clearly stood on opposite sides of the aisle.

"I like the things you took out," Robin said slowly, trying to find the right words to agree with both of them. She felt like she was dealing with an irrational teenager, and one wrong step would land her in hot water.

"I think it's fine if you want to say he's not perfect, but I'm not sure it's...best if you say he drove you from the cove."

"He *did* drive us from the cove." Clara's dark eyes flashed with dangerous lightning.

"I understand that," Robin said, refusing to look at Kristen. "But I think everyone at the funeral will already know that. They saw you two leave and not come back. I don't think it needs to be said quite so blatantly." She glanced at Kristen, who had started nodding. "Some things are better to let people just assume, and everyone at the funeral tomorrow will already have an opinion of Joel that nothing you say will change anyway." She swallowed, needing a big glass of water.

"Okay," Clara said, stepping forward and taking the paper. "That's actually a really good point."

Relief filled Robin, and she reached for another cookie. She now knew there would be peanut butter and chocolate chunks at the end of the world, because she'd just survived it, and she definitely needed at least three more of these cookies.

"Thank you for coming to check on me," Kristen said, stepping into Robin and hugging her.

"Of course," Robin said. She hugged Clara too, and Robin made her escape with a cookie in each hand.

ROBIN STARTED CRYING BEFORE SHE EVEN LEFT THE HOUSE. Duke said nothing, because he was used to Robin weeping for reasons she couldn't name. She'd calmed herself enough to tame the tears by the time they'd arrived at the funeral home.

Eloise pulled in immediately after them, and Robin joined her family with all of the others. She reached for Alice's hand and squeezed it as they walked inside. The foyer held a podium for people to leave condolences before they moved into the chapel, and Robin let Duke do that so she could glance around at all the details.

Everything seemed to be going well, and by the time everyone had signed the book, Robin's lungs shuddered as she breathed. She took one of the individual tissue packs from the basket beside the door.

Duke put his hand on her lower back, and Robin's next step really hit the ground. She sat in the first row behind the roped-off family rows, and slipped her hand into Duke's as he sat beside her. Alice came down the other side, positioning herself right next to Robin. They all fit on the single row, and Robin hoped they would be a solid foundation of support for Kristen.

She'd wanted to arrive early so she could get this spot, so they had to wait for a while until a man wearing a black suit stepped up to the microphone and said, "Please stand."

Robin did, taking a moment to find her balance in her heels, and she turned to watch the pallbearers bring in the casket. It was already closed, with a huge splay of red roses at the head of it.

The heat built behind her eyes again, and she didn't fight it. Thankfully, she wasn't the only one sniffling and opening her packet of tissues. Joel's family wasn't very big, and they filed onto the bench in front of Robin.

Kristen, Clara, Scott, Lena, Rueben, Jean. Joel's younger brother. That was it.

Robin reached forward and squeezed Kristen's shoulder, and the older woman reached back and patted her hand. After that, Robin settled down, and she only had one moment where she pulled in a breath and held it, and that was when Clara got behind the mic and stood there for what felt like a very long time without saying anything.

She'd eventually been able to begin, and she'd read a kind version of the eulogy Robin had read last night. She stood as the casket left, the family following. She rode in the car with the lights on to the cemetery.

The threat of rain oozed over the island at the cemetery, and Robin liked to think it was heaven weeping over Joel's death. At the same time, she wasn't sure he was the type of man that deserved tears from heaven. Her mind went back and forth, and Robin wished she could just turn off her thoughts completely.

"Home?" Duke asked as they all piled back into the car.

"We're invited to the luncheon," Robin said. "I'd like to go, but you can drop me off. I'm sure Eloise can take me back to the house."

"We'll come," Duke said, and a rush of affection for the man washed over her. She didn't normally think morbid thoughts, but she hoped she passed before Duke, because she did not want to live without him.

She walked into the church with blue siding, her family trailing her, the scent of freshly baked bread hanging in the air. The first person she saw was Kristen, and she stood by herself amidst all the activity in the gymnasium. And Robin did not ever want to be in that position. She nodded toward Kristen, and Duke pointed to some seats at a table near the back and on the side.

That was all the conversation they needed, and Robin went to make sure Kristen wasn't alone on the day she'd buried her husband.

CHAPTER THIRTY

Kristen stood on the very edge of the rocks, the dark water in front of her invisible. She could feel the power of it, though, as it washed through her soul. The ocean possessed something unrelenting and magical, and Kristen wanted to be like the ocean.

She wanted to crash through obstacles. She wanted to continue on, no matter what challenges stood in her way. She wanted to roll through wave after wave of punches and still arrive on the shore.

She breathed in, feeling the power of the sea air fill her from top to bottom. Right now, she felt like the waves had sucked her under, and they were tossing her up and down and around. She didn't know which way to swim to break the surface, but she knew she'd find her way.

Maybe not tomorrow, maybe not even next week or

next month. But she'd figure out how to live in this world without Joel, and she'd learn how to accept who he was and how he was different than the man she'd believed him to be.

The lighthouse beamed into the distance, and Kristen felt like there was another one clear across the ocean, drawing her home, guiding her back to a new definition of normal.

The wind blew up the cliffs, and Kristen rubbed her hands up her jacketed arms. She needed to get back to the house, but she didn't move. Clara and her family were staying in the lighthouse, and they had not invited Kristen to come over after the funeral.

She'd tried not to be hurt by it. She knew Clara had a lot of healing to do, and she whispered into the sky, "Please help her come to a place of peace." Kristen wished the same thing for herself, but she didn't vocalize anything.

When her nose tingled with cold, she finally turned from the edge of the world and made the solitary walk back to her cottage. Behind the closed, locked door, she paused, trying to find how she felt. Perhaps she should be crying now. She could break down, take a few pills to help her sleep, and not get out of bed in the morning.

Kristen didn't do any of that. She drew in a long, deep breath and looked around the starkness of the house as compared to what it had once been. "I miss you, Joel," she said, talking to him for the first time since he'd died. "I wish you would've told me the truth about a lot of things before you left, but I can't change the past."

She'd been alive long enough to know that. But knowing something and doing it were two very different things.

So when Kristen woke the next morning, she didn't get out of bed. She lay there, staring at the ceiling as the daylight turned from gray to yellow to gold. Her mind seemed to race at times, remembering summers on the beach with Joel and the kids, rugby games for Rueben and dance recitals for Clara.

Other times, she lost her train of thought and let her mind drift into blankness as she searched for the next memory to occupy herself with. She remembered Thanksgiving dinners, and Christmas trees that lit the small living room with colorful lights. The report cards that had earned the kids doughnuts, and the Sunday night movies with popcorn and soda. It had been one of the only times she'd allowed the kids to have carbonation.

Her brain halted, and she realized it hadn't been her that had disliked the children drinking soda, but Joel. How she'd put that on herself, she didn't know.

"Mom?" Clara called, and Kristen pushed herself up with a groan. A moment later, her daughter poked her head into the bedroom. Kristen hated that she hadn't been happy in the cove, but she smiled at her. She'd come, she'd read a good eulogy, and Kristen could appreciate how hard that was for her daughter.

"Are you okay?" Clara asked, coming into the room.

"Yeah." Kristen nodded as her smile slipped away. "Just tried already."

"Well, you have lots of time to rest." She sat down on the mattress beside Kristen and put her arm around her shoulders.

"I love you, Clara," Kristen said. "Thank you for coming."

"I love you, too, Mom." She leaned into Kristen, and so much more was said.

After a couple of minutes, Kristen asked, "Are you headed out?"

"Yeah, our plane leaves in a little bit."

"All right." Kristen sighed as she got up. "I packed up some cookies for you. Let me get them." Clara didn't protest, and when she took the zipper bag of cookies, she also took Kristen into a hug.

"Maybe we could come visit this summer. Lena does love the beach."

Clara and Scott's only child had been born with Down Syndrome, and she'd never married. She lived with her parents, and she worked twenty hours at the local grocery store in Vermont, where they lived.

"Come any time," Kristen said. "I'm sure Rueben wouldn't mind hosting you, or we can rent a house closer to the beach. Maybe on Bell Island."

"I'd love to go to a different island," she said. "Especially in the summer. Diamond is always so crowded."

Kristen nodded, out of things to say. "Well." She hugged her daughter again, and she followed her daughter outside and down the sidewalk to the parking lot. She hugged Scott and then Lena, and they all got into the car. Kristen waved and waved and waved until the car turned out of the parking lot and went down the hill.

Once they were out of sight, Kristen turned back to the lighthouse. She wanted to go see what Rueben and Jean were doing, but she didn't want to impose. Jean had come into town on Friday afternoon, and she'd only said a handful of words to Kristen.

She'd mind her business, and she'd taken a couple of steps down the sidewalk back to her own house. She paused, though, wondering that if she'd stuck her neck out more, maybe she would've known about some of the stuff Joel had done.

Perhaps she should've asked more questions when he came home late, or stayed quiet when she asked questions. Perhaps she should've been more involved in paying the bills, so she would've seen him buy the glassworks shop out from under Guy. Or looked at the computer screen when he sat in front of it.

She changed direction and headed toward the lighthouse. She didn't normally go somewhere uninvited, but she thought maybe she could simply invite herself in to visit with her son and his wife.

After arriving at the navy blue door, she knocked and waited, something she hadn't done before. She had to ring the bell before Rueben came up the steps and peered through the window. He smiled at her, unlocked the lighthouse, and said, "Morning, Mom."

He came all the way outside and enveloped her in a hug, and Kristen clung to her son as if her life depended on having her arms around him.

"Come in," he said, stepping behind her. "Jean just pulled a loaf of bread out to make French toast."

"All right." Kristen entered the lighthouse, everything about it fused to her soul. She went down the two flights of narrow stairs and emerged into the living area of the lighthouse. "Morning, Jean," she said to the petite brunette whisking eggs in a glass bowl in the kitchen.

She flashed a smile so brief that Kristen barely saw it. "Morning." She turned her back on Kristen and bent to get the griddle out. A chill definitely radiated off her shoulders, and Kristen didn't know what to do about it.

She sank into a chair in the living room with a sigh, thinking she should offer to help Jean. But she didn't know how, and the woman would tell her no anyway. She thought of Alice, and how she'd told Kristen no several times as a surly teenager. AJ had a stubborn streak that was as strong as gravity, and Kristen had tamed her.

So she pushed herself back to her feet and headed toward the kitchen. "What can I do to help? Heat up the syrup?"

"I'm fine," Jean said, opening another cupboard like she didn't know where anything was.

Behind her, Rueben's anxiety bled into the air, but Kristen ignored them both. She'd been around the block enough to know a situation was only awkward if she allowed it to be.

Kristen stepped into the kitchen and opened the second drawer down in the cabinets, pulled out the power cord for the griddle, and plugged it into the outlet on the end of the counter.

"Here it is," Jean said, and she tapped several shakes of cinnamon into the bowl. She looked at Kristen, and their eyes hooked together.

"I'll heat the syrup," Kristen said. "Get out the plates and all of that." She tried for a warm smile and felt like she'd achieved it when Jean noticeably softened. They moved around each other in the kitchen then, and Kristen finally asked, "How's your mother, Jean?"

"She's doing okay," Jean said. "This last round of chemo was really hard on her."

"I know what that looks like," Kristen said quietly, and she kept her head down though she felt both Rueben's and Jean's eyes on her. "Mint leaves helped Joel quite a bit with the tongue sores."

"I'll tell her," Jean said just as quietly. She dipped a piece of bread and placed it on the hot griddle. Kristen put plates on the table, laid a knife and fork next to it, and took the syrup from the microwave. With a plate of butter on the table too, Jean flipped the last piece of French toast and unplugged the griddle.

"Mom," Rueben said, stepping next to his wife. "We have something we want to tell you."

Kristen put her hand on the back of one of the kitchen chairs and leaned into it. A trickle of trepidation bubbled inside her, because Rueben could say anything. Kristen would deal with whatever it was.

Just like the ocean, she told herself.

"Jean and I have talked, and we want to re-commit to the lighthouse for at least another year." He looked at his wife and put his arm around her. "Her mother is sick, but she's not going to leave for very long periods of time, as she has in the past."

Kristen's heart beat wildly in her chest, even though he'd said what she'd wanted to hear. "Oh, that's wonderful," she said.

"Just a year," Jean said. "And then we're going to re-evaluate. My son is in Texas, and we've talked about relocating there."

And do what? Kristen wanted to ask, but she kept the question beneath her tongue. Rueben hadn't married Jean until six years ago, and she'd been divorced for ten at that point. She had one son, and Rueben had never been married and had no children.

"You two will make the right decision for you," she said. "I'm just glad I'll get to have you here for another year." She beamed at both of them, truly glad she'd deviated from her original plan to go hide in her cottage.

Rueben picked up the spatula. "All right," he said. "Let's eat."

CHAPTER THIRTY-ONE

Robin stood in the kitchen, frying bacon, when the first sounds of someone lugging their suitcase down the steps met her ears. She hated that sound, though even she could admit she was ready to have her house be hers again.

She also needed to get back to work, as she had events coming up as the weather continued to warm that she'd put off since Joel's death.

But not today, she told herself as heel clicks sounded in the hall. Alice, then.

Sure enough, Alice rounded the corner and entered the kitchen, her hair perfectly coiffed and every stitch of clothing and makeup precisely perfect. How she put herself together like that by seven a.m. made Robin tired.

"Morning," Alice chirped, and Robin simply smiled at her. Alice poured herself a cup of coffee and sat at the bar while Robin started putting the crisp bacon on a plate lined with a paper towel. "Do you think I'm being silly about the summer sand pact?"

Robin switched off the burner and turned to Alice. "Not at all." She looked at Alice, the anxiety easy to find in her light eyes. "We did say we'd come spend time together every summer, and you know, I think we believed we would at the time."

Alice nodded, and Robin had never been able to tell exactly what she was thinking. "Things change a lot when you leave the cove."

"That they do," Robin said. "Eggs?"

Alice waved her hand as she shook her head. "I don't eat breakfast."

"What about the twins?"

"They're coming," she said. "And they do like eggs, though you'll have them so spoiled that my attempts to make sure they're properly fed in the morning will make them laugh."

Robin smiled, because Alice had, and she knew Alice didn't hold any ill will toward her. "I don't always make breakfast," Robin said, leaving the kitchen for now. Eggs were best eaten hot, and she heard no noise upstairs. "Just sometimes."

"Sure," Alice said, nudging her with her shoulder as Robin sat. She sipped her coffee and fell silent.

"I'm going to miss you, Alice."

Alice looked at her then, and Robin saw backward

thirty-plus years to the first time they'd met. Her eyes harbored the same vulnerability, the same strength, the same fear, now as they had then. Alice was a very complex person, and Robin couldn't even begin to understand why she'd want to return to her loveless marriage in the Hamptons. She wouldn't ask—at least not this morning.

Bumping came down the stairs, echoing through the house, and Alice said, "We'll call, Robin. It won't be like before."

"Okay," Robin said as she recognized the footsteps. "That'll be Eloise."

She came into the kitchen, and she too was ready to go, though not nearly as polished as Alice. Still, she wore a cute pair of black slacks with bright white and pink flowers on them, with a white blouse. "I'm headed out in about five minutes," she said. "I just want to say good-bye to Aaron this morning."

She conveniently turned away from Robin and Alice to get a coffee mug.

"Robin is taking us to the airport," Alice said, glancing up at the ceiling. "But they better get a move on if we're going to be on time."

Robin wasn't sure how she was going to fit five people and their luggage in her SUV, but Alice had assured her that, while not technically legal or safe, one of the twins could ride in the back with the suitcases. Robin had her doubts, but she didn't have another car to take, and no one wanted her to make two trips.

Duke had gone to the harbor last night, and he would've been out on his boat for about seven hours by now. Robin thought of the day ahead of her, of what would happen after she dropped everyone off at the airport.

Then what? she wondered.

Her life felt altered now, as if she'd jumped from one path to a completely new one in the past couple of weeks.

Eloise sighed and faced Alice and Robin. "Tell me I'm not being stupid by having this long-distance relationship. If you tell me to break up with him this morning and get on a plane to go back to my life in Boston, I'll do it." She sipped her coffee calmly, as if this was normal over-coffee conversation.

"Don't be silly," Alice said. "People do this kind of stuff all the time."

"It's a hopper flight," Robin said. "Forty-five minutes. I can't even get to Rocky Ridge that fast." She exchanged a glance with Alice. "Besides, it's still new. When you're back in Boston, you'll know how you really feel."

"What I feel is like I'm fifteen, with my first boyfriend." Eloise shook her head, though she didn't look terribly upset. "He has kids."

"Hey, having some excitement in your love life isn't a crime," Robin said.

"Especially at our age," Alice added, trilling out a giggle afterward. Robin and Eloise laughed with her, and Eloise finally nodded.

"Okay, you're right."

More commotion started then, and Kelli and AJ came downstairs with their luggage. Kelli alone reached for the bacon upon entering the kitchen, and Robin was glad she hadn't concerned herself with making scrambled eggs.

"Are we ready?" AJ asked.

"I'm waiting on the twins," Alice said.

"Only Ginny is up there," Kelli said. "Oh, I need to get my curling iron out of the bathroom down here."

It had been all mirrors and outlets on-deck yesterday morning to get ready for the funeral, and Kelli bustled down the hall to get her appliance.

Alice frowned, and then she turned toward the back door. "Maybe Charlie went outside this morning. I swear he was in the bedroom when I got in the shower."

"Okay, I'm headed out," Eloise announced, and Robin leapt from the barstool to embrace her. She held her tight, the emotions storming in her chest and about to explode out. Maybe if she hugged Eloise long enough, she wouldn't leave.

At the same time, Robin knew she had to go. She knew it wasn't the end. Things had changed between the five of them, and the next thing she knew, Alice had joined the embrace. Then AJ, and finally Kelli after she returned to the kitchen.

With the five of them huddled up, Robin let the love and acceptance of their friendship—their life-long friendship—wash over her.

"Okay," Eloise said, clearing her throat. "Don't make me cry. I did my makeup for Aaron and everything."

They chuckled together, and the group broke up. Robin stepped out of the way, so she was the first to notice the back door open.

Charlie came through it first, followed closely by Mandie.

Robin's heartbeat stuttered in her chest, and one look at her daughter's face told her that Eloise wasn't the only one involved in a long-distance relationship. Her eyes flew to Alice, who was watching Charlie too.

"You better go get your bag," she told him. "And get Ginny down here."

"Okay." He walked away from Mandie without looking at her, but something had definitely happened.

"There's bacon," Robin said weakly, trying to figure out how she felt about this new development. Charlie was a good boy, and Mandie had had crushes on other guys. So it was probably fine. It would likely fade in his absence anyway.

"No, thanks, Mom." Mandie put a smile on her face, which had returned to its normal color. "Can we go to the beach today?"

"Maybe," Robin said, because she wasn't sure how she was going to be feeling when she got home from the airport. She watched Mandie nod and go down the hall, and everyone waited until they heard the click of the bedroom door before giggling.

"I'll talk to him," Alice said, setting her empty coffee mug in the sink.

"How are you going to do that?" Robin asked, hoping she'd get some hints. "What are you going to say?"

"I have no idea." Alice grinned and shrugged one elegant shoulder, the deep eggplant blouse she wore rippling with the movement. "But I'll make sure he knows he can't mess around with her."

Robin simply nodded, but she thought she should say something to Mandie too. Girls could hurt boys just as easily as they got hurt by them, and Mandie wasn't particularly well-versed with boys or boyfriends.

She followed them all down the hall and held open the garage door as they went through with their suitcases. She puzzled through where to put bags and people, finally getting everyone into the SUV who needed to go to the airport, with everything they needed to take with them.

Yes, AJ had to hold her carryon on her lap, and Alice had a suitcase by her feet in the front passenger seat. But everyone and everything made it in, and Robin backed out of the driveway.

She had no idea what to say, and apparently neither did anyone else. Silence draped them for the first few blocks, and then Kelli started to sing. Her voice began low, though she had a soprano singing voice, and grew in volume as she progressed toward the chorus of the Seafaring Girls song.

Alice joined in first, and then AJ came in on the chorus. Robin's voice felt stuck behind her vocal cords, and she simply listened to the others, a ray of sunshine moving through her.

They erupted into laughter at the end of the song, and Robin joined in then.

"That was great," Alice said. "I can't believe I remembered those words."

Robin couldn't either, because Alice had always said she hated that song Kristen had made them memorize and sing. Robin had loved it, because she'd loved everything about her days in the Seafaring Girls.

As she drove toward the airport, she tried to identify the comfortable, easy feeling within her, and it wasn't until she pulled up to the only terminal at the Five Island Cove airport that she realized she was content.

Purely content.

"All right," she said, getting out. "Let's get everything out."

Busyness and chaos ensued, while suitcases got switched around and people double-checked the car to make sure they had everything. Then the five of them stood on the sidewalk, and Robin wasn't going with them.

She hugged Alice first, then both of her twins. "You guys help your mother, okay?" she whispered, and funnily enough, both Ginny and Charlie nodded.

She hugged AJ while Kelli hugged Alice, and then she hugged Kelli while AJ hugged Alice. With everyone properly good-byed, Robin retreated around the front of the SUV and waved one last time.

They turned, all of them, and went into the airport. She got behind the wheel of the car, knowing she couldn't stay long in the drop-off zone. But she couldn't go just yet.

She took a deep breath, searching for the place of contentment again. It manifested itself quickly, and she murmured to herself, "I love you guys. See you in June," before pulling away from the curb.

She had a ton to do before Duke left for Alaska too, and now she'd added a talk with Mandie to her list.

But that was okay. Robin was okay. She was strong, and smart, and sexy, and she and Duke would weather their time apart just fine. Life this summer might not look the way Robin had thought it would—or even how she thought it *should*—but as she drove home and thought back on her life until this point, it had rarely been the way she'd imagined.

And her life was still good, still happy, and still worth having.

As she passed the road that led up to the lighthouse, she looked that way, seeing the top half of the structure that had defined her for so long. It was strong. It shone light into the world. It guided people to safety.

She wanted to be all of those things, for her friends, her husband, and her girls.

So when she got home, she opened the door, and

called, "Mandie? Jamie? Get your beach stuff together, and let's get going."

After all, it was a beautiful day, and Robin did not want to waste it inside, feeling sorry for herself that she was the only one left in Five Island Cove.

Mandie came down the hall, already wearing her bikini top and a pair of cutoff shorts. "Jamie's changing."

"Great," Robin said. "You get the towels and some water. I'm going to change, and then I'm going to call Kristen and see if she wants to come sit with us."

Because she wasn't the only one left in Five Island Cove, and she didn't want Kristen to think she was either.

Read on for the first couple chapters of **The Summer Sand Pact, the next book in the Five Island Cove women's fiction series**, for more secrets, more romance, and more great friendship and sisterhood fiction that brings women together and celebrates the female relationship.

THE SUMMER SAND PACT - CHAPTER ONE

Alice Kelton signed the paperwork on the clipboard and handed the keys to the sedan to the man who'd be driving it onto the ship. She tucked her arms into a fold as she watched, the wind coming off the harbor bringing the scent of summer with it. Sunshine, and ice cream, and an easier time was what Alice imagined summer to smell like, and she drew in a deep breath as she pressed her eyes closed.

In her mind, she saw Frank sitting behind his desk in his home office. She'd asked him for a meeting, but he hadn't looked up when she'd entered. Until then, she'd second- and triple-guessed her decision to talk to him about a mutual split.

A divorce, she told herself as Charlie stepped to her side. Alice gave him a faint smile and put her arm around his shoulders. "That's almost everything," she said.

Her son said nothing, because the move from the Hamptons to Five Island Cove had been hard on all of them. Alice had spoken with the twins first, and they'd both agreed to move to the vacation home on Rocky Ridge.

"Where's Ginny?"

"Waiting in the office," Charlie said, his eyes focused out on the ship that would take everything they owned across the waters to the cove. "She said she doesn't feel well."

Alice didn't either, and she watched the men on the ship too, thinking they looked remarkably like little dolls among all the huge shipping containers. Until recently, Alice had hosted one of those bright, vibrant shipping containers in her front driveway.

She'd dealt with half a dozen visitors asking questions before she'd texted the most gossipy woman in the community and told her to spread the word that Alice wasn't entertaining visitors, nor did she need any help going through things or packing.

In that moment, Alice panicked, wondering what she was doing here, standing in front of a waist-high wall made of gray stone, watching her life get loaded onto a ship.

Another breath, and the scene in Frank's office played through her mind again.

"Frank," she'd said, settling into the wingback chair in

front of his desk. She placed the agreement she'd put together herself over a two-week time period on his desk and inched it closer to him. "I'd like to talk about splitting our assets."

That had got him to look up from the small tablet he used to do literally everything. "What?"

"I've put together a proposal," she said, staring straight at him. She'd been attending law school when she'd met Frank, and she still knew plenty of people in the industry. She'd worked in a family law firm for two years before the twins had been born. She also knew how to use the Internet, and she had all her facts lined up.

Facts, not emotions. She wasn't stupid, and neither was Frank.

Frank reached for the eleven-page proposal and began to read it. Alice's heart tapped out an extra beat every third second, but she folded her legs like boredom might overtake her before Frank finished reading.

"You're going to move to Rocky Ridge?" He lifted his eyebrows but didn't look up at her.

"That's right," Alice said, knowing the next paragraph down laid out her request for him to either pay off the mortgage or provide the monthly payment to her.

She knew when he'd reached that part of the proposal, because the air hissed out of his lungs. He put the packet down and looked at her. "You write very well," he'd said.

"Thank you." Alice didn't miss a beat, because the time for praising her legal writing skills had come and gone twenty years ago. Of course, Frank was used to charming his way back into her good graces with compliments and gifts, but Alice would not be swayed this time.

"Mom," Ginny called, and Alice pulled herself back to the shipyard. She turned toward Ginny, who approached from the direction of the office. "He said we can go."

"We better do it," Charlie said. "We don't have much time."

"All right," Alice said, turning completely away from the ship that would take a week to arrive at the industrial dock on Diamond Island. Then came the task of moving the cars and her belongings out of the storage container.

She'd paid for six months of storage at the dock, because the vacation home was fully furnished, and she didn't really need anything she'd packed.

"Did they call a cab?" she asked.

"Yes," Ginny said. "He's two minutes out."

Alice joined her, thinking of their tight itinerary. She'd booked their drop-off at the shipyard and their flight close together on purpose, because she didn't want any opportunity for any of them to back out of their plan.

She walked with her children back to the office, through the back door, the office, and then the front door. By the time they arrived, a bright yellow cab waited at the curb. Alice waited for the driver to say her name, and then he loaded the few suitcases where she and the children had packed their immediate needs into the trunk.

He opened the back door, and Charlie slid in first. Alice rode in the middle, with Ginny the last to enter the car. Alice had tried to keep herself between the twins as the split had happened, because they needed her. She needed them.

Honestly, life for the three of them had not changed all that much, and Alice wanted to keep it that way. The only real difference was that everyone now knew Frank wouldn't be coming home from the city. Before, there'd been the hope, the tiny glimmer of hope, that they'd see him in the kitchen on Saturday morning.

Ginny leaned against the window and closed her eyes. Alice didn't, but the memories ran through her head anyway as the cab started navigating the streets farther inland.

After she'd thanked Frank for the compliment on her legal drafting, she'd said, "I'm being very fair. I don't want this house. If you'd like to keep it, that's fine. If you want to sell it, I'm requesting an even split on profit, as outlined on page four."

He hadn't gotten to page four, but Alice didn't care. He was a huge corporate lawyer, but Alice had never gotten below an A in college, and her proposal *was* more than fair—and iron clad for any divorce lawyer.

"I want my car," she said. "And you have the same choices with it as you do the house in the cove. I'd also like the Toyota for the twins." Two cars—one of which no one had driven in months. But the twins would be getting their licenses soon, and the white Camry just collected dust in the expansive garage in the Hamptons. Frank would have no need of it in the city.

"All the other vehicles, you can do what you wish with," she said. She didn't care if she got an even split of the sale of them. She'd also been very careful to leave many decisions like that up to Frank, because he loved making decisions for her and the children. He excelled at it, and he'd already be reeling from her requests for car payments and house payments, child support...and alimony.

Alice had given him several seconds to say something, but he didn't. He didn't move toward the paperwork either, and Alice uncrossed her legs, and put the right over her left. "I'm asking for full custody. The children will move to Five Island Cove with me, and I've already discussed it with them, so you won't have to."

She hated that she'd sounded like she was doing him a favor, but they both knew she was. Frank barely spoke to the twins when he was home, and she couldn't remember the last time he'd called or texted them during the week.

"You'll be free to speak with them whenever you wish," she said. "Texts, calls, video, chat. They have phones, and we'll have the Internet." She wanted to shift, but she remained absolutely still.

"The alimony is an average of payments judges across

the state of New York have awarded in cases like ours, in the past twelve months," she said. "I'm asking for twenty-one years, the same number of years we've been married, as I started supporting you as you finished law school, and then quit everything when the twins were born."

Alice hated the weakness in her stomach, but she did need the alimony. She could do anything, but she hadn't been employed in over fifteen years.

"I'm aware of what you've done," Frank said, his voice icy.

Alice nodded, schooled her face into complete passivity, and reminded herself not to make anything she said sound like an accusation. "The child support is the same as the alimony. The twins are in high school, with the activities, opportunities, and expenses that requires."

Frank tapped the papers but made no effort to pick them up again. "So the beach house, the Lincoln SUV, the Toyota, alimony, and child support."

"Full custody," Alice said. "You can, of course, see them whenever you wish. It's a forty-five-minute flight, and we don't need to be so strict with visitation. We don't need to go through the courts." She stared at him, and he lifted his eyes to hers. Her message had gotten through. She didn't want a nasty divorce, and she didn't want to take him to court. Nothing about this needed to be made public.

"We'll be out of the house by June tenth," she'd said. "If you want to take them to Disneyworld for a week, just text me the dates. I'm sure we can work out those kinds of things."

Frank would want to take them during Homecoming week, or when they had finals, Alice was sure. He didn't pay attention to that kind of stuff, because he'd never had to before.

"And then you'll be free," she'd said. "To move to the city. Sell the house. Keep it. Do what you want."

And she'd be free too, and she'd inhaled and held her breath.

She repeated the gesture in the cab too, pushing the hardest conversation she'd ever had out of her mind.

"What's the first thing you're going to do when we get there?" Charlie asked, looking at her.

Alice smiled at him, her sweet, strong son. He looked so much like Frank, but his square jaw had been softened by Alice's genes. He did sport the same dark hair and eyes, and when he kept the scraggly facial hair that had started to grow in patches along his chin shaved, Charlie was downright handsome.

"Go to the grocery store," Alice said, grinning now. "There's nothing to eat at the house."

"We should get one of those island burgers," he said, returning the smile. "Then we can go to the beach when we get there."

"You and Ginny can go," Alice said, patting his knee.

"We're going to have a great summer," he said, and it sounded like he was trying to convince himself. His phone chimed, and Alice caught the name of the girl who'd texted him. Mandie. No last name, but Alice knew Mandie Grover. Her best friend, Robin, was Mandie's mother.

Alice had sat Charlie down and talked to him about the girl he'd started a little relationship with the last time they'd been in the cove. Charlie had rolled his eyes through most of it, then he'd said he wouldn't "mess with Mandie," and he'd gone to Jessica's.

Alice had been distracted enough by Ginny, who'd needed an extraordinary amount of help getting ready for the prom. Her first. She'd been beautiful in a bright blue dress that had layers and layers of fabric for the skirt. She'd gotten more of Alice's fair features, with skin that would rather turn pink than tan.

When Alice had suggested that Charlie take Jessica to the prom, he'd once again rolled his eyes, and said, "No. We're just friends." He hadn't gone at all, but he had hung out with her that night.

"Friends can go to the prom together," Alice said.

"No, they can't, Mom," Charlie informed her, which hadn't settled her stomach at all about sending Ginny with her date. Not with her shoulders bare and her makeup adding at least five years to her age.

But Matheson Turner had been very gentlemanly when he'd come to pick up Ginny. Afterward, Ginny said she'd had to dodge his attempts to hold her hand and kiss her for the whole night, and Alice had half a mind to march over to Sandra Turner's house and tell her to keep her son in line.

But the shipping container had arrived the next day—a week early—and Matheson stopped texting. Apparently, he was not interested in a long-distance relationship with someone who was moving.

"Mom," Ginny said, and Alice turned her head to see her daughter had gotten out of the car. Everyone had, except for Alice, and she quickly scooted to the end of the seat and stood up. She paid the cab driver, took her suitcase by the handle, and faced the airport entrance.

She'd given up her position on the library board, the HOA presidency, and a prominent fundraising position on the PTA, all with simple texts. Just like that, positions she'd campaigned for aggressively were gone.

With a couple strokes of a pen, Frank had agreed to her proposal. The divorce wasn't final yet, but neither of them would contest it, and she wasn't planning to come to the hearing at all.

"Okay," she said, gripping the handle on her suitcase until her knuckles ached. "Tell me our summer sand pact."

"Not a word about the divorce," Ginny said, facing the doors with the same tenacity Alice felt rising through her. She looked at her son, her eyebrows going up.

"Be good with Mandie," Charlie said, rolling his eyes.

She nodded and squared her shoulders. "Mine is to do something new every day." And today, that thing was leaving behind the life she'd worked so hard to get. The life she'd thought she wanted. The life that had been suffocating her for years.

She took the first step, and the second was easier. The third landed smoothly, and the doors opened automatically, and Alice Kelton moved into a future without a housekeeper, the biggest house on the block, or a husband.

THE SUMMER SAND PACT -
CHAPTER TWO

Kelli Thompson saw the man with the light brown hair and freckles across his face sitting in the area for the gate next to hers. She'd seen him at the market yesterday too, and this morning, on her block as she and Parker had left the house to come to the airport.

Her skin prickled, but Kelli told herself not to over-react. She watched a lot of crime dramas, that was all. This man wasn't following her.

She stared at him for several minutes, and he never once looked up from his tablet. Someone bumped into her leg, and Kelli's attention diverted from the man to her son, who had taken off his headphones and opened his backpack to put them away.

"Done?" she asked, reaching over to smooth Parker's loose hair off his forehead. He'd gotten kissed by some of her strawberry blonde hair, but his eyes were much darker than hers, a trait that had come from Julian.

"Yeah," Parker said. "Can we get a cinnamon roll?"

"Yes," Kelli said, some relief moving through her. "Let's go get a cinnamon roll." They shouldered their packs and walked away from the man sitting a few rows over. A slip of unease moved through Kelli to turn her back on the man, but no one grabbed her from behind.

Calm down, she told herself, and she glanced over her shoulder. The man still studied his screen as if his life depended on memorizing whatever sat there.

She bought a cinnamon roll and a bottle of milk for her son, skipping everything except a bottle of water for herself. They walked slowly back to the gate, and it had grown even more crowded as their flight's departure time grew closer.

After scanning the waiting area and the one for the next gate over, Kelli didn't see the man. Further relief seeped into her muscles, and soon after that, she and Parker boarded the plane, found their seats, and settled in.

The flight from Jersey to Five Island Cove only took eighty minutes, and the plane was full this time where Kelli had enjoyed her choice of seat the last time she'd gone. Seven weeks made a big difference on the island, and the summer vacationers had obviously already started to flood the cove.

She disembarked behind Parker, taking his hand in

hers once they could walk side-by-side so they wouldn't get separated among the masses of people making their way to the baggage claim area. "So," she said, smiling down at him. "What did you think? Your first flight."

"It was great," he said, smiling. "I wasn't even scared."

A rush of love for the eight-year-old moved through Kelli, and she led him to the baggage claim only to find other people four deep, waiting for their bags.

Kelli never was one to push her way to the front, so she hung back, waiting for others to get their bags and go. She'd told Robin she could get herself to Rocky Ridge, because she was coming in a day after everyone else.

Delaying her trip by one day had allowed her to finish the week at the gym without having to get someone to cover for her for too long. And Julian had been able to get a huge order out yesterday while Kelli laundered every-thing she and Parker owned, packed, and scrubbed the townhome from top to bottom so Julian would have a clean house while she was gone.

When Kelli had proposed the idea of a two-week vaca-tion in a luxury home in Five Island Cove for the three of them, Julian had frowned. Actually frowned. Kelli could still see the drawn-down eyebrows, the way small lines appeared on the outer edges of his mouth as his chin drooped.

She pushed the image of her unhappy husband out of her mind. She'd been unhappy when they hadn't taken the vacation he'd promised they would. His mother hadn't known about taking Parker so Julian and Kelli could reconnect.

Parker didn't have school, and other than her few aerobics classes each week, Kelli wasn't tied to New Jersey during the summer. So she'd boldly told Julian she'd take Parker herself, and they'd see him on the twenty-fifth.

Done. Simple as that.

Her phone dinged, and Kelli rummaged in her purse to find it as it continued to chime over and over. Embarrassment heated her face, and she quickly silenced her phone as if the people around her cared that it had made a few noises.

Julian had texted several times, saying he missed her already and he couldn't wait until she got home. A sigh gathered in the back of her throat. She wasn't sure how to interpret the messages. He could simply miss her and wish she'd hurry home. That would be the sweet assumption, the one that made her smile softly at how romantic her husband was.

But Kelli suspected he'd sent them to make her feel guilty for leaving at all. The back of her throat burned, and familiar bitterness gathered there.

Miss you too, she sent back, adding a smiley face emoji to the text before shoving her phone back in her purse. The crowd inched forward, and Kelli looked up to see if she could get closer to the rotating baggage belt.

Her eyes met those of the man who'd been sitting in the airport in Jersey. They were a darker blue than hers, but just as bright and just as...electric. He lifted his hand in a wave, and Kelli turned to look at the people around her. He couldn't be waving at her; she didn't know him.

When she looked back at him, he'd moved, and Kelli frantically searched to find where he'd gone. Who was he? Why was—?

She found him heading out the door, towing a single, black piece of luggage behind him. She glanced around at the others beside her, sure they could protect her. He wouldn't dare try to hurt her or Parker with so many people around.

"That's mine," Parker said, and Kelli blinked her way back to the present.

She said, "Stay here," and went to get his bag. It too was black, with a bright green duct tape turtle on the front of it. She hefted it off the moving belt and took it to him. She turned back and got her own bag, pulling out the handle so she could walk with the bag beside her.

"All right," she said, refusing to scan for the stranger. "Let's go get in line for a car."

Five Island Cove had an amazing summer transportation system, as no one could drive to the cove. At the airport and every ferry station, a station for RideShare could be found, and all she had to do was get in line and say how many people she had and where she was going. They'd drive her there, and if she bought a monthly pass, she could ride as much as she wanted.

Since she and Parker would only be there for a couple

of weeks, Alice had said she had two cars, Eloise had volunteered to rent one so she could go see Aaron whenever she wanted, and Robin said she'd have her SUV, Kelli hadn't bothered with a pass. But she still needed to get to the house on Rocky Ridge.

The line stretched down the sidewalk, and Kelli joined it, noting that it was moving quickly, as cars were lined up to get people already. It was just a matter of loading as quickly as possible, and only a few minutes later, she and Parker had a car headed for the north ferry station.

Parker's eyes stayed round as dinner plates as he took in the island, the ferry, the water that seemed to stretch in every direction. Kelli kept a smile in her heart at the way he wondered and experienced everything, confident in her decision to bring him to the cove this summer. They rarely went anywhere, and she'd taken him to every park and museum in their Jersey suburb. They'd gone into the city several times, and Kelli did her best to make sure Parker had plenty of opportunities for play dates. He had no siblings, and Kelli wasn't the best playmate for him, she knew that.

"This is Sanctuary Island," she told him as the ferry approached the dock. "We're not getting off here. This ferry will continue around the west end of the island and go on to Rocky Ridge."

"That's the last island on this side of the cove," Parker said. "Right?" He looked up at her.

"That's right," she said. "We flew into the middle

island. On the south side is Bell Island, and then Pearl Island."

"I heard they were going to build a highway to connect Bell and Pearl," someone said, and Kelli's anxiety spiked as she turned toward the woman standing there. She seemed familiar, but Kelli couldn't place her light green eyes and washed out brown hair.

"Really?" she asked, wishing talking to new people didn't freak her out so much. She was far too old to have a fight or flight response over making small talk on the ferry. "I didn't know that."

"Been some rumors among the locals," she said with a smile.

"Are you a local?" Kelli asked.

"Born and raised." The woman smiled, her eyes filling with pride. She was probably five years younger than Kelli, but the locals on Five Island Cove all knew each other.

"Do you know Robin Grover?" Kelli asked. "Her younger sister, Rosalee, still lives here too."

The woman's face lit up. "Sure," she said. "Rosalee and I were in the same class."

Surprise hit Kelli right between the eyes. "Really? What's your name?"

"Leslie Norman," she said. "Well, I was Otto, back in those days."

"Leslie Otto?" Kelli said, putting the name together with the girl she'd gone to high school with. "I'm Kelli

Watkins." She touched her chest, wondering if anyone from her younger days would remember her.

Kelli had the kind of face that was forgettable. She didn't speak up the way Alice did, and she hadn't been perky and popular like Robin. She didn't play sports and have boys fawning over her like AJ, and she didn't stick out academically like Eloise. Yes, Kelli was entirely able to disappear from memories as if she'd never existed.

"Kelli Watkins," the woman said, clearly trying to find the right memory with Kelli in it.

"I'm older than you," Kelli said. "I'm sure you don't remember me." She glanced back out over the railing of the ferry, the sunshine so bright today. No wonder so many people came to the cove in the summer. Everything about it soothed her soul, and again, Kelli was glad she'd decided to come.

"Did you have siblings?" Leslie asked, and Kelli nodded.

"Two sisters," she said, cutting a look at Leslie. "One older and one younger."

"Watkins..." Leslie made the connection, Kelli could tell, and she wanted to move away from the other woman.

"Heather?"

"Yes," Kelli said.

"I didn't know her very well," Leslie said, and at least her voice was kind.

Kelli nodded again, and thankfully, Leslie didn't try to strike up more conversation. Heather had not finished high school, so it wasn't surprising that someone like Leslie didn't know her. She'd left the cove when she was fifteen, and to Kelli's knowledge she'd never come back.

Everyone handled the demise of their family differently, and Kelli thought Heather had hung on for as long as she could.

Thankfully, the smudge of island on the horizon came into view, growing larger with every passing minute. "Here we are," Kelli said as the ferry pulled up to the dock. "One more car ride, and we're there."

She tugged her luggage along beside her, ready to be done with the travel already. Parker went in front of her, and Kelli edged her way off the boat and over to the line for a ride. She tapped on her phone and pulled up the address Alice had given her, and she read it to the driver while he loaded their suitcases in the trunk.

He peered at her phone, and then nodded. "I know where this is."

"Great." Kelli ushered Parker into the car, turning back to the line of people waiting for their car, her eyes catching on someone standing there.

Her feet stumbled as she realized that man had followed her to Rocky Ridge.

This couldn't be a coincidence.

Her breath froze in her lungs, but she managed to hurry into the car behind Parker and close the door. "Hurry, please," she said, and the driver pulled away from the curb. She turned around to see if he'd follow them, but he hadn't even been next in line. There was no way he could follow them.

Coincidence, she told herself, but her pulse would not settle down. Could it really be a coincidence? She'd never seen him in her neighborhood before yesterday, and she would've remembered those blazing eyes.

She felt like she had ants crawling all over her body, and she couldn't hold still for more than a few seconds. Alice owned a home clear up on the ridge, of course, as that was premium land, and nothing Alice did came in second.

"Thank you," Kelli said, passing the driver a tip. He unloaded their bags, and Kelli started up the front sidewalk to the mansion's front door.

"Wow, Mom," Parker said. "This place is huge."

"Isn't it?" Kelli said, peering up at the two-story giant in front of her. The exterior sported gray siding above a darker gray stone that looked very expensive. The front door probably weighed a thousand pounds, as it looked thick and sturdy.

She'd just made it to the top of the six steps to the porch when someone called her name. She turned, her heartbeat ricocheting around her chest.

That man stood there, trying to get his bag, pay the driver, and walk toward her at the same time.

"Parker," Kelli said, her voice quivering. "Hurry." She didn't bother to knock or ring the doorbell. She ran the few steps to the door and opened it, herding her son inside. She heaved his bag in after him, ignoring his question, and turned back to the man.

He'd left his bag on the sidewalk, and Kelli abandoned hers too. It was just a suitcase. She launched herself into the house and pushed the door closed with a deafening slam, twisting the lock immediately afterward.

"Kelli?" someone said behind her. A man.

A yelp came out of her mouth, because she didn't think there would be any men here. Honestly, anything would've made her cry out at this point. She could barely hear anything past her own heart beating in her ears.

Aaron Sherman stood there, concern on his face, and Kelli almost started crying in relief.

"What's going on?" he asked.

Kelli looked from Parker to Aaron, to Eloise, who came into the foyer too. "There's this guy following me," he said.

"What?" Eloise asked.

"I know it sounds crazy, but he's been everywhere I've been for the past two days."

As if to prove her point, the doorbell rang, and a fist pounded on the door several times.

Kelli once again cried out as she leapt away from the door. Eloise caught her arm and pulled her to her side with the word, "Aaron."

"You guys take the boy into the kitchen," Aaron said authoritatively. "Tell everyone to stay out of sight."

"What are you going to do?" Eloise asked.

Kelli reached for her son's hand, ready to hide in whatever closet, under whatever bed, she had to in order to keep him safe.

Aaron turned toward them, and somehow gave a smile that was both confident and curt at the same time. "I'm going to talk to him and find out who he is and what he wants." But as the doorbell rang again, and Eloise, Kelli, and Parker hurried into the kitchen, Aaron took his radio off his belt, and said, "I need backup to Upper Ridge Road, number 42357."

The Summer Sand Pact is available now! Get your copy today to continue the journey with the women in Five Island Cove.

BOOKS IN THE FIVE ISLAND COVE SERIES

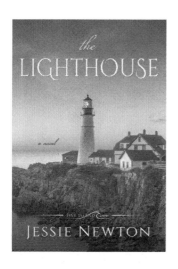

The Lighthouse, Book 1: As these 5 best friends work together to find the truth, they learn to let go of what doesn't matter and cling to what does: faith, family, and most of all, friendship.

Secrets, safety, and sisterhood...it all happens at the lighthouse on Five Island Cove.

The Summer Sand Pact, Book 2: These five best friends made a Summer Sand Pact as teens and have only kept it once or twice—until they reunite decades later and renew their agreement to meet in Five Island Cove every summer.

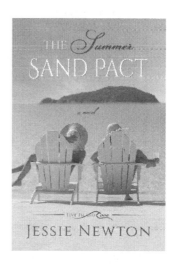

BOOKS IN THE FIVE ISLAND COVE SERIES

The Cliffside Inn, Book 3: Spend another month in Five Island Cove and experience an amazing adventure between five best friends, the challenges they face, the secrets threatening to come between them, and their undying support of each other.

Christmas at the Cove, Book 4: Secrets are never discovered during the holidays, right? That's what these five best friends are banking on as they gather once again to Five Island Cove for what they hope will be a Christmas to remember.

BOOKS IN THE FIVE ISLAND COVE SERIES

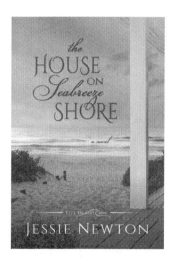

The House on Seabreeze Shore, Book 5: One last trip to Five Island Cove...this time to face a fresh future and leave all the secrets and fears in the past.

ABOUT JESSIE

Jessie Newton is a saleswoman during the day and escapes into romance and women's fiction in the evening, usually with a cat and a cup of tea nearby. The Lighthouse is her first women's fiction novel. Find out more at www. authorjessienewton.com.

Made in the USA
Coppell, TX
29 November 2021

66732277R00233